Get It
and
Get It Again

Other titles by Kimberly T. Matthews

The Perfect Shoe

Ninety-Nine and a Half Just Won't Do

Before I Let Go

A Little Hurt Ain't Never Hurt Nobody

Good Money

Promise You Won't Tell Nobody

Fruit of My Womb

After You've Done All You Can (Vols. 1–3)

Get It
and
Get It Again

Kimberly T. Matthews

URBAN BOOKS
http://www.urbanbooks.net

This is a work of fiction. Any references or similarities to actual events, real people, living or dead, or to real locales are intended to give the novel a sense of reality. Any similarity in other names, characters, places, and incidents is entirely coincidental.

URBAN SOUL is published by

Urban Books
1199 Straight Path
West Babylon, NY 11704

ISBN-13: 978-1-59983-094-0
ISBN-10: 1-59983-094-9

First Printing: May 2010

10 9 8 7 6 5 4 3 2 1

Printed in the United States of America

Dedication

    This novel is dedicated to every person who has ever made the decision to get up and get it, whatever *it* may be:

Your education	Your weight-loss goal	Your children
Your career	Your family	Your relationship
Your marriage	Your dream	Your happiness
Your peace	Your freedom	Your success

Your _____

Fill in your IT here!

Not only can you get it—you can get it again!

Acknowledgments

Thanks be to God Almighty, who has given me the gift of creativity and imagination! Thank You for lighting my path and guiding my way and putting people in my path to share, laugh, and brainstorm with. Without You I can do nothing, and without You I am completely nothing. It is to You that I am truly and ultimately grateful.

This is for the people: What a great time I had writing this one!

First, thanks to Clay R. Hooker Jr., my wonderful husband, who went hungry on several Friday nights to let me work on this book. Actually, he didn't go hungry—he just went to Chick-fil-A. But he wasn't happy about it. He wanted meat loaf or chicken or spaghetti or pork chops. In other words, he wanted me to actually cook! I had forgot about that part of being a wife, but only because Clay wines and dines me like royalty. He's the best like that! As a matter of fact, at the time of my writing this, it's Friday night. I'm in trouble! This is the first book that I've had to write from beginning to end since he made me a Hooker, and I'm still struggling to find that balance.

To Davion, thanks for helping me to think like an eight-year-old. Actually, because of you, I didn't have to think at all—I just had to ask the right questions and capture your responses. I've never heard divorce described quite like that.

To Anthony, Terrell, and Wayne, and every other

man who wanted to see Jerrafine brought to some level of justice involving physical pain, thanks for your thoughts. Anthony, you will be disappointed to know that her brake lines did not get cut. Terrell, no one had to pay a ton of money, and, Wayne, no one got punched in the face. Or choked. Oh yeah, Ant, no cousins got called, either. Sorry!

And thanks to Tamara, who acted out every crying, gasping, belly-holding, getting-sick, throwing-up, and forehead- and neck-sweating scene in the book. My gratitude to Trineka, who guided me through what the Wal-Mart conversation should sound like, which still makes me laugh today. Thanks to Shermori and Machelle, who had some great sneak-attack strategies, although none of them involved stealing money. And I am grateful to Kenyatta (who so graciously played Nadia Mitchell at the *Good Money* book release party in May of 2009) for agreeing with every idea that I ran past her, by giving her signature stamp of approval, "I don't mind!" Thanks to Tanya for the bacon grease recommendation (and it's still funny as I don't know what!). Bacon grease?

And finally, thanks to everyone who has ever supported me on any level by reading my books, my blogs, my Facebook comments, my Twitter postings, and my MySpace bulletins. Thanks for your e-mails, your review postings, and your feedback. Thank you for attending my book signings and parties, and for thinking enough of me to want my autograph!

To everyone, thanks for traveling with me on this part of the journey! You make the trip worthwhile!

1

The cool air felt good against Jerrafine "Feenie" Trotter's skin as she walked alongside of several other female inmates, identically dressed in bright yellow jumpsuits. She was thankful that it wasn't predicted to be as hot as it had been for the past few days, which had been unbearable for picking up trash by the roadside. Instead of making small talk with the others, she kept to herself, thinking about how much her life had changed in the course of just a few months. It seemed like a lifetime ago that she'd had her freedom, her home, a nice monthly check, and her girls. Now she'd been reduced to a few items: plain white undergarments and a journal and pen. She'd played things over and over again in her mind, remembering how she'd gotten there. Let her tell it, and it wasn't her fault. Had her girls done what she'd told them to do, she would have never landed in such a place as the Baltimore City

Correctional Center. It was a minimum-security facility, but still jail.

Feenie had spent the first few months of her sentence in a cussing, fussing rage, angry at the world. She'd hated life and everything it now presented to her on a daily basis, not wanting to take ownership of the fact that she'd brought this situation upon herself. She'd spent two days crying her eyes out, trying to get over the initial shock and disbelief of having to serve sixteen months behind bars. Then anger had crept in. First, she'd been angry at Mary Trotter, her mother, for limiting her visits to just the first two weekends of her incarceration, dropping off the socks, briefs, bras, and T-shirts and not returning.

"I've been trying to get by there to see you," Mary had declared during Feenie's one and only accepted collect call. "But Saturday is my only day off, and I got so much stuff to do."

"But, Ma, it's only one day a week for twenty minutes. You could at least come once a month. And it ain't like you gotta drive fifty hours away. You ain't even right, Ma."

"What? How am I not right? You got yourself in this mess, but then I ain't right for not taking the time outta my life to run behind you. Jerrafine, you more than forty years old. You a grown woman, and I'll be doggone if I let . . ."

"Just forget it, Ma." Rolling her eyes and not wanting to hear another word, Feenie had slammed the phone down, even though she hadn't asked Mary to send money for commissary purchases. She'd returned to her cell, nestled as close as she could to the wall, and silently cried for the rest of the evening, feeling lonelier than she'd ever had in her whole life. She'd known then that she'd be walking her road alone.

Feenie's first friend, dare she call her that, was Angela Pierce, a twenty-eight-year-old who had been close to completing her degree when she got caught up with the wrong man, Demarco Franklin, who mesmerized her with materialistic things purchased with drug money. Once Feenie had made it through her initial month, it became easier for the two cell mates to talk, as neither of them had ever been in a cell before, and both were scared out of their minds.

"So do you still talk to ol' boy?" Feenie asked, referring to Demarco, as the two women sat down to breakfast, which consisted of a cold piece of fried bologna served with grits and water.

"Nah. He came up here once or twice, but that's it." Angela shrugged. "I still can't believe he did me like this." This time she shook her head slowly, reliving her decision to do a few runs for her then boyfriend.

"Girl, that's how people will do you," Feenie threw in. "You doing everything you can for them, and they turn around and stab you right in your back. That's how them two little brats of mine did me," she spat.

"Oh, you have two kids? That had to be hard, leaving them to come here."

"Yeah, whatever." Feenie rolled her eyes. "Their selfish behinds was pro'lly glad to see me go." Feenie talked a few minutes about how her daughters, Mia and Cara, had been playing on the phone, dialing 9-1-1 while she wasn't home, which led to a Child Protective Services investigation. "They know they ain't have no business on the phone. I'm out there breaking my back to put a roof over their head," she lied, "and they ain't have nothing better to do."

Feenie had Angela believe that she had been out working a second job for a couple of hours and had been unable to find a babysitter for the twin girls when they became curious about emergency services, but Feenie had actually been running around town, shopping and getting her nails done. "And I don't know what it was that they told the social worker when she came to talk to them. Whatever it was, it got my hips sitting behind bars. They my babies, but I wanted to choke slam those little wenches."

"Man. That's tough. They should have given you a break since you were working," Angela offered, buying into Feenie's story. "It would have been different if you were at the club or something. I'm glad I don't have any kids. I'd probably be real messed up right about now, having to leave them."

"You did yourself a favor. Don't have none, 'cause they ain't nothing but headaches and hardships."

"So who has your kids while you're here?"

"Their stupid daddy," Feenie grumbled.

"That's good that he took 'em," Angela replied. "Most men don't be tryin' to keep no kids. They don't even be wantin' to baby-sit. Were y'all together?"

"Girl, please. We won't never together. This

honeypot was just too good and sweet for him to let go of," Feenie answered, looking over her right shoulder and cutting her eyes down at her behind. She wiggled a bit in her seat, to clarify what she meant by honeypot.

"You ain't put it on him, did you, girl?" Angela chortled.

"Think I didn't when I did?" Feenie stood and seductively gyrated her hips. "Girl, that man ain't been right since. Started hittin' this like it was crack or somethin', and as long as he was paying, I was givin'. I was ridin' that joker like bam! Bam!" she exclaimed, forcefully thrusting her pelvis forward. The two women broke into full laughter. "Girl, that man put me in a house and was paying my rent *eh-ver-eee* month. He was taking good care of all three of us." Feenie's laughter faded as she collapsed back into her seat.

"You think he's gonna give them back to you when you get out?" Angela used a tine of her fork to clean black lines of dirt from under her nails.

"I 'on't know. The question is, am I gonna take them back? After they got me in this mess, humph! I 'on't know about all that. I think they need to stay right where they at," Feenie snapped.

"I'm sure they miss you, though. Every child wants their mother."

"They shouda thought about that before they lied to Social Services," Feenie replied, rolling her eyes and standing to drop off her tray for cleaning.

Feenie had always felt like the twins were in her way and the only thing they were good for was netting her a healthy income each month from Rance. It had been ten years ago that Rance had taken Feenie on as a client for what he thought would be a normal divorce proceeding, but he had got much more than he had bargained for when the two became intimate, not knowing that Feenie had ulterior motives from the onset. Once she'd determined that Rance had a pretty sizeable income, was married, with children of his own, and was not likely to leave his wife, Feenie had written her own ticket.

After several months of midday and late-night rendezvous, Rance became too comfortable. He'd already begun to fork over varied amounts of cash at Feenie's request, providing her with shopping and pampering money, which gave Feenie the green light to move forward with her plan to never have to work again another day in her life. And when she was ready, she set her plan in motion.

It wasn't long after Feenie stopped swallowing hormone-filled pills that her body responded just like she had planned by receiving Rance's fluids and allowing conception. She didn't even wait for her period to be officially late, but anxiously tested her urine two weeks ahead of time, looking for positive results. Rather than having to wait the full three minutes the package stated, almost instantly, Feenie watched a pastel-colored plus sign manifest itself on the end of the testing wand, and an uncontrollable and conniving smile spread across her face.

She arrived at his office after hours that same evening in a trench coat, with very little underneath. "Mr. Alexander, I'm sorry I'm late. My car broke down," she began in full character as Mimi, an underperforming secretary.

"I thought I told you one more tardy would come with severe consequences," Rance replied sternly, but with excitement. His manhood was already beginning to rise.

"I know but . . ." Feenie rushed through the office, taking off her trench coat on the way, revealing all flesh and curves and just a small triangle of fabric attached to a silk ribbon that circled her waist. "I promise this is the last time," she added. "If you just let me get started, I can get all my work done."

"Yeah, you need to get started right away. I have a *long* list of tasks for you on top of my desk, so you better get there fast," he answered. "It might take you a while to do all that needs to be done." He followed her to his desk, already beginning to unfasten his pants.

"Yes, sir," she answered subserviently. "I'm willing to stay all night if I have to." She bent over his desk, exaggerating her attempt to pick up a pen. "I just might need a little bit of help reaching those files I need. You keep them in such a tight spot," she teased, turning her back to Rance. "Oops!" Feenie exclaimed, purposely dropping the pen on the floor, only to bend at the waist, her feet spread wide in a pair of silver glitter pumps, and slowly pick it up again.

"Sorry about that, Mr. Alexander." She smirked, watching Rance's eyes and boxers bulge. "I will be more careful with the office supplies."

"Yeah. I'll need you to be more cautious," he panted. "Sometimes you need to start off taking your time until you get in a groove."

"Yes, sir. I'm ready to get started now. I think if you stand right here behind me and lift me up a little bit, I might be able to reach those files you need for tomorrow morning."

"I'll be glad to help you. As your boss, it's the least I could do."

After a full role-play session, with a bonus round celebrating an imaginary win of a large case, Feenie was ready to spring her trap.

"Rance, we need to talk," she stated after easing down off his desktop. Rance was hot, sweaty, and exhausted from the labor he'd just put in, and had all but collapsed into his chair. He motioned with a wave of his fingers for Feenie to come closer to him. She straddled his lap, and he, like a newborn baby, latched on to her breast and let out a satisfied moan.

"What is it?" he mumbled, his mouth full of her flesh.

"Rance." She paused, as if she was struggling to get her words together. "Rance, I'm late."

Immediately, his suckling stopped, and he leaned back in his chair. "What do you mean?"

"I mean I'm late," she repeated. "My cycle hasn't started." Feenie bit into her lower lip and studied Rance's face, which was now filled with worry.

"So . . . so what are you going to do?" he asked, knowing there was no way on the green earth he wanted her to have his baby.

Feenie shrugged, although her plan was in full effect. "You know I've always longed for a baby, and I thought after Marvin did what he did to me that it would never happen."

Rance kept silent, reflecting on what Feenie had shared with him when she'd come seeking his professional services in divorcing her then husband, Marvin. Starting with the lie that Marvin had simply expressed that he didn't love her anymore and had complained about her weight, among many other things, Feenie had convinced Rance that Marvin had caused her to miscarry her first baby. However, nothing was further from the truth.

The only reason why Feenie had ever given Marvin the time of day in the first place was that he was being scouted by the National Basketball Association. She'd never had any true interest in or feelings for Marvin, other than disdain, but with the promise of becoming a millionaire's wife, Feenie masked her greed with what she pretended was love. They wasted no time getting married right out of high school, Marvin none the wiser of Feenie's true feelings. But Feenie, wanting to always enjoy millionaire status whether the marriage was successful or not, right away stopped taking her prescribed contraceptives and let her husband deposit his seed deep inside of her to produce a child. When her pregnancy was confirmed, Feenie knew she was financially set for life but didn't share the news with Marvin right away.

In the meantime, Marvin couldn't have been a happier newlywed. He believed he had a beautiful, sexy, loving wife, and he was on the cusp of launching into the extremely well-paying profession of his passion. It wasn't until he shattered his ankle, thereby voiding his NBA career before it even had a chance to leave the ground, that he realized Feenie had only been in it for a free ticket to ride.

Feenie showed her concern, waiting on Marvin hand and foot, until a team of doctors determined that although his ankle would heal, it would never be strong enough to meet the demands of professional ball playing. It was then that Feenie's true colors blazed through. Marvin was devastated as he came to know that everything that he thought he knew about the character and personality of his wife had been a lie. He needed her to love and support him, to comfort him, and to help him discover other areas where he could be successful and support both of them. What he got instead was a wife who refused to wait on him despite his injury, forcing him to hobble on crutches around their small apartment, a flurry of curse words just about every time Feenie looked his way, and a pair of locked legs, though she swore that she'd never hold sex back from her man and allow another woman to take her place.

Even so, he loved Feenie and wanted the marriage to work and told her as much with each passing day. "We won't be millionaires, but we can still make it, Feenie. I mean, we both love each other, and that's all we need to make this thing work. Forget about the money. We don't have to be rich to live. We both have jobs and make enough together to pay the rent and eat. I can work two or three jobs once my ankle heals." Most days the only response she'd give was the rolling of her eyes. If she did open her mouth, Marvin would always regret that he'd summoned her to speak at all.

When Feenie was alone, she would cry for hours at a time, despising her situation as well as the baby in her belly, and wishing she'd have at least waited until Marvin began cashing NBA checks before she'd upped and tied the knot. She bawled even more profusely when she realized she was pregnant by a man who had suddenly been reduced to working part-time at 7-Eleven. So Feenie made an appointment to terminate the pregnancy. And when the time was right, she laid out the perfect lie.

Marvin had come home one evening, once again pleading for his wife's help.

"Babe, I'm just saying, if you go full-time instead of part-time, we could make a little bit of extra money. It's supposed to be you and me against the world, baby. We supposed to be in it together."

"See, that's where you're wrong," she replied nonchalantly as she sat on her feet, nestled in a corner of the couch, painting her fingernails. "What it is supposed to be is you bringing home the bacon and taking care of me, not me breaking my back, slaving my life away, waitin' tables to help you pay bills. It is supposed to be me being able to shop wherever I want to, not me looking at the clearance rack at Target."

"I thought when we got married, it was for better or for worse. That is what I heard you say before the minister, your mamma, my mamma, and the Lord."

Feenie sucked her teeth. "Don't nobody mean that mess. And you crazy in your head if you think I'ma sit here and baby you and pat you up when you supposed to be a man. And a real man takes care of his woman."

"So what are you trying to say, Feenie? I'm not a real man, just because I broke my ankle? Just because I'm asking my wife to help me, like a wife is supposed to do?"

"I ain't supposed to do jack smack but give you somma dis right here," she snapped, jerking her legs open and pointing to her crotch. "And I can tell you right now, I ain't free and I ain't cheap! And if you think I'ma keep on wasting my good stuff on you, you best think again! What I got is gold, and truth be told, I supposed to be married to and givin' it up to a millionaire, not to some broke-tailed, jackleg, tryna-make-a-dollar-outta-fifteen-cents, cain't-half-pay-the-bills joker like you!"

Marvin was initially stunned as he watched Feenie bring her knees together and begin attending to her fingernails again. Marvin's hands balled into tight, angry knobs as for the first time he recognized Feenie for what she really was. "You ain't nothin' but a materialistic, gold-diggin', ghetto ho!"

Like an attacking tiger, Feenie leapt to her feet in lightning speed, made a near-twelve-inch reach to Marvin's face, and slapped him so hard, his head did a quarter turn. In an instant and without thinking, he retaliated by shoving her in the face, so that she stumbled backward over the coffee table. She landed on her butt, but her right arm slammed against the table's edge, while her head landed on a cushion of the couch. Shrieking out in pain, Feenie scrambled to her feet, grabbing her arm, then fell to the floor, crying hysterically.

"I'm sorry, baby. I'm sorry," Marvin said, remorsefully falling to his knees. He tried to take her in his arms, but Feenie was having none of it.

"Get away from me!" she cried, jerking at his touch.

"Feenie, please. I didn't mean that."

"Yes, you did!" She looked up into her husband's face and saw her chance to completely manipulate the situation. Feenie suddenly moved her hand from her arm to her belly. "Oww!"

Marvin's look changed from remorse to confusion. "What? What is it?" Marvin leaned forward to reach out a second time to his wife.

"Get away from me, Marvin!" She dug her feet into the carpet, wildly scooting away from him like a wounded and terrified animal. Leaning against the couch, Feenie began panting heavily as she let her tears flow.

"What is wrong?" Marvin asked again, becoming panicked.

Feenie sat silent for close to two minutes, while tears seeped through her closed lids. Not knowing what else to do, Marvin sat beside her, wishing he could undo the mess he'd created. Cautiously, while Feenie's eyes were still shut, he reached up and stroked her hair. This time Feenie didn't pull away.

"Gimme my purse," she said between sobs.

Without question, Marvin moved at her command, went to their bedroom, and came back with a large faux Coach bag, which she'd received as a graduation gift.

Still sobbing, she dug around in the bag for a few seconds, until she pulled out a folded sheet of paper, then handed it to her husband. "I was going to wait until our three-month anniversary to tell you," she whispered.

Marvin unfolded the paper and glanced over the writing, which confirmed Feenie's positive pregnancy test. "You're pregnant?" he asked gently as his eyes watered with tears.

Feenie nodded, although she knew their baby had long been gone.

Once they arrived at the emergency room, and the doctor could find no traces of a heartbeat, Feenie feigned hysteria and, with a slew of curse words, put Marvin out. Remorseful and incredibly guilt ridden, Marvin, like a dog who'd lost a fight, tucked his tail and ran. And just like Feenie had planned, he wasn't present to hear the doctor tell Feenie what she already knew—there was no baby. Feenie used the situation to manipulate Marvin every way she could.

And now after his money, Feenie pulled the same card deck of lies out for Rance. The very last thing Rance needed was a child produced outside of the sanctity of his marriage to his devoted wife, Laiken. Nonetheless, he kept silent and listened to Feenie's tears and pleading.

"I mean, I tried to get pregnant a whole bunch of times after that, but I never could," she lied further. "And I just accepted the fact that I would never be a mother and know a life outside of my own body." Feenie lay her hands on her still flat abdomen, although she truly was pregnant this time. "I just feel like this is a second chance for me."

In a low tone and as gently as possible, Rance replied, "Feenie, you know I can't tell Laiken that you're . . . we're having a baby." He rubbed a hand over his face, now wanting Feenie off his lap, but thought more strategically than to push her off, knowing full well that she could easily blow his cover. He tilted his head back and studied the ceiling tiles above them.

"I really want this baby, Rance. I don't expect you to leave your wife and kids, but I really want this baby." Feenie began to cry. "Please don't ask me to get rid of it, because I just can't do that."

Rance cursed himself silently.

"This baby means more than anything to me, and if it means staying out of your life in order to keep it, then that is what I'm willing to do." At that, Feenie pulled away from Rance, standing to her feet. "I don't mind giving you up, Rance, but I can't give up my baby," she said through tears as she slid her arms into the sleeves of the trench coat she'd arrived in, tightened its belt around her waist, and headed for the door. Before leaving, she turned back to say some final words. "I'll send you the doctors' bills and what we'll need financially, but other than that, you don't have to worry about me ruining your life."

That was what Feenie had promised, and she even honored it for several years, as Rance sent her a healthy check every month to support his clandestine twin daughters, but it was a promise that Feenie couldn't keep now that she was behind bars. The day she was sentenced, Rance took Mia and Cara home to live with him . . . and his wife and two sons.

2

Rance pulled into his driveway and let out a heavy sigh before letting himself out of his car. His decision to take Mia and Cara into his home chipped away at his marriage each day. And how could he expect it not to? He'd betrayed his wife by not just sleeping with another woman, but by getting her pregnant, and lying by omission for several years. Laiken hadn't left him. "At least not yet," he uttered to himself as he fumbled with his keys at the front door. He'd come to no longer expect the aroma of a cooked meal as he entered his home. The evenings that Laiken would greet him with a kiss and a drink to help him unwind were over. Now she'd barely even look at her husband, let alone speak to him or serve him anything. He couldn't blame her. Nonetheless, he'd speak each evening when he came in.

He slid his key in the door, let himself in, and sat his briefcase in the foyer, like he did every night. Walking past the family room, where

Laiken was curled on the couch, watching Lifetime, he spoke, but expecting no response, he didn't even bother to look her way or slow his stride to the kitchen with hopes of there being leftovers, which he'd no doubt have to reheat himself. As usual there were none.

He pulled lettuce, a tomato, and a package of deli cold cuts from the refrigerator, along with a jar of mayonnaise, made himself a sandwich, took a seat at the breakfast-nook table, and stared out the window, focusing his attention on his four children, who were involved in a game of BlongoBall, which entailed tossing a pair of balls connected with a short rope toward a ladder-shaped goal. They looked to be working up a healthy sweat, as well as fostering friendly competition, high-fiving each other every time any of them scored.

Rance shook his head, wishing his life could be so simple. Mia and Cara had been with him for just a year now, and despite counseling sessions and his acceptance of several verbal assaults from Laiken, their relationship had not improved. They were distantly cordial at best; Laiken would allow no more. She was miserable, and she made it known each time she opened her mouth, which was mostly limited to when they both sat in front of their marriage counselor.

"Tell me what you'd like to accomplish by coming here, Rance," Sandra Melton asked calmly, studying Rance's nonverbal reaction.

He sniffed, ran his hand across his chin, leaned forward, resting his elbows against his knees, and turned his head toward Laiken. "I'd like to save my marriage," he replied, steadying his eyes on hers.

A sarcastic chuckle escaped Laiken's lips while she shook her head from side to side.

"And how do you feel about that?" Sandra asked, shifting her eyes to the opposite side of the sofa, where Laiken sat.

With her arms folded tightly across her chest, Laiken focused an angry stare on her husband. "How do you expect me to embrace you, Rance, after what you did to me? How do you even think I can look at you? You are saying you want to save your marriage, but were you thinking about your marriage when you did what you did?" she spat.

"No." Rance paused momentarily. "I wasn't." He paused a second time. "I wasn't and I'm sorry."

"And you expect me to believe that? You actually expect me to believe that you're sorry?" Laiken snarled.

"What exactly did Rance do, Laiken?" Sandra inquired as she jotted down a few notes.

"Let's let him tell you. Tell her what you did! Tell her how you've destroyed our family," Laiken shot at her husband.

After a deep inhale and release, Rance spilled details of his illicit affair with Feenie, and of the twins, whom he'd managed to keep hidden for more than eight years. He couldn't fault Laiken for what she felt, betrayal, mistrust, anger, and deep pain. Nor could he justify what he'd done, so he didn't try to. "I'm just willing to do whatever it'll take to repair the damage and keep my family."

"I think you want to hold on to us only because

you know I will take you for every dime you have!"
Laiken growled.

*Rance would never admit it, but that very thought
had run through his head more than a few times.*

Still staring out of the kitchen window, he
chuckled at the kids' antics, wondering what
was really going on in their heads. He and
Laiken kept their disagreements from them as
best they could, and they'd not asked too many
questions. Most nights he was up long after the
children went to bed, so he hoped they hadn't
noticed that he'd been sleeping in the guest
room, since Laiken had banished him from
the master suite. It certainly wasn't the best of
situations, but one thing he could say was he'd
never observed Laiken mistreating the girls, as
hard as accepting them had been. He reasoned that it was the day-care coordinator in
her. Laiken was continuously surrounded by
children and was very comfortable with inter-
acting with them in a variety of settings. For
the most part, the girls were well behaved, respectable, and obedient and gave neither of
them any trouble.

"I guess Feenie did something halfway right,"
he mumbled to himself as he stood to his feet
and headed for his home office. More and
more each day he accepted the reality that his
marriage was over; it all was just a matter of
time. He pondered what it was he thought he'd
be able to do with the kids, his girls especially,
not knowing if Jerrafine would ever get her life

together enough to regain custody. How would he be able to manage a single-father role and still maintain his law practice? Laiken had always been a great mother to the boys, involving herself in extracurricular activities, going to parent and teacher meetings, checking homework, helping with projects, and the like. Not to mention just keeping the house clean and preparing meals. Now that he thought about it, he wondered if he'd taken Laiken for granted, his affair with Feenie notwithstanding.

"I'd be up a creek," he mumbled, imagining how hectic his life would automatically become if Laiken walked out. Yet and still, he felt like it was right on the horizon. He toyed with the thought of hiring a nanny if he needed to, then snickered a laugh, thinking about actor Robin Williams in the movie *Mrs. Doubtfire.*

3

It had been a long, hard sixteen months for Feenie, confined in the walls of a Baltimore correctional facility, but finally, with nothing to her name but a handful of letters, she was free again and ready to start over. Somehow. Someway.

Glad to see her mother's face, she gave Mary a hug, then took a seat in the car. "It's so good to be out of there," she commented as she leaned back against the headrest. "All I want to do is sleep in my own bed."

"Well, that ain't gon' happen, unless you talking about the bed you used to sleep in in my house. I had to sell just about all your stuff. Couldn't afford to store it," Mary announced.

"What? Ma!"

"Chile, that storage won't free!" Mary snapped. "And you won't in a position to pay for nothin'. I did keep some of it, but I didn't have nowhere to keep all that furniture and whatnot."

"Well, what did you do with my other stuff?

Not furniture, but my clothes, books, and pictures, and stuff like that."

"Most of it's in my garage, but somma that mess got thrown out," Mary answered, wheeling her Camry onto the highway. "Now, how long you plan on staying at my house?" she continued, conveying that it wouldn't be long before she expected her daughter to be on her own again.

"A couple of months, I guess. I'ma need to get a job at least."

"Where you thinking 'bout lookin'? McDonald's is hiring every day," Mary advised, setting another expectation. "I can't let you just sit up in the house and do nothing. Not in my house. I don't take care of grown folks."

"I know, Ma." Feenie turned her head to look out the window, already growing irritated with just the thought of having to live temporarily with her mother. "I'ma start looking this week."

"Too bad you don't still have that nice place."

"Yeah." Feenie had only been renting the home she and her girls had lived in prior to her going to jail. "I don't know where I'ma go, but I'ma try to have something by the end of next month."

"You heard from the girls lately?"

"Yeah. They wrote not too long ago and sent pictures."

"They daddy act like them girls ain't got no other family. I ain't seen them girls since you been gone."

"It wasn't like you was coming around too much in the first place, Ma."

"Even so, I'm still they grandma, and I got a right to see them girls."

"Whatever," Feenie mumbled under her breath, remembering how Mary had refused to take the girls while she was incarcerated. Now, all of a sudden, she was the faithful grandmother who deserved and had a right to see the twins.

"Now, I know you a grown woman, Feenie, but let me go on ahead and explain the house rules to you."

"Ma," Feenie began.

"Don't 'Ma' me, unless you got somewhere else to sleep tonight."

Feenie bit her tongue.

"You ain't gon' be hanging out all times of the night and bringing all kinda men up in my house." She paused, pursing her lips together and cutting her eyes away from the road for a few seconds to look Feenie's way. She was well aware of Jerrafine's history of using and abusing men to get whatever she wanted. "Now, on Sunday mornings we going to church. I got something in my closet you can wear until you get some money to pick you up a few things."

"All right, Ma." Feenie knew there was no point in challenging her mother; she had nowhere else to go for now.

"Don't expect me to be cooking and cleaning up behind you. You want something to eat, go on in the kitchen and cook it yourself. Clean your mess up if you make one, 'cause I'm too old to be picking up behind folks. You hear me?"

"Yeah."

"Now once you get a job, you gon' have to pay me something. I'ma give you a few weeks to find somewhere to work, but you can't live free, baby."

"Pay you?" Feenie hadn't been prepared for that one. "Ma, once I get a job, I'ma need all my money to move out."

"Oh yeah, you will be doing that, ain't no doubt about it, but you gon' have to pay me something in the meantime. Times is too tight for me to just be taking care of grown folks. I seen too many grown kids come back home, talkin' 'bout they need help just for a little while, and end up almost runnin' they parents crazy. Jean Louise ain't never got her son back out of her house once he got kicked out of the military and came back home. Don't make nobody's sense how that big, old, crusty grown man like that living up under his momma and making babies all over town."

By the time Mary pulled into the driveway at her home, Feenie was already sick of being there. She lifted herself from the car, stretched, went inside, and headed for her old bedroom.

"I'm just gonna go 'head to bed, Ma. I hope you don't mind."

"It's still back there." Mary waved her hand. "You're welcome to it."

Once inside her bedroom, Feenie lay back on her bed. It offered the same comfort that she remembered from more than twenty years before, except now it was much smaller than what her memory had preserved. At any rate, it was one thousand times better than sleeping on a flat and worn-out jail-cell cot.

Realizing she was still holding on to the envelopes, Feenie sat up and spread them across the comforter, then sorted them by date. Each envelope held two handwritten letters, one from each of her daughters, and a photo or two. As angry as she'd been with the girls a year and a half ago, it hadn't taken her long to begin to sincerely miss them. Most days their faces, captured in a moment of time and printed on four-by-six rectangles of photo paper, had been what kept her going while locked away. There had been lots of time for her to personally reflect on what kind of mother she'd been to the girls, and Feenie was ashamed to admit that she hadn't been the best. Not even close to it. Even when she tried to give herself credit, she knew most of it wasn't deserved. Just the way she'd come about having them in the first place had been completely sneaky and underhanded. She'd sprung a trap on their father once she'd realized he had deep pockets. For Feenie, it had always been about finding someone to take care of her, even at the price of pushing two kids from her womb.

When the girls were babies, Mary was so proud and wanted to brag every chance she got, so it was nothing for her to keep them for days on end while Feenie ran the streets, partying, clubbing, and looking for her next financial victim. It wasn't until the girls got to be of school age that they became a chore and a bother to Feenie. She lived across the city from Mary, in a townhome that Rance paid the rent on faithfully, which was where the girls were registered to attend school. Feenie felt like a caged wild tiger, having to be home every afternoon to meet the school bus and every night to put the girls to bed. She felt like she still had lots of living to do, and twin girls were seriously in the way.

Desperate for night life and freedom, Feenie began leaving the girls home alone once they were tucked into bed and sleeping. Then after a while, she began leaving them home for short periods after school. Each time she'd come home and there was no hurt done to the kids, it was that much easier to leave them home again. As she grew more comfortable but careless with leaving them alone, her short periods turned into longer periods of time when the girls were left to fend for themselves, with a set of strict rules: don't open the door for anybody, don't use the stove, and don't answer the phone, unless they saw her cell phone number.

Randomly selecting an envelope, she read the letters to herself.

Dear Mommy,
   Thank you for being the best mom ever. You have been there for me all the time, and I hope that you can come home soon so that we can live together again very soon.
               I love you,
               Mirance Diana Alexander

Dear Mommy,
   I love you very much. I hope we can spend

*time together very soon. You have done very
much things for me, and you have done so much
for me.*

                    xoxoxoxoxoxoxoxoxoxox,
                    Carance

A lump of guilt slowly rose within Feenie's
throat as she realized the unconditional love her
children had for her in spite of her substandard
level of basic parenting. Feenie looked at one of
the photos that had come with the letters. In it
both girls had huge smiles on their faces, and
their heads were pressed closely together for the
camera. Instead of their hair being in long, neat,
and shiny plaits, like she had normally kept it, it
was dry looking, loose, wild, and all over their
heads. She assumed that Rance's wife had no
idea how to manage it. When she'd received the
photo a year prior, she'd been so angry with the
twins and with the world, she'd come close to
tearing it in two. Now reflecting on where she
was, she was glad her emotions had not gotten
the best of her. She missed her daughters and
wanted badly to see them. Rance hadn't brought
them a single time to visit her while she was incarcerated, and while it hurt her on one hand,
on the other, she was glad that her girls had
never seen her in her jailed condition.

Picking up the phone, she contemplated calling them but at the same time was very cognizant
that Laiken could answer the phone and probably wouldn't take too kindly to the call. Feenie
thought through the possible scenarios of what

she imagined could happen and narrowed them down to three responses:

"Jerrafine? Oh! Umm . . . hold on. I'll get the girls for you."

"Jerrafine, you've disrupted—no destroyed—my entire family life. How dare you dial this number? Don't you ever call here again!"

"Jerrafine! You've got some nerve calling my home after you slept with my husband, extorted his money, then dumped your children off on me, expecting me to take care of them. You have the audacity to call my house! Who do you think you are?"

No matter how Laiken would respond, Feenie was willing to accept it. After all, Laiken had every right to be angry. The worse thing that could happen was that Laiken would slam the phone down in her ear, and that was bearable. Without further thought, she dialed the number to the Alexander home.

"We're sorry. The number you have dialed, 301-555-3850, has been changed to an unpublished number. Please make a note of it. 301-555 . . ."

She hadn't meant to, but from out of nowhere, Feenie began to cry, responding to the void she felt in missing her girls. The flow of tears forced her thoughts down a path of various decisions she'd made in her life, starting with her ploy to become pregnant and trickling back to her very first pregnancy with Marvin's baby. Again, she felt overwhelmed by guilt and shame, feelings she'd become familiar with as her jail time passed each day. Slowly Feenie slid off the bed and to her knees, something she couldn't remember doing since first grade.

"God," she whispered, then paused, not really knowing how to verbalize what was in her heart. "Help me." Feenie paused again, trying to make sense of her thoughts. "I can't think of anything I've ever done right. I've not been the best mother to my children. I've not done right by them, and they don't even realize it. I don't even deserve it, but they love me anyway. I know that I've always done the wrong thing. But, God . . . please help me. Help me to change." She gulped, then sniffed, hoping that God would understand what she was really trying to say. "I can't continue to live like this. Tricking and manipulating people. I'm sick of it, Lord," she uttered sincerely. "I'm sick of myself." Feenie fell silent for a moment, biting into her bottom lip, crying even the more. "I'm so ashamed of myself about what I did to Marvin. He didn't deserve that," she sobbed. "Just help me, God. Please. If you give me a chance, I'll do the right thing this time."

She didn't bother to lift herself from her knees after she ended her prayer, but instead, slid downward to sit on the floor, crossed her arms on the bed, and cradled her head. She sat silent for several minutes, wondering if there were a way she'd ever be able to get in contact with Marvin. She hadn't seen or heard from him since July 9, 2000, not that they had any reason to keep in contact. She had no idea what he was now doing with his life, if he'd re-married, if he had children and a successful career, or if he was sleeping in a cardboard box on the streets.

She reached over to the nightstand and grabbed the television remote, trying to find something to distract her mind from what currently weighed upon it. Flicking through the channels, she stopped on HGTV and watched a few room makeovers. "I could do that," she said to herself. Feenie had always had a knack for decorating and could convert any cave into a castle. When she had her own place, her friends and visitors would compliment her constantly on how great her home looked, and often asked her opinion on decorating tips. It was effortless for Feenie, and she enjoyed it. Picking up an envelope from the bed, she jotted on the back a note to herself to look for interior-decorating jobs. She figured since she had to find a job, she might as well find one she was going to like.

With a press of her thumb, Feenie scanned more channels, pausing for two seconds on each one. She wasn't looking for anything in particular but came to a screeching halt on Channel Twelve. The NCAA tournament was on, and as a team in white jerseys with light blue lettering cheered over a three-pointer shot, the camera switched to the coach on the sidelines. Feenie found herself staring at the face of none other than Marvin O'Neil Temple.

She gasped out loud, with widened eyes soaking in her ex-husband's features. Not much had changed since she'd seen him last, although he was far more polished and mature looking. His hair was neat and close, and a goatee framed his lips. The skin on his face was smooth and youthful, not revealing to the naked eye that he, like Jerrafine, was quickly approaching forty-five. Feenie couldn't have cared less about the actual game, but her eyes stayed glued, watching for all the shots of Marvin, which were few and far between. Each time they showed him yelling, cheering, or silently looking on from the sidelines, her heart leapt.

Feenie scribbled on the envelope "Marvin Temple—Old Dominion University," not that she would need a reminder; his place of employment was already committed to her memory. As soon as the game went off, she took a seat at her mother's computer to do a search on the college and in seconds had Marvin's work address. It was time to put together a plan.

4

Mia and Cara lay in their beds behind their closed bedroom door, having their usual nightly chat before drifting off to sleep.

"I'll be glad when Mommy gets out of jail," Mia said.

"Me too. I want to see her."

"Do you think she will let us still live here?"

"I don't know. She might if we tell her we have more fun and stuff over here. It's so boring over there. Plus, we won't have any brothers to play with. I'ma ask her if we can live here," Cara answered.

"I don't wanna live here, though. I only wanna come visit sometimes."

"Why not? We got everything over here, and it's way more fun."

"Because I miss Mommy," Mia whispered across the room.

"I do too. But she did used to yell at us all the time, though. And we always had to stay home by ourself."

"Yeah, you're right."

"Miss Laiken don't hardly say nothing to us, and she be here to watch us, but she don't care what we do."

"I think she don't like us," said Mia.

"I do, 'cause she lets us do everything," Cara replied.

"We got to do a lot of stuff at home, though."

"But we always had to wait until Mommy won't there. Ms. Laiken don't care," Cara noted. "The other day I heard Michael tell her to shut up."

"Ohh!" Mia gasped. "She didn't say anything?"

"Nope. She was like, 'Don't you talk to me like that,'" Cara answered, mocking Laiken. "But he just walked right out the room."

"For real?"

"Yep. Both of them be saying stuff to her like that," Cara added, referring to Jonathan as well as Michael. "We woulda got smacked for saying that and woulda got smacked again for walking out while Mommy was talking."

"I know!" Mia confirmed.

"They don't talk to Daddy that way. He probably would beat their butts!"

"I don't think so. He's too nice."

"He always look sad. I think him and Miss Laiken are gonna get a divorce."

"What is that?" asked Mia.

"That is when two people have to go to court for something, and it was too bad for the police to handle, so they have to tell a judge. Then, after they talk to the judge, he gets to say who the bad person was so they can go to jail."

"So what do you think they did that was so bad?"

"I don't know. I think he did something that was real, real hardheaded or something, 'cause I heard him say, 'I'll do whatever you say from now on—whatever it takes.' That's what you always supposed to say if you didn't do what somebody told you to do. He probably didn't take out the trash or something. That what husbands are supposed to do."

"That's not what husbands do, 'cause Mommy used to make us do it all the time," Mia declared.

"Because if you don't have a husband, then the kids supposed to do it, but if you married, then it's the husband's job," Cara informed her.

"If you're a wife, then you're supposed to cook," Mia added.

"You're supposed to do that if you're a mom, too. Miss Laiken cooks all the time. Mommy didn't cook that much, though."

"Yes, she did," Mia said, defending her mother. "She fixed us hot dogs and noodles and stuff."

"Yeah, but Miss Laiken cooks rich people food, like steak and them skinny green things that's pointy on the end. I think it's asparagus or something."

"Mommy cooked stuff like that sometimes, too."

"But not for us. Only for her boyfriends. Miss Laiken cook stuff like that for us almost every day," said Cara.

"Sometimes I just want hot dogs, though."

"Me too. That green stuff is nasty!" Both girls giggled.

"Do you think Mommy and Daddy got a divorce? 'Cause they had to go to court," Mia asked, basing her reasoning on her sister's definition of divorce.

"Yep. That's why she had to go to jail."

5

Marvin watched from the sidelines as his team ran the court, crushing their opponents. Due to Marvin's coaching ability and the team's dedication, they were undefeated for the season and were headed for another win.

"Coach Temple, you have quite an impressive track record with creating dynamic, winning teams. We've seen you do it over and over again. Can you share with us what is at the core of your success?"

Marvin placed his hands on his hips and seemed to study the floorboards as he answered the interviewer's questions right after a winning performance at an NCAA play-off game.

"Well, first of all, I work with a tremendous team of young men who are all committed and dedicated to the profession of basketball. Not only are they incredible athletes, but they are incredible students, which is first and foremost. I've always driven home that principle for every team I've ever coached. Then we're a family off the court first, then on the court. In addition to that, I encourage them to have strong support systems, both on and off the team."

"And who is your support system off the court?" the interviewer asked, prying.

Marvin smiled, like he always did when Dominique came to his mind. "Well, of course, God makes all things possible, and my amazing wife makes all things bearable and enjoyable."

"And it seems to be working very well for you. Congratulations to you and the team," the interviewer said, ending the interview.

Exhausted but exhilarated, Marvin drove home. It was late, but he hoped Dominique would be up waiting for him. She generally would greet him when he came home after a game, whether the team had won or lost, but since she was pregnant, he understood that she needed her rest and was operating with a new bedtime curfew.

Quietly he eased into their bedroom, where she lay sleeping silently. He smiled at his angel, brushed his teeth, then slid into bed, easing his arms around her. Instinctively she nestled against him, letting out a comforting moan.

"Great job, baby," she commented, easily waking.

"You caught us?" He pressed his lips against her forehead.

"Of course. Wouldn't have miss it. I saw your interview, too," she said with a sleepy grin. "You give me too much credit."

"I couldn't do it without you, babe. You deserve that credit and more. You're my backbone." Marvin kissed his wife again.

"And you're my sweetest love," she replied.

"How are you feeling?" he asked, rubbing her swollen middle.

"Pretty good. She's been kicking today."

"She?" Marvin asked excitedly.

"I don't know for sure, but I think she's a she."

"And that's fine with me." He chuckled. There was a brief moment of silence before Marvin spoke again. "You asleep?"

"Almost," she whispered.

"You're the best part of my day," he whispered back.

"Better than you guys winning tonight?" she teased.

"I've won games all my life." He paused pensively. "I've gotten all kinds of trophies, won championships, and all that, but it's never completed me. Winning games has always been great, but I still had a void in my life—until I met you."

Dominique tilted her head upward and kissed Marvin's lips. "You're the best husband ever," she commented.

"That's because I love you." His arms tightened around her. "You're the inspiration behind everything I do."

"So when is your next game?"

"We hit the road tomorrow, babe. On our way to Kansas City. Then if we win, we go to Maryland."

"You'll do it. You always do."

"Jerrafine, what you plan on doing today?" Mary asked from the stove, where she stood scrambling a couple of eggs. She was still in a thin cotton house robe, slippers, and rollers. "Now, I know it ain't easy, but you can find a job doing something!"

"Ma, I been looking," Feenie whined like a teenager, which was exactly how she felt her mother was treating her. "Ain't nobody calling me back." It had been more than fifteen years since Feenie had held a job, and that wasn't working in her favor.

"Where have you applied?" Mary's question was rhetorical; she didn't pause for an answer. "Seem like to me, if I was really looking for a job, I'd be down at the unemployment office, meeting them there every morning."

"And what good is that gonna do, Ma, if I don't have no résumé and no job experience? What? You think they gonna get tired of looking at me and just let me start working there?"

"You never know how God gone move, chile," Mary said, trying to be encouraging, but Feenie didn't take it as such. She rolled her eyes behind her mother's turned back. "If them people saw your persistence, they won't be able to help but find you something." Mary put a plate of cheese eggs, grits, link sausage, and toast on a plate, then offered it to her daughter, and then piled the same on another plate for herself. "You gonna have to do something."

"I'm working on it, Ma."

"If I gotta work, you gotta work."

Feenie gave no response. She was tired of hearing the same speech almost daily. And she was tired of waiting for the phone to ring with a minimum-wage job offer. On top of that, her frustration was consuming more and more emotional energy, fueled by staying in her mother's home, having to ask for money every time she needed something, and having to get a lecture right after.

The two ate silently at the table for several minutes while Mary watched *Good Morning America* on a small TV nestled into a corner on the kitchen counter, but Feenie's thoughts were elsewhere. The game of manipulating men out of their cash was still fresh in her mind, and if anybody knew how to play the game, she certainly did. The only thing was, Feenie didn't want to go back to her old ways.

"Well, I've got to be at Dillard's in about an hour," Mary said, rising from the table and placing her plate in the sink.

Thirty minutes later, dressed in casual slacks and a blouse, Mary headed out for work. "I hope by the time I get home, you'll be done finding something to do wit yourself."

"Love you, too, Ma," Feenie replied sarcastically.

She retreated to her bedroom, plopped on the bed, and stared upward. "What can I do? What can I do!" she yelled, slapping a hand across her eyes. Stripping came to mind, but if Mary ever found out, Feenie would be on the streets for sure. Drugs were just out of the question. Selling Mary Kay and Avon both required up-front financial investments, not to mention doing face-to-face sales, which Feenie wasn't confident enough to do. She lay in thought for about ten minutes, then jumped to her feet with an idea.

Feenie headed to the garage, found an old tattered box, from which she tore off a panel, walked into the kitchen, then dug through a kitchen drawer until she found a black marker. After a few minutes of thought, she used her sloppiest handwriting to pen the words: "Homeless. Don't want my daughters sleeping on the street. Please help."

Panhandlers were common where she lived, and she couldn't count the times she'd seen cars pause for a moment at a light, with whoever was doing the begging for the day running to the window to grab a dollar bill or two. Feenie figured it would at least help her get the money she needed for the security deposit and first month's rent for an apartment.

Already dressed in tattered jeans and an oversize, faded blue T-shirt and a zippered sweat jacket, Feenie slid into a pair of flip-flops. With twenty-two dollars to her name, Feenie folded her sign, stuffed it in a backpack with a few bottles of water and a ball cap, called a cab, and waited. When it arrived, she asked to be taken to the Port Covington Drive Wal-Mart, which was far enough from where she lived that she felt no one she knew would see or recognize her. During the ride, she undid the two braids that circled each side of her head, then ran her fingers through her hair to further dishevel it. She pulled the ball cap from her backpack and fit it over her mane, leaving tufts of hair poofing out from underneath.

"Here is good," she instructed the driver just as he pulled into the lot. He moved out of the flow of traffic and came to a stop. "Thanks." Feenie handed him a twenty, waited for her dollar and five cents change, slid out of the backseat, then walked to the lot's entrance. In seconds her shop was open and turning a profit. She stood, shifting her weight from side to side, holding her sign, collecting dollars and coins, and dropping them into her backpack, which now hung from her front, instead of her back, for easy access.

"Thank you. God bless you," she said to every single person who held money out toward her. Feenie was both humbled and grateful, but embarrassed to a certain degree. Several cars flew by, donating obscenities and harsh looks instead of money.

"Get a freakin' job, crackhead!"

"Even a ho gotta do some work for the money!"

"Welfare tramp!"

Within a few hours, Feenie had heard it all, but she did not move from her post. She fed dollar after dollar into the open mouth of her backpack, encouraged by its slowly growing weight. She took a break only to use the bathroom, folding up her sign and dashing into a nearby Taco Bell. While inside the stall, she quickly counted out the bills, which totaled more than two hundred dollars. She glanced at her watch and did some quick calculations in her head, figuring if she stayed in place for another four hours, through what was likely to be peak store hours, she could ride home with an easy five hundred tax-free dollars. She folded the paper money together, placed the bills across the crotch of her jeans, where she felt they would be most secure, zipped her jeans up, and headed back to her corner, thanking strangers for their random contributions.

One person even brought her a sandwich and a canned soda, and while food was not what she was after, she graciously accepted, sat on the ground with folded legs while the car's passengers looked on, and began to eat. She positioned the sign so that it remained propped up and visible to other passersby and wasted no time jumping to her feet, sandwich in hand, to collect whatever they were willing to hand her. It wasn't the best of jobs—really, it wasn't a job at all—but she felt good about it since she felt her efforts were honest. She was down on her luck and needed help to bring her girls home, just like her sign stated, which was the truth.

Several hours later Feenie pulled herself from the backseat of another cab, toting the backpack, which was now full of change, canned goods, and a few bags of fast food, along with some toiletries and personal items she'd picked up on the way home.

"Where you been, looking like that?" Mary asked as soon as Feenie stepped back in the door. Although Feenie had combed her hair back into place on her ride home, Mary knew that her overall look was not typical of her daughter.

"The library," Feenie stated. It was believable. "Found a few leads. I'll be out again tomorrow, too."

"That's good. See how God works?" Mary smiled. "I told you He could work it out."

"Yeah. I'm going to take a bath right quick." Feenie pulled the backpack up farther on her shoulder as she passed through the living room.

"Well, I left you something in there to eat."

"I'm not hungry, Ma, but thanks," Feenie replied, already halfway down the hall.

She went into the bathroom and closed the door behind her and began to draw her bath. She pulled a bottle of bath oil from her backpack and poured it by the capful under the running water. In an instant the fragrance of a soft vanilla musk filled the air. Feenie peeled off her jeans and collected the money from between her legs, took a seat on the closed toilet, and exhaled. The bills had absorbed the scent of her body, soaked by both the sun and sweat, and she crinkled her nose. "They can still be spent," she whispered, running the bills through her fingers, counting her "earnings." She stopped at 435 dollars and smiled to herself; the total didn't include the loose change all over the bottom of the backpack, which she planned to count later. She placed the bills in a side pocket.

With her clothes piled on the floor, Feenie slipped into the tub of hot water, lay back, and closed her eyes, thinking of how she could present herself as more needy. Maybe a tattered T-shirt, instead of a simple faded one, and a couple more rips in her jeans. *What I really need is one of the girls, with their hair all over the place, to stand with me,* she thought. *I'd probably make twice as much then. Maybe I can offer to baby-sit the girls.* She dismissed the thought after pondering it for a few minutes, knowing that having the girls out on the street, begging, would not help her reach her goal of regaining custody.

Nonetheless, visions of dollar bills floated across her mind, followed by things she'd be able to purchase easily. On the way home, her eyes had caught sight of Symphony Center, a luxury apartment complex in downtown Baltimore. She had visited the building when she was dating a former lover and had been awed by the upscale amenities. The spacious apartments featured up to 1,447 square feet of comfortable living space, and the complex had free garage parking, secured entrances, a business center, and a fitness center. What begging couldn't pay for, Rance could, once she reestablished child-support payments. She imagined coming home to a front-desk clerk who'd hand her any messages, and sitting in a marbled foyer, complete with a coffee bar and fireplace, which would be perfect for entertaining company that she didn't want in her personal living space. "A glass of wine would be so good right now," she whispered, further imagining herself in a new home.

Thinking about her next-day strategy, Feenie sank lower in the tub, allowing her hair to get wet. She fully immersed her head for two seconds, then came up for air. She planned to towel the excess moisture from her hair, then let it air-dry while she slept. By morning it would be a half-matted, half-bushy mess. Maybe it would be good for an extra hundred dollars.

"How long you plan on being in there?" Mary called through the door, interrupting Feenine's peace.

Feenie sighed long and hard.

"Other folks gotta get in there, too!"

"I'm coming." Using her toes, Feenie pulled the stopper from the tub's drain, causing it to belch and echo throughout the bathroom. She pulled herself up from the cooling water, wrapped a towel around her still shapely body, gathered her clothes and backpack from the floor, and exited to her bedroom.

Reaching into the backpack again, she pulled out a package containing three pairs of hip-hugger panties, pulled one from the plastic, and slipped into them, then pulled on a clean T-shirt. Sitting on her bed, she counted out sixteen dollars in change, raked the coins into a shoe box, and nestled beneath her covers with a smile on her face. It wouldn't be long before she was back.

6

Church was the last place Feenie wanted to be that morning. Nonetheless, she dragged herself from bed, got in and out of the shower before Mary could start hollering about her water bill, and put on a black pencil skirt with a ruffled fuchsia blouse. She poured herself a cup of coffee as she waited for the toaster to brown and return the two slices of bread she'd entered into its slots.

Two weeks had passed since she'd left the walls of a cell, but work was slow in coming. With the Sunday paper spread out on the table, Feenie browsed the employment section of the classifieds, circling ads, although this method of job searching was far outdated. Mary did have a computer and a broadband connection, but she seemed to be much holier and sanctified than Feenie remembered and wouldn't allow her on the Internet before church. It was easier to comply than to argue, so Feenie would do her real job searching later that afternoon.

"You 'bout ready?" Mary called from her bedroom.

"Yeah. I'm in the kitchen," Feenie answered back, although she knew her mom was well aware of her whereabouts in the house.

Mary emerged from her room as sharp as a tack, dressed in a powder blue suit featuring silk panels and rhinestone trim, with a matching hat and purse. "That's what you wearing? I know I had a coupla suits back there in that closet you could have put on. That skirt a little bit short for a Sunday, ain't it?"

"I'm fine just like this," Feenie answered, ignoring her mother's disapproving look. Boy, had Mary changed over the years. She thought back to what she'd worn the day she married Marvin at eighteen. It had been so little fabric, it could hardly be called a dress. It had had just a bit more fabric than a tankini, and Mary had thought it was beautiful. Feenie shrugged it off, concluding that it was an aftereffect of getting old and getting saved.

"Well, let's go. I don't wanna be late."

Sunday morning service started off in a way that Feenie considered typical, yet she found it refreshing. Initially she felt ashamed and condemned. From what she remembered, Mary didn't have the smallest mouth in the world; on the contrary, there was little that her mother knew that she didn't share with the world. As Feenie caught the occasional glances of random parishioners, she wondered how many of them knew her story. "But today's a new day," she whispered to herself. Deciding to be less concerned about what others might or might not know, Feenie focused on the lyrics of the songs sung during the praise and worship portion of the service. It wasn't long before she forgot about the others and began to engage in the charismatic atmosphere. She even stood and clapped. Right before the pastor took the pulpit, the choir sang a well-executed rendition of Donnie McClurkin's "We Fall Down," which brought tears to Jerrafine's eyes. She dabbed her face with a tissue, thinking about the words that the group ministered.

"We fall down, but we get up," the lead singer crooned, causing Feenie to realize how far she'd fallen. For no reason that she could point out, Marvin popped into her mind. She remembered how cruel she'd been to him during their marriage, and because she had never loved Marvin, her despicable actions had come easy, as if she were without a conscience. Until now. Suddenly she was overwhelmed with feelings of guilt and remorse. The lies she'd told, the damage she'd caused, the torture she'd inflicted. For the first time in her life, she regretted her actions.

"Open your Bibles with me to Acts, the ninth chapter," the pastor began. "We're going to look at how God is not just the God of a second chance, but of a third, fourth, fifth, even one hundred and fifth chance." He gained a few amens from the congregation, then continued. "Now if anybody in the Bible deserved a lightning bolt from the Lord God Almighty to burn him up him on the spot, it was Saul of Tarsus.

Now, you all know the story. Saul was running from town to town, torturing and killing Christians, as many as he could round up. Now, don't you think Saul should have been punished for his blatant treachery against God?" A few words of agreement were shouted in response. "If some of us were God, we would have knocked Saul out, and put him six feet under. Am I right about it, church?"

"Amen!"

"But God, in his infinite mercy and grace, didn't do that. What God does instead is give Saul a second chance. Not only did God save him and convert him, but He went on to change his name and use him as an apostle. He used the man who was formerly Saul, but now was Paul, to preach His word. Now, if you read the rest of the story, you'll see that that didn't stop Paul from experiencing troublesome times in his life. Even after his great meeting with the Lord, Paul was shipwrecked, beaten, stoned, robbed, and imprisoned, yet God kept him from death, giving him chance after chance to complete the task He had destined for Paul.

"Now, church, I came to tell somebody today that you don't have to be Saul, converted to Paul, to receive a second chance—or third chance or millionth chance—from God. No. Christ has a second chance for anyone who needs it, including you. Maybe you've made some bad decisions that have taken you on a long, winding, twisted path. You feel like you have failed at life, and you think that dream is lost. I can tell you, though, from my own experience that we serve the God of second chances. I believe I'm 'bout on my fiftieth chance. But guess what, church? God don't keep score!"

The church went up in a frenzy of clapping and shouting.

"Whether it's a job, your marriage, your kids, or your finances, you might have made a mess of things, but God hasn't given up on you. He wants to heal you. He wants to turn that thing around for you and guide you into the purpose He has for your life. Not the purpose you thought you had, but His purpose! Nine times out of ten, what you have planned for your life is completely different from what God has mapped out for you. And if you just give him control, church, I'm a living witness that God will give you every tool and circumstance you need to accomplish His purpose.

"Now, a lot of times we look at the mess we done made and we think, 'Oh, God cain't do nothing with me. He cain't use me. He don't want me.' We think that God is too angry to forgive us, but, church, I'm so glad that God don't carry no grudges. He's quick to forgive us and give us that second chance. Jesus was always reaching out to people like you and me, people who needed a second chance. Some had enough faith to receive it, like the woman from the well or the woman caught up in adultery. They recognized their second chance and grabbed it! Recognize your second chance today, church. God wants to mend those broken places in your life if you let Him. Your life isn't wrecked for good. Paul went through a shipwreck, and

God still used him. God the Father is offering you a second chance today, and He has the power and creativity to do it. If you will say yes to the God of second chances today, I want you to make your way down to the altar."

Moved by the sermon, Feenie didn't tarry. With tears in her eyes, she pushed past Mary's knees and those of the others on her row and headed to the front of the church, ready to turn over a new leaf. She had to talk to Marvin.

7

Marvin Temple sat at the desk in his home office, sorting through the mail and going through his monthly ritual of reviewing his income versus expenses. Money for the Temple family was not tight by any means, not anymore, though he wasn't earning millions, which had once been right at his fingertips. He had spent several months volunteering as a basketball coach at his local Boys and Girls Clubs, then had gone on to put together and manage a few community leagues. With a couple of years' experience under his belt, he'd been able to be compensated for his passion when he took a job coaching on the high school level, which eventually paved the way for his position as the men's basketball coach of Old Dominion University. It had been a long time coming, and it was hardly the NBA, but Marvin had learned to count every blessing with a grateful heart.

With budgeting software pulled up on his computer monitor, he opened one envelope at a time, keyed in figures and due dates if necessary, and watched the numbers change on the screen. He went through seven envelopes before he got to a standard business envelope with no return address. Without a thought, he sliced through the paper with his letter opener and pulled out a single sheet of legal paper, covered with blue ink.

Dear Marvin,

I know you must be shocked to hear from me after all these years. I didn't put my name on the outside of the envelope, because I didn't want you to tear up or burn this letter without reading it first. I hope that you will take the time to do that, although I'm sure you've looked at the last page by now and realized it is from me.

Marvin paused right then and glanced at the writer's signature.

I really hope the years have been kind to you, because I did some really ugly things to screw your life up, and it's only through some serious reflection, prayer, and meditation that I have gotten to this point where I know it's necessary for me to give you my most humble and sincere apology.

There is nothing I can say to change the past and undo all the wrongs I've done to you. I was a sick individual, Marvin. Selfish, self-centered, egotistical, and conniving. I don't want to start trying to justify my actions, because truly I can say nothing in my defense.

I treated you horribly, and I regret it so much now. Back then I never gave your feelings a second thought, because I thought the world should and did revolve around me. I lived my life for several years believing that, but now I know better. I can hardly believe what a rotten, horrible person I was, and again, I am very sorry.

There is one other thing that I must tell you—a terrible secret that I've kept for many, many years. As I attempt to make peace with myself, I cannot continue to let you live a lie. I'd like to see you—just one time—to talk with you face-to-face. What I have to share shouldn't be shared through ink smeared on paper. Please, please call me so that we can set up a time to meet. I swear to you, I am not the same person that you knew years ago. I just want to meet to clear the record.

Jerrafine
301-555-1579

Marvin reread Feenie's letter three times, then stared at the phone number printed beneath her signature until his eyes blended and blurred the digits together. The day he and Feenie left the courthouse, depositions completed and divorce granted, he had promised himself that he would never, ever speak to Feenie again. Never.

His fingers toyed with the paper, folding and unfolding it again and again, while his mind journeyed back to his younger years, when he'd been in love with Feenie. It hadn't taken long after they'd said "I do" for Marvin to realize that it wasn't love that had brought them together. Not for Feenie, anyway. It was his promising NBA future she'd been after, the money, the notoriety, the fame, and the status of being a millionaire's wife. Marvin had felt incredibly stupid for not being able to see it before, thinking that what he and Feenie had was truly special—that she loved him for him. But once his NBA career was derailed by an ankle injury, Feenie had made her true feelings crystal clear.

What could this woman possibly have to tell me? he asked himself. He thought about every horrible, shocking thing he could imagine, but there was nothing that he could think of that somewhere along the course of their ten-year sham of a marriage Feenie hadn't done or tried. She'd refused him sex, dated and slept with other men, brought home sexually transmitted diseases, spent the bill money, damaged his property, cut his car tires, bleached his clothes, refused to clean up or cook, spewed words of hatred, and even pulled a gun on him once. He'd dealt with it all. And if there was something out there that he had not dealt with—something new that Feenie had done that she now wanted to come clean about— well, Marvin would just rather not know. He crumpled the letter in his palm and tossed it in the wastebasket. Even then, he still found it hard to focus on what he'd been doing before, so he sat, reliving and rethinking experience after dreadful experience with his first wife, Jerrafine Trotter.

The memories were painful, which was why

Marvin had kept them as far from his remembrance as he possibly could. Some wounds had not healed, and Feenie's letter was like salt. "She got me one time. She won't get me again."

"Babe." Dominique, Marvin's second wife of now three years, stood in the doorway, holding a glass of wine and a small plate of strawberries, cheese, and crackers. "I brought you something." Right away she noticed the pensive look on her husband's face. "What's wrong?"

"Nothin'." He pushed thoughts of Feenie from the forefront of his mind and gave Dominique a half smile. "Come here."

She stepped toward him, her slightly rounded belly leading the way. Marvin took the plate and glass from her hands, sat them on the desk, then wrapped his arms around her waist. Still seated, he was able to lay his head against her belly and enjoy her warmth and at the same time listen for the tiny heartbeat within his wife's womb. Dominique in turn rubbed Marvin's head, neck, and shoulders.

"I love you, baby," he whispered.

"And I love you back," Dominique replied without hesitation.

Marvin lifted her shirt and planted kisses on her smooth flesh, then rubbed a gentle hand over her stomach before giving a little squeeze. "How are you feeling today?" he asked.

Dominique had just gotten through her first trimester, during which her bouts of morning sickness had Marvin experiencing a type of morning sickness of his own. While Dominique's doctor had assured him that nausea and vomiting were par for the course, it didn't relieve his anxieties about his wife's health and that of the baby she carried.

"I feel fine, honey," she said, comforting him. She had to admit that Marvin's constant worrying irritated her sometimes, but she never took his caring for granted. "I think the worst is over. At least until July gets here and I go into labor." She giggled.

"I just don't want anything to happen to you two." Marvin had stated this more times than Dominique could count.

"And that's why I love you."

Marvin pulled his wife down on his lap and tilted his head up to kiss her. He reached for a strawberry and offered it to her lips, then kissed her again. "You didn't sip from this glass, did you?" he teased, knowing Dominique would rarely have a drink before she was expecting.

"You know me better than that." This time she reached for a strawberry and fed her husband.

Marvin thought about her words, and how much he had thought he knew Feenie years ago. Anytime Feenie crossed his mind, it made him appreciate and love Dominique even more. It had taken a while before he would even let himself think about a woman after he had finally ended things with Feenie. For four solid years, he had stayed completely to himself and focused solely on work, developing every team he touched into champions. There had been a few women who sought his attention, but he had been too broken to be open to any relationship, and too much of a gentleman to play with a woman's emotions. And there had been one or two that had caught his eye, but he'd always speculate about what could possibly be wrong with them, and thus he wouldn't let himself be interested. But the day he met Dominique that all changed.

Marvin hadn't been looking for anything or anyone when he walked into the barbershop for his weekly shaping. Dominique had just gotten out of the chair, for she wore her hair close, faded, and tapered, but distinctly feminine. That, along with her stature of just a quarter inch over five foot seven and a shapely 140 pounds, immediately captured his attention like no one before her ever had. She was strikingly beautiful; even still he was slow to act and said nothing. It wasn't until he happened to run into her later that day at Starbucks that he decided not to let the opportunity pass a second time.

"Excuse me," he greeted after clearing a bit of nervousness from his throat. As she looked up, he continued. "Your hair is very nice."

"Thank you," Dominique replied with a slight smile.

"You know, I think we have the same barber. Don't you go to the shop right there on Old Courthouse Way?" He took note of her open laptop, a small journal, and a pen that featured a lavender carnation on its end.

"Umm . . . yeah." She slightly raised her brow in a second of uncomfortable silence.

"Yeah, I thought I saw you there earlier today.

That cut is very becoming." Marvin realized he didn't have much else to say.

"Thanks."

"So what is your name?" he asked, stuttering.

"I don't give my name out to strangers," she replied after an intermittent pause, but she kept her tone cordial.

"Well, we're not really strangers, because we have the same barber," he countered.

Dominique pressed a finger to her lip in thought, then spoke. "Our affiliation at the barbershop does not negate the fact that I don't know you from a can of blue paint."

"Well, I can assure you I'm not a can of paint," Marvin said with a chuckle, which made Dominique giggle a bit. Once he saw that, he took his chances. "Would you like something to drink? I was just about to grab a cappuccino or something."

"I actually have a drink right here."

"How about a Danish? A muffin? A cookie?"

His bit of persistence caused Dominique to chuckle again. "I try to stay away from sweets."

"Oh, okay. Well, do you mind if I join you?"

He watched as she rolled her eyes upward, then answered, "Sure. Why not?"

Marvin cracked a small smile. "Okay. I'll be right back."

Minutes later he joined Dominique at her table, but then thought better of it as he noted how diligently she was working. "You know, if this is a bad time for you, I understand. But if you're not too busy tomorrow night, I'd love to take you to dinner."

Is this man crazy? He doesn't even know my name, Dominique thought. "No thank you. You're welcome to sit down while I'm here, but I'm not interested in dinner."

"Fair enough."

Marvin took a seat, and Dominique closed her laptop, stared directly at him, and flatly stated: "So now what?"

"How about we start with introductions. I'm Marvin." He extended a hand for a shake.

"Dominique," she said, accepting his hand.

"That's nice. So, are you in school?"

"I guess you could say that. I'm not a student. I teach English."

"Oh. What grade?"

"College level."

Marvin nodded.

"So what do you do?" she asked.

"Coach basketball at ODU."

Dominique's brows shot up. "Old Dominion?"

"That's it." He lifted his cup to his mouth and sipped.

"I've never seen you on campus," Dominique said with suspicion.

"Likewise. Do you go to the games?" he asked.

"Not really. I generally don't have time."

"You're missing some good stuff," he bragged. "I've gotten those boys tight this year."

"So I've heard. Basketball games just aren't my cup of tea, I guess."

"And what exactly is?"

"The arts. Writing, singing, plays, books and literature, libraries. That kind of thing."

Marvin nodded silently. "How about eating? Do you like to eat?"

"Excuse me?"

"You know, chicken, macaroni and cheese, lobster tail, baked potatoes, string beans, ham, rice pilaf . . . things that go in your mouth."

Dominique couldn't help but laugh. "You are too funny."

"What? Why?" Marvin questioned. "I'm serious." He chuckled.

She humored him with a response. "It's not one of my favorite pastimes, but I guess you could say I like to eat."

"That's great, because I like to cook, and I'd love to cook dinner for you."

Dominique gave it a few seconds of thought before she answered. "I don't know about that. You cooking would mean me coming to your place or you coming to mine, and I'm just not open to that right now."

"Understood. So how about I take you to dinner? Your favorite place, and you can meet me there. That way I won't know where you live, if you're uncomfortable with that, although it would be an honor to pick you up."

"I'll meet you," she immediately threw in.

They agreed upon a place, a date and a time, and Marvin handed her his business card, confirming to her that he was indeed the men's basketball coach at Old Dominion, then rose to his feet. "You enjoy the rest of your day, and I look forward to seeing you again."

Dominique simply nodded with a smile and watched Marvin's back as he left. Right away she pulled out her cell phone and called her sister, Tamara.

"What's up, sis?" Tamara answered.

"Nothing. Sitting here in Starbucks, catching a man." Dominique giggled.

"You make me sick doing that," Tamara replied, pouting. "I can stand outside buck naked with a sign that says SLEEP HERE FREE and not get as much attention as you on your worst-looking day."

"That's because you're so mean and focused. I keep telling you it doesn't hurt to smile every now and then. Smiling gets you a dinner date."

"Yeah, and it also gets me behind on my studying. But, anyway, who'd you catch?"

"Some dude named Marvin. He's actually the men's basketball coach at the school." Dominique flipped Marvin's card between her fingers while she spoke.

"What does he look like?"

"Like a basketball coach. Tall, athletic," Dominique said, describing him.

"What are his vitals?" Tamara asked, referring to his age and the number of kids he had.

"I don't know. We didn't get all into that."

"You're supposed to find all that out up front."

"I'll find out over dinner next week," Dominique promised. "We're going to Macaroni Grill."

"Girl, you need to go to Ruth's Chris Steak House. Now, that's a dinner date."

"You know what? You got a point there," Dominique agreed. "We can go to Macaroni Grill any old time, huh? I think I *will* go to Ruth's Chris."

"So you're going to call him, then?"

"I guess so." Dominique shrugged. "It's been a while since I've been entertained by man antics."

"Glad to know you have time for it. When's the date?"

"Next week."

"Let me know how it goes."

"For sure!"

By the time the following Friday rolled around, Dominique had nearly forgotten about her dinner date but found an unexpected re-minder in her in-box. Her e-mail had been easy for Marvin to find since they both were staff members at the same university.

From: martemp@oduu.com
To: Domisharpe@oduu.com
Subject: Dinner—Saturday at 7

Ms. Sharpe,
I look forward to seeing you tomorrow night. ☺
Marvin

Dominique smiled to herself, thought a bit, then clicked REPLY.

From: Domisharpe@oduu.com
To: martemp@oduu.com
Subject: Re: Dinner—Saturday at 7

Hello Mr. Temple,
Hope you don't mind the change in location.
Ruth's Chris Steak House? The address is 205
Central Park Avenue, Virginia Beach, VA 23462.

From: martemp@oduu.com
To: Domisharpe@oduu.com
Subject: RE: RE: Dinner—Saturday at 7

See you there!
M. Temple

The next evening Dominique dressed in a
white, draped, strapless dress, accented with
deep red accessories. Four inches were added
to her stature as she slipped into a pair of
Christian Louboutin petaled stilettos. Her hair
had a beautiful sheen courtesy of Miss Jessie's
Curly Buttercreme, and her skin had a glowing
bronze tone. A sheer gloss coated her lips, and
she touched her lashes with just a bit of brown
mascara, which opened her eyes but didn't give
her a made-up look. She looked like a natural-
born queen.

Marvin immediately stood to his feet when
he caught sight of her, completely mesmerized. Dominique smiled her greeting as she
approached.

"Wow," he said. "You look amazing."

"Thanks" she said, taking a seat in the chair
Marvin had chivalrously pulled out for her.
"You don't look too shabby yourself," she joked
glancing over Marvin's standard black slacks,

his pale yellow shirt, neatly tucked into his slacks, and his tweed sports jacket.

Dominique ordered lamb chops served with fresh mint, along with sweet potato casserole embellished with a pecan crust. Marvin chose oven-roasted, free-range double chicken breast stuffed with garlic-herb cheese and served with lemon butter, along with a side of creamed spinach topped with melted cheddar cheese. They both selected a salad of crisp romaine lettuce tossed with Romano cheese, garlic croutons, and creamy Caesar dressing, topped with shaved Parmesan cheese and sprinkled with fresh ground pepper.

"I'm glad you came," Marvin shared, a grin overtaking his face.

"Thanks for asking me."

"You're welcome. I can't believe that I've never run into you before," he stated as they shared an appetizer of barbecued shrimp. "You're not seeing anyone?" Marvin thought it better to ask now and be safe than to not ask and be sorry later.

"Don't you think you should have asked me that before now? Suppose my husband came bursting in the door, ready to jack you up?"

"I assumed you didn't have a husband, because there was no ring on your finger, but a boyfriend and sometimes a fiancé are a little bit more difficult to detect." He paused momentarily as he dabbed his mouth with his napkin. "So are you married?"

"No, I'm not," Dominique replied right away. "Nor do I have a boyfriend or a fiancé. What about you?"

"I definitely don't have a boyfriend," Marvin answered. "Never had one of those."

"Glad to know that!"

"I don't have a girlfriend, either, but I do have an ex-wife," he said honestly.

"When was the last time you saw her?" Dominique questioned, wondering if Marvin was truly a free man.

"The day our divorce was finalized, which was about ten years ago."

"Do you still talk to her?"

"Never," he answered.

"No kids' report cards to discuss?"

"Nope. No kids."

Dominique nodded slightly.

"What about you? Do you have children?" he asked.

"Not anymore." She pressed her lips together for a few seconds, then gave a sad smile. "I delivered my daughter two months too early, and she didn't make it. She only lived for a couple of hours, and I only got to hold her for a couple of minutes."

"I'm sorry to hear that, Dominique," he said with compassion.

"Thanks. I appreciate that. It was a long time ago, but sometimes it feels like just yesterday."

Marvin thought about the child he had never got to hold and wondered which situation was more painful. He thought that asking her how long ago it had been was insensitive, so he left it alone, figuring it would come up in a future conversation.

"What about your daughter's father? Do you still see him?"

"No. He got into drugs, and I just didn't have the desire to endure the effects that drug activity tends to have on people's lives. He almost cost me mine a couple of times, and I simply cannot live like that."

"I can understand that," Marvin commented.

"I don't know if you know what it's like to have a gun pressed to your head, but let me tell you, my experience with it wasn't pleasant," she added.

With perfect timing, the server presented them with their meals, allowing for the conversational tone to lighten.

"Mmm, this looks so good," she commented, looking down at her plate.

"It sure does. Yours looks better than mine. You wanna trade?" Marvin chuckled, bouncing his eyes back and forth between both plates.

"Your eyes may shine, and your teeth may grit . . ."

"Yeah, yeah, yeah, I know the rest. But none of that I'm gonna get," Marvin said, finishing the rhyme with a snicker. "Classic."

There had been no looking back since then. Within a few weeks, they began dating exclusively. Dominique found Marvin to be the most adoring and caring man she'd ever met and couldn't think of a time when she'd seen a better gentleman. Marvin saw Dominique as a queen and never treated her like anything less. Before long, Dominique made time in her schedule to attend more and more basketball games, becoming known as "the coach's girl-friend." When Marvin wasn't on the court, with love, he was preparing gourmet meals in either of their homes, massaging her feet, and show-ering her with gifts.

"The world's yours for the asking," he told her one hot and muggy July evening as they sat on the beach, in the sand. Dominique sat between his legs and leaned back on his chest, and he wrapped his arms tightly around her. Gentle waves washed ashore, momentarily cov-ering their feet and hips.

She turned and tilted her head toward him and pecked his jawline.

"There was a time in my life when I thought I had nothing in this world to live for." Marvin had long before shared with Dominique his most disappointing moments, so he didn't have to elaborate. Dominique knew from where his statement stemmed. "But then you came along."

She rubbed a handful of sand against her thighs as water rushed back toward the Atlantic Ocean as quickly as it had come forward.

"And now I have everything. Well, maybe not everything, but almost everything that's ever been important to me, because I have you in my life," he added.

After two years of blissful courtship, he made Dominique his wife, and he believed it was the best thing he'd ever done.

8

Marvin studied his phone's keypad for several minutes before slowly maneuvering his thumb to the digits that would connect him with his ex-wife. Not wanting her to have his number, no matter what her reason was for needing to speak to him, he first dialed *67, which meant his would be a private call on a caller ID system. His mind raced as the phone rang three times. Then Feenie answered.

"It's Marvin." He felt that anything more than that was unnecessary.

"Oh my goodness," Feenie gasped. "Marvin, I'm so glad you called."

It had been ten years, but her voice was familiar. Her tone had changed, though, he noted. The snappy, razor-sharp voice he still remembered from years before had been significantly softened. Her mellowness caught him off guard, yet he dared not let his defenses down.

"What do you want with me?"

"Marvin, there's something I need to tell you."

"You made that clear in your letter. What is it, Feenie?"

"I can't tell you on the phone. I need to see you."

"Listen, I don't have the time or the patience for this. Whatever it is you need to tell me, you better spit it out now."

"Please, Marvin. Not over the phone."

Becoming irritated, Marvin began to raise his voice. "I know you don't think I'm crazy enough to actually agree to see you!"

"I know it's asking a lot, considering our past, but I swear to you, Marvin, I am not the same person."

"And you expect me to believe that?" Marvin guffawed. "Are you on crack or something?"

Feenie gave no response.

"You have got to be out of your mind to even think . . . No, I have got to be out of *my* mind for even dialing your number. What the hell am *I* doing? Psshhh." He pushed a long breath through his barely parted lips. "Don't send me no more letters. Bye."

"Marvin, please don't hang up. Please," Feenie blurted but kept her tone even and low.

"Then what is it, Jerrafine? Speak now or forever hold your peace, and I do mean forever!"

"I really don't want to tell you this over the phone, Marvin. I need . . ."

Before she could finish her sentence, Marvin slammed his phone closed, ending the call. "Maniac," he uttered. Shaking his head, he stuffed the cell phone into his pocket, heaved his bag over his shoulder, and left the gym.

Feenie couldn't hold back the tears as she stared at the face of her cell phone. They trickled from her eyes but didn't make it far beyond that before she smudged them away, thinking about what had just happened. There was so much she wanted to say to redeem herself if given the chance. She didn't know why she expected this to be so easy. Why she expected Marvin and Rance and the rest of the world to simply accept and believe her.

Pulling the cord, she signaled to the driver to slow the bus for the next stop. The Social Services building was just up the street, and the walk there would give her enough time to try to clear her thoughts and compose herself. During her walk, she quoted a few scriptures out loud in an attempt to lift her spirits. "Let us not be weary in well doing, for in due season we shall reap, if we faint not."

She must have said it more than fifty times before she made it to the office doors. Feenie took a seat in the lobby and waited for thirty minutes past her appointment time, listening for her name to be called. A magazine article on preparing quick meals kept her mind fairly occupied in the meantime. When she finished it, she stormed to the counter out of turn.

"When is someone going to call my name? I been sittin' out here all morning, waiting for my appointment, and ain't nobody came out here yet," she declared.

"Ma'am, we will get to you as soon as we can. Please have a seat," said the clerk.

"No, I'ma stand right here and worry you to death until somebody come get me. This don't make no sense how y'all got people waiting in here all day, then got the nerve to treat us like we trash when we do get back there."

"Ma'am, I'm going to have to ask you to have a seat."

"I will, after you call who ever supposed to be talking to me and tell them to get their sorry behinds down here," Feenie stormed.

"Ma'am, if you don't take a seat, I'm going to have to call security," the clerk warned.

"Call them then. I don't care. . . ."

"Jerrafine Trotter," a voice called from behind her.

Feenie whipped her head around and identified herself. "Right here." She waved. "It took you long enough." She left the clerk's desk and followed behind her caseworker.

"Have a seat, Mrs. Trotter," Bernice McMahn offered to her client. "Now, how can I help you?"

"I just really want to get my children back." Feenie sat, explaining to Bernice how it came to be that she no longer had custody of her children. She knew that the social worker had this information at her disposal with just a few keystrokes on her computer; nonetheless, Feenie was cooperative.

"And where is it that they're currently residing?"

"They've been with their father ever since I went to jail."

"And was he supporting them financially before that?" Bernice asked, assuming that Feenie was a welfare recipient.

"Yes, he was," Feenie answered flatly.

"Were you receiving any benefits at all, like food stamps or Medicaid?"

"No."

"Were you on Section Eight?"

Feenie struggled to not take offense. "Not at all."

"Where were you working?"

"I didn't work. My girls' father supported us fully."

"Were you married to him?"

"No, I wasn't," Feenie answered, still struggling to not take offense. "Look, I need to know what I need to do to get them back."

"Would your children's father be opposed to releasing the children back to you?"

"I don't think so. He is married and has other kids, so I'm sure he won't have a problem with them coming back home to me."

"Well, many times in a situation where a parent has been absent for several months and the children have been living with the other parent, that other parent is not so anxious to release the kids."

"I'm pretty sure he won't have a problem giving them back to me. I just need to know what all I need to do."

"Well, we need to ensure that these girls can be properly supported. Looking over your file,

I see you were charged with neglect. What were the details regarding that?"

Feenie sighed, again knowing that the full details no doubt had been recorded and kept on file. "I left the girls home alone a few times."

"But you said you weren't working. Why were they left alone?"

"I can't justify my behavior," Feenie answered, shaking her head. She was too embarrassed to be forthcoming about her whereabouts when she left her two eight-year-olds home by themselves. "It was foolish decision making on my part."

"And where are you living?" Bernice asked.

"I've not secured a place yet. Right now I'm living at my mom's house, but I was hoping that you all could possibly help me out with that."

"I do have some subsidized-housing complexes that I can send you to, but usually they have lengthy waiting lists. Do you plan on getting a job?"

"Yes. I've been looking every day, but I haven't found anything yet," Feenie confessed.

"So you really don't have any means of supporting your children? Nor do you have a home for them?"

"Like I said, I'm living with my mom, and she has room for the three of us," Feenie stated, although she knew Mary was not looking for or encouraging any roommates. "She's helping me to get on my feet."

"Well, to be honest with you, until you are on your feet, not getting on your feet, I can't see your children being returned to you. Especially given that you have a neglect charge on your record. Now, with you seeking employment, are you going to have proper child care lined up for your girls?"

"I don't right now, but I will."

"Uh-huh," Bernice commented, looking over her glasses. "I suggest you go ahead and get a job and find a home, and in the meantime, talk to their father to see if he's comfortable with releasing the children back to you."

"Yes, ma'am."

"I'm also going to suggest you take a parenting class to learn how to interact with your girls on a more positive level. I saw some of the comments that were made, and what your girls had to say about you and your discipline methods is very interesting." She paused, peering at Feenie over her glasses again. "Would you be opposed to that?"

"No, I'm open to doing whatever it takes to bring my babies home. I've got to get them back again," Feenie replied.

"That's good to hear. Let me give you this information packet so that you can read over the course details and make whatever adjustments necessary for you to attend the classes." Bernice handed Feenie a brochure and gave her a few minutes to look over it. "Which session do you want to start attending?"

"As soon as the next one starts. How soon is that?"

"I believe there is one starting up in about two weeks. It's a thirteen-week course, so you will be going one night a week for the next few months."

"That's no problem."

"Now, will you be applying for benefits?"

Feenie hadn't given much thought to applying for welfare. She had always taken advantage of utilizing other people's money and had never needed to live off of "the system." For a split second, she thought about who she could manipulate out of some immediate cash, but she quickly came to herself. If she was going to make it, she knew she had to stand on her own two feet, even if it meant getting government assistance temporarily.

"Yes, I'll be applying. I just need a little help until I can get more established," she replied.

"Okay, well, after you leave my office, go ahead and stop downstairs so you can see a caseworker today. I'm going to go ahead and get you registered in the next Strengthening Families class, and someone should be calling to confirm that with you in the next week or so."

"Thank you, Ms. McMahn." Feenie stood to her feet and extended her hand. "Hopefully, I can get my girls back real soon."

"It's going to take some work, but you can do it." Bernice smiled as she shook Feenie's hand. "Give me a call if you have any questions or anything."

Feenie left the office with mixed emotions. On one hand, she felt she was making a tiny bit of progress toward getting Mia and Cara back into her possession. On the other hand, the goal seemed so far away. She reasoned that during the thirteen weeks that she'd be taking the parenting class, she would use that time to find a job and an apartment.

9

These weeks should fly by, Feenie told herself as she boarded the city bus to take the scenic route home. On the way, she decided to get off and walk to Symphony Center, just to take a look around. Knowing that the building's entrance was secured, she tried to time her approach to coincide with any resident who would be coming in for the day. As a cover, she pulled an *Essence* magazine from her bag, pretending to read as she walked. It wasn't long before she noticed a man in a suit walking up, approaching the door. She quickened her steps, trying to keep her nose partially buried between the pages, but timing her stride to make it inside the door.

"Feenie, is that you?" the gentleman called.

Surprised, Jerrafine looked up and saw the face of Bryan West, a former lover she'd put it on so good, she couldn't get rid of him when she was done using him.

"Hey, Bryan!" She feigned excitement.

He extended his arms toward her for a cordial hug. "Hey, girl, long time no see, no call, no nothing!" He laughed. "What are you doing here? You live out here now or just visiting somebody?" he asked, sizing her up with his eyes as he punched an entrance code into the door's electronic keypad.

"No, I was actually looking into getting a place out here," she answered and flashed him a smile that made him remember old times. "I've passed by here a couple of times and looked it up online. It looks like a pretty nice place to live. I thought I'd check it out."

"Well, let me let you in." He nodded and licked his lips. "I see you still keepin' it tight and everything," he complimented, more for his selfish gain than out of sincerity.

Mentally Feenie rolled her eyes, thinking back on how unattractive and unfulfilling she had found Bryan to be. She had spent two years privately entertaining him strictly for the benefits, making him think he performed like Superman. But Feenie's reality had been that he left a lot to be desired.

"You look good," Bryan added.

"Thanks." Feenie's eyes bucked as they absorbed the posh lobby, which contained exquisite furnishings, a large-screen TV, and a coffee bar. "This is nice," she commented. "So, you rent here?"

"Yeah, I got a place here. I've been out here about three years now."

"So I take it you like it then?"

"It's all right. It's all right." He nodded again.

"They got coffee and everything," she said, almost in a trance, walking over to the bar. "I'm 'bout to get somma this. Is it free?" she asked just before pouring the java into a mug provided on the bar.

"It's complimentary." Bryan chuckled. "Help yourself. Matter of fact, I think I'll join you so we can catch up a bit." Bryan pulled a mug from the mug rack and poured himself a cup of decaf. He added a bit of hazelnut creamer, but no sugar, and circled a stirrer around the inside perimeter of his mug, perfectly blending the liquids.

Feenie had already taken a seat on a sofa facing the TV and blew into her mug to slightly cool her coffee.

Bryan sat on the opposite end of the sofa, not wanting to crowd her. "So what are you doing these days? You must be doing all right for yourself if you thinking about living here," he said between sips. "'Cause they're not asking for chump change."

"I do okay, I guess." Feenie shrugged. She wasn't about to share with her former lover that she'd become a full-time professional beggar. "Just making it work for me, you know?"

"Yeah, I heard that."

"What about you? Are you still down at city hall?"

"Yep, still there doing what I do."

"Which is what now?"

"I'm actually the city manager now," he bragged. The title explained the expensive but standard gray business suit he wore.

"Oh, you're doing big things!" she replied, impressed. "Ain't nobody scooped you up and took you home to meet they daddy yet?" she teased, leaning a bit to her left and looking around at his left hand, in search of a ring.

"Nah. I'm not there yet. You ain't got no man, either, I see, or do you?"

"I'm still flying solo. Haven't found Mr. Right yet, I guess."

"Cool." Bryan paused and bit into his lower lip. "Maybe we can get together and chill." He shrugged nonchalantly. "Especially if we're gonna be neighbors."

"Maybe." Feenie winked, then glanced down at her wrist. "Well, I only have a few minutes to get to my tour appointment."

"If you want, I can show you my place. That way you don't have to rush."

She thought about it momentarily so as not to seem so anxious.

"I mean, wouldn't you rather see a furnished place instead of a big old empty one?" he asked.

"I'm sure they have a furnished unit to show."

"But it's not as nice as mine," he coaxed.

What's in this for me? Feenie thought to herself. She was working on changing, but she still had a few tricks saved in her memory bank. *I may need a cosigner or a recommendation to get in this place.*

"I guess I could do that," she agreed with a shrug. "That is, if you're not doing anything."

This time it was Bryan who glanced at his wrist. "I got a few minutes before my next appointment.

Come on up," he said, stepping toward the elevator.

"Thanks, Bryan."

Feenie's heels clicked across the marble tile floor keeping in perfect step with Bryan. She was thankful that because she'd had an appointment that morning, she wasn't clad in her begging jeans and ragged wife beater. Instead, she wore a turquoise knee-length dress accented with cocoa brown pumps and wooden beaded jewelry. She'd used gel to create sista twists in her hair, then pushed them back from her face with a headband, which gave her the look of an eclectic natural beauty. Cocoa butter gave her skin a radiant and healthy glow, which Bryan took note of.

After a quick ride in the elevator, he led her to his apartment door, slid the key in its lock, and with a twist of the knob, offered his home to her for a visit. Just as she had suspected, Bryan's apartment was impeccable.

He led her from room to room, pointing out features as if he worked in the leasing office, saving his bedroom for last. "And this is the master suite." He motioned her to enter with an outstretched hand.

The large room was split in the center by a three-sided fireplace enclosed by glass. His king-size cherrywood bed, covered with a luxury comforter set and matching pillows, sat to the right, while a work and sitting area was to the left. Feenie sauntered over to take a seat in one of the two armchairs that faced the fireplace, crossed her legs, and picked up a copy of *Forbes* magazine for just a few seconds.

"This is nice, Bryan," she commented, imagining how she'd decorate her own bedroom once she received approval for a unit.

"It's just a little something," he responded, busying himself in front of his dresser, then turning to open the doors of an expansive walk-in closet.

"Oooh!" Feenie cooed. "I love a man who knows how to keep a closet."

She entered behind him and ran a hand across several suits that had been neatly hung to her upper right. Below them, hanging just as neatly, were slacks. Long-sleeved shirts were arranged by color, starting with white and trickling through the rainbow and ending at black, and rows of shoes were on display on several tilted shelves. Bryan followed Feenie back to the far end of the closet, standing closely behind her.

"Remember what we used to do in here?" he asked, beginning to press against her backside. "Well, not in here, but in the closet at my old place." He placed his hands on Feenie's hips, allowing her to feel the pulse of his manhood.

"Yeah, I remember."

"I think this closet might need to be broken in," he whispered in her ear, letting his hands travel up her body to caress her breasts.

Feenie laughed and pulled away. "I thought you were going to show me your place."

"Oh, I got something to show you," he said, tugging at her arm, but Feenie wriggled a bit to free herself and strolled toward a huge floor-to-ceiling window.

"Great view," she commented, looking down at the city.

"Not as great as the one I have from back here," Bryan slyly replied, soaking in Feenie's curves first with his eyes only, but then nestling up behind her again and draping his arms around her waist. "Mmm, mmm, mmm," he exclaimed softly.

Feenie knew the game well, so she played along, slightly and subtly pushing her behind back against his manhood, which he pushed forward in response.

"What building is that over there?" she asked, pointing randomly. She knew Bryan couldn't care less, but it was part of the act.

"What building?" he whispered, beginning to place kisses on her neck. "I don't see any building."

"That one right there." She pushed back into him even more, slowly circling her hips.

"Where?" he asked, not bothering to look up.

"Down the street," she said, bending her knees just a bit, then standing straight again.

Bryan moaned in response.

"And around the corner," she added as she circled her hips seductively.

"Girl, you 'bout to find out," he panted lowly. "Tell me some more about it."

"Well, it looks like it's all brick. You know, something solid that I could lean on." Bryan held Feenie's hips and pressed forward. "Yeah, solid like that," she coached. "It's a big building, too."

"Is it now?" Bryan huffed, lapping at her neck.

"Uh-huh. I'm just wondering if it's as big as it seems, because from here it looks like it has some size, but if I look closer, it might just be a trick."

"Maybe you need to look a little closer. You need to see it right in your face," he suggested greedily.

"Do you think it has an elevator shaft? I sure would like to ride up and down." Again, Feenie lowered, then raised herself slightly against Bryan a few times.

"Girl," he drawled in a long breath. "Come on and ride." He took a step backward and pulled on Feenie's hips, encouraging her to follow him to his bed, but Feenie resisted. "Come on now. Stop playing." He tugged again.

"Uh-uh," she teased. "I got too much to do today and not enough time."

"What do you have to do? This ain't gonna take that long."

"A quick trip ain't what I'm after on this go-round. You got something to do and so do I." She pulled away from Bryan's grasp. "So we both need to take a rain check and get moving," she added, exiting the bedroom and heading for the bathroom.

Bryan let out a defeated sigh. "All right. Let's go." Quickly he straightened his clothes and stomped down the hallway. "Tease," he muttered under his breath as he passed the closed bathroom door. "Come on!" He yelled in frustration when he felt Feenie was dragging her feet.

Feenie stood in the bathroom, nearing tears as she stared at her reflection. More and more, she liked herself less and less. The woman who stared back at her was nothing more than a whore—selling herself over and over again for a paid cell-phone bill, a steak dinner, a pair of shoes, or a car payment. Feenie wanted to stop, but using her body was all she knew. She knew that the right man would pay the right price for the feeling of flesh wrapped around his own. Feenie used to love that feeling of power and control, maneuvering her body to bring a man to his knees. But now all Feenie felt was shame.

"This is the last time," she promised in a whisper. She splashed water over her face to wash away her trickling tears, then took a deep breath and closed her eyes. "Lord, please forgive me for what I'm about to do. Help me to change my ways. I don't want to keep doing this. I can't keep doing this. So please help me to stop." She stared into her own eyes. "This is the last time."

Feenie emerged from the bathroom completely naked, with the exception of her shoes and jewelry.

A grin spread across Bryan's face, and in an instant his erection began to bulge through his pants a second time. "I forgot how much you like to play." He chuckled.

"I want to see a bit more of the view," she said, turning back toward the bedroom. "I know you got somewhere to be, but do you mind staying with me for just a few minutes?"

"I think I can do that." Bryan began disrobing on his way toward her.

"Open the curtains," she instructed as she lay back on Bryan's bed. "I wanna look from here."

Silently Bryan walked to the window, drew the curtains back, then finished removing his clothes before approaching her. "This elevator 'bout to take you to the top, girl."

"So what do you think? Are you gonna try to move in?" Bryan held Feenie's body close to his own, exhausted but satisfied.

"I'ma try. I think I might need a recommendation, though. I got the money, but I haven't been working at my job very long."

"Where do you work at again?"

"Just at Wal-Mart right now," she answered semi-honestly. "I need something else though, especially if I'ma live out here."

"I'll help you," Bryan said, easily committing. "There's a couple of positions open for the city you could probably get with my reference."

"What kinda jobs they got?" she asked, hiding her frown. Collecting tax-free money from generous givers was the best thing going in her mind.

"I can check the job board and let you know, or you can just go online to look and apply. Just call me and let me know what you're interested in."

"Well, if I could just get a place first, that would help most. I gotta get my girls back, and I'm not gonna be able to get them until I do that." Feenie pulled away from Bryan, taking the sheet with her. "I need to go ahead on down here and at least fill out the application. I'm just scared they are going to deny it once they see my income."

"Well, let me ask you this," Bryan began but paused to measure his words. "Don't take this the wrong way, but how are you planning to pay rent?"

"I told you I got money."

"From where, if you don't mind me asking?"

"My daddy died a couple of months ago," she lied, then mentally blurted a prayer for forgiveness. "He left me a little something."

"Oh. I'm sorry to hear that. You okay?"

"Yeah. Some days are harder than others," she said, mimicking what she'd heard several bereaved people say. The truth was, Jerrafine's father had never been around. He and Mary had broken up shortly after Feenie was born, and he had found several things to do other than raise his daughter. If she ran smack-dab into him on the street and their eyes met, she wouldn't recognize him, but the lie came easily. "The money helps, but it doesn't even come close to filling the void, you know?"

"I can't even imagine," he answered apologetically.

"I wouldn't wish it on my worst enemy." Feenie forced a single tear to roll down her face.

"Let me know what I can do to help," Bryan offered.

Bingo! She paused before she spoke, gazing pensively out of the window. "Well, if you could just help me get this place, I would really appreciate it."

Within one week Feenie had the keys to her new apartment at Symphony Center, with the first three months paid in full, despite the fact that she didn't even have a checking account.

10

Taking a seat at the desk in his home office, Rance turned his computer on to reply to a few e-mails that required his attention and was surprised to find a message from Jerrafine.

From: feeniefinesse@yahoo.com
To: rjalexander@thealexanderlawgroup.com
Subject: Mia and Cara

Rance,
I hope this e-mail finds you and your family in the best of health. I just wanted to let you know that I've been released and I'd like to get the girls back. I'm sure your wife has not been appreciative of their presence, but I can't thank you enough for seeing after them while I've been away.
Please contact me at 301-555-1579 so that we can discuss making this transition. I am not opposed to your wife being a part of these conversations if she'd like to be.
Jerrafine

Rance had been aware of Feenie's release time frame but hadn't particularly anticipated her wanting the girls back, being that she had not provided the best care while they were with her. His feelings were mixed. He loved Mia and Cara, and even more so now that they'd lived in his home, but knew having them out of his home would give him a better chance of patching things up with Laiken. Then again, he was sure Feenie wasn't going to take the kids without an agreement of exorbitant financial support from him. And who was to say that Feenie wouldn't do something else to endanger the girls' lives? What kind of woman was she now that she'd spent time behind bars? What kind of company would she keep? Thugs covered with tattoos, toting pockets full of marijuana, cocaine, crack, or other substances that he wouldn't want his daughters near? Would his girls be safe? He chewed his bottom lip in contemplation, weighing the factors. He knew Cara and Mia missed their mother terribly and probably would have no reservations about going back to live with her. But would it be the right thing to do?

And what was the reality of Laiken truly forgiving him and them being able to move on? There definitely were no guarantees where that was concerned. For the here and now, Rance felt like he was doing everything he could to hold on to the fragments of their shattered marriage, and while Laiken was still there, he saw no effort on her part. Maybe his expectations were unrealistic. If it were she that had done the unthinkable, he could admit to himself he probably wouldn't be quick to forgive.

He wasn't sure how long he'd be able to hold on to the invisible hope of reconciliation. All he could do was take things one day at a time and wait for Laiken to come around—if she ever would. In the meantime, he tried doing everything he knew how to give her no further concerns. That meant updating her on his whereabouts every single minute of the day. It meant striving to take her calls each and every time she called the office or his cell. And sometimes she called both in succession just to see if he would pick up. It meant giving her a key to his office so that she could drop by anytime, after hours included. It meant surrendering his cell phone upon request and allowing her to scroll through his text messages, e-mails, address book, contacts, and anything else she wanted to inspect. Laiken would often ask, "Who was that?" after he ended any phone call, regardless of the business tone in his voice or the legal jargon he'd use. She questioned everything he did, no matter how small and seemingly innocent. A loosened tie at the end of his workday was an indicator to Laiken that at some point in his day a woman had helped him become a little more comfortable. A neat tie was a sign that he'd gotten completely undressed during his day for illicit sex, then redressed. Every late meeting was suspect; every lunch engagement was questionable.

He'd submitted to all Laiken's scrutiny for the past year and a half, and some days he felt like it just wasn't worth it. In his opinion, she wasn't interested in working things out; she was more consumed with catching him doing something wrong. He thought he'd be able to take it all, but every day it became more and more unbearable.

Were his girls worth his marriage, or was his marriage worth his girls? He didn't know the answer to that, sitting at his computer, rereading Feenie's request. Even trying to reply was hard. Surely if he responded via e-mail, and if he copied Laiken on his response, she would come with a flurry of questions and accusations about how long they'd been in contact. If he hid it from her and she found out, any progress he'd made, which he was sure was very little, would instantly be undone. He started to just jot the number down to give Feenie a call later but thought better of it. That was all he needed, a random number jotted on a sticky note that connected him to Feenie. Rance let out a heavy sigh and shook his head slowly. He concluded that no matter how he decided to handle the situation, the results would not be favorable. He could do nothing else but be honest.

Clicking on REPLY, then adding his wife's e-mail address in the CC line, he started on his response.

From: jalexander@thealexanderlawgroup.com
To: feeniefinesse@yahoo.com
Subject: RE: Mia and Cara

Jerrafine,
Are you working with a counselor or social worker?

Please have her contact me via e-mail to establish a
meeting time to discuss this matter. It is imperative
that my wife is included in all communication. I've
included her in this response for that reason.

He didn't bother with a signature line before
clicking SEND. Now, what was Laiken going to say
about this? In that instant, he wished he could
recall his reply to Feenie, realizing that a better
strategy might have been to talk to Laiken first.
He couldn't imagine that she would want to care
for the girls longer than necessary, but he still
should have given her the respect of presenting
the options to her and having some level of dis-
cussion around them. Rance stood to his feet
and trod to the kitchen, where she was preparing breakfast for the children.

They'd long gotten out of the habit of greeting each other with "Good morning," so while
this was his first time laying eyes on his wife
that morning, he skipped the niceties and
cut to the chase. "We need to talk." He leaned
back against the countertop and folded his arms
across his chest.

Initially Laiken didn't respond, but before
long she commented, "About what, Rance?
You've been hiding more kids across town, and
all of a sudden they need a home?"

Ignoring her cynical question, Rance moved
on. "Jerrafine wants the girls back."

This time Laiken's arms crossed her chest.
"How do you know that?"

"She sent me an e-mail saying that she has been
released and would like the girls to come home."

"Oh." Her response was less defensive than before.

"Well, what are your thoughts?"

"What are my thoughts?" she repeated. "What do you mean, what are my thoughts? You tell me what you would think if you were me. Suppose I came home carrying not one but two of some other man's kids and dumped them in your lap and asked you to freaking take care of them every day while I waited for him to get out of prison. How do you think you would feel about me talking to him after he got out so we could probably make plans to start our little secret rendezvous all over again while you stay home and see after our kids." She paused only to tighten her lips in a ball for a few seconds. "Do you think you'd be ready for them to go back with their dad? Or would you say, 'Oh that's all right, honey. I want to take care of your little bastard children forever!'" she mocked as she dried her hand on a dish towel, slammed it as best she could on the countertop, and stormed from the room.

Rance remained in the kitchen, his feet seemingly frozen in one place. In retrospect, it was a loaded question, he admitted silently to himself. He couldn't have expected anything different than Laiken's tirade, although he had hoped for a more peaceable response.

He sighed, wondering if there was any solution to the situation. He was nearing his breaking point, feeling that there would never be any resolution or compromise, but the last thing he wanted to do was walk out on his family under the conditions that he'd put them under. He certainly couldn't leave his daughters and expect his wife to care for them. And if he did leave, he knew it would mean living in an extended-stay hotel room. That was certainly no place to bring two girls.

Walking out was too expensive to consider. Laiken would be sure to get him on abandonment, on top of squeezing him for every copper penny she'd be able to get. So with all things considered, Rance figured he'd have to tough it out a while longer. Maybe Jerrafine would really pull it together and be able to provide a wholesome, safe, and nurturing environment for the girls. It would take an incredible amount of stress off of his head.

"But for now, it is what it is," Rance muttered.

11

Content with a small patch of grass beneath her feet, Feenie, dressed in her usual tattered jeans, a T-shirt, jacket, and flip-flops, held up her sign for passersby to see. She kept her countenance solemn and lowly, but inwardly she smiled to herself. She'd "upgraded" her sign to include the photo of the girls with their hair Afroed on their heads. That one change resulted in Feenie accepting nearly a third more donations of folded cash, in larger denominations.

The day was long and boring, but the money was easy. And between her ball cap and poofed hair, the earbuds to her MP3 player weren't even noticeable. She listened to a mix of John Legend, Mary J. Blige, and Raheem Devaughn, who all seemed to make the day pass a bit quicker.

So far Feenie had saved up just about five grand in the three weeks she'd been panhandling, and she was planning on continuing until she had about four times that, or at least until she could buy a car.

She sang a few songs out loud and thanked people in between, while spending money in her head. She'd already picked out her living-room and bedroom furniture, which would be delivered in the next few days. Every evening Feenie stopped somewhere to pick up some-thing to furnish her new home. Today would be Wal-Mart so she could pick up a few gro-ceries, along with her housewares.

Once inside the store later that day, she grabbed a shopping cart and slowly walked the aisles, selecting items. She made it to the cereal aisle and stopped to compare a few brands of toaster pastries. With only a second of warning, which was a burst of laughter, she felt her right ankle explode in pain as a child slammed into her with a cart.

"Ouch!" Feenie shrieked, dropping the boxes she held to reach down to grasp her leg. She glared at the child with twisted lips and fur-rowed brows, wishing she could retaliate.

"Sorry," the boy blurted, pulling away and speeding down the aisle, still in laughter, being chased by another boy, who was close behind with a cart of his own.

"Where is your mother!" Feenie yelled be-hind him, but he didn't stop. She puffed out a sigh, then stood again, highly irritated, to resume her shopping. She made her way, filling her cart with items from the next few aisles, then turned to the snack aisle and stopped in her tracks.

At one end the boy was coming nearly full speed with the cart, but in the middle of the aisle stood a woman, who was trying to convince a girl to put back several bags of chips. "Will you guys please stop!" she yelled at both kids, clearly frustrated.

"No!" the female child yelled, running forward to grab more bags of chips. Right away Feenie recognized the unkempt hair.

"Carance! Put those chips down right now!" Feenie ordered in a way that only a reprimanding mother could.

Cara halted immediately, and her head spun to meet her mother's eyes. "Mommy!" Cara exclaimed both in shock and joy. She put the bags down and ran to her mother, instantly wrapping her arms around her waist as Laiken only looked on in surprise. "Mommy, how'd you get here?"

Feenie hugged her daughter tightly for several seconds, while her heart beat wildly in her chest, excited and overwhelmed and taken completely by surprise at their chance meeting. Fighting back tears and clearing her throat, she pulled back a bit and made a failed attempt to smooth Cara's hair down with her hands. "I drove. Where is your sister?"

"She went to get some milk for Miss Laiken. We 'bout to go home with you?" Cara inquired.

"Not today. Why are you talking to Miss Laiken like that?" Feenie asked. "You know goodness well that that is not the way you talk to grown-ups, don't you?"

"Yes," Cara answered. She was several inches

taller than she'd been a year and a half ago. Right away Cara turned to Laiken. "I'm sorry, Miss Laiken," she mumbled, then turned back to her mother. "You still live in the same house?"

Before Feenie could provide a brief update, Mia rounded the corner, toting a gallon jug in both arms. She shrieked with delight when she saw Feenie, quickly dropped the milk into the cart at Laiken's side, then ran toward her mom.

"Mommy!" Like her twin before her, Mia tightened her arms around Feenie's waist. "You outta jail?" she asked in a loud voice, which seemed to Feenie to resonate throughout the entire store.

"What I tell you about your mouth?" Feenie whispered sternly.

"Sorry," Mia murmured.

"Mommy, why do you look like that?" Cara asked with furrowed brows, expressing confusion. She had never seen her mother look so disheveled in her whole life.

Feenie hadn't even given a thought to her appearance and would have been embarrassed if not for the wad of cash sandwiched between her legs.

"I just moved into a new apartment." The lie rushed forward from her lips before she could even think twice about it. "I've been pushing boxes, lifting stuff, and moving furniture all day. Why does your hair look like that?" Feenie reached into her backpack and pulled out her comb and brush right there in the middle of the aisle. "Come here," she ordered, although both children stood right by her.

Without delay, Cara subjected herself to her mother's hand by moving one step closer.

Laiken stood by, speechless at Feenie's power of command and control of her daughters. She had mixed emotions about coming face-to-face with the woman that her husband had had an affair and two illegitimate kids with. Laiken looked her over, soaking in every detail, disbelieving that Rance had found this ratty-looking woman with a bird's nest of a hairdo attractive enough to sleep with. It was difficult for her to see past the costumed facade and notice anything becoming about Feenie. She was offended, to say the least, and wanted to say something confrontational but couldn't find the words, having been caught off guard, so she stood with her arms folded across her chest, saying nothing at all.

"I hope you don't mind," Feenie said, glancing at Laiken for a brief second. "But they heads is a mess. What do you be puttin' in them?"

"What do you mean? Like shampoo and conditioner?" asked Laiken.

"No, I mean like hair grease and gel," Feenie replied.

Laiken shrugged. "Hair grease? What is that?"

"You got these girls' heads looking like straw."

"Excuse me?" Laiken narrowed her eyes incredulously. "You've got some nerve judging! You come whipping in here . . ." Laiken abruptly stopped her diatribe when she suddenly became aware of the two little girls, whose faces stared at her and who hung on her words.

Her eyes darted between both the girls, then at Feenie's eyes, and she bit her tongue. "Their hair was the least of my worries," she said, trying to keep her tone and language appropriate for the kids.

"I didn't mean any harm, Laiken." Feenie's softened pitch suggested sincerity. "I really didn't. I'm sorry for the way that came out. Please forgive me." Feenie whipped her daughter's hair into two braids that traced the perimeter of her head while she waited for Laiken's acceptance or refusal of her apology.

Laiken stood silent for several seconds, studying Feenie's face, then shrugged her shoulders and looked away. "I just didn't know what to do with it."

"I can show you," Feenie offered. "You gonna have to put something in it, some moisturizer or something."

"Well, can you show me while you're here?" Laiken asked.

Feenie nodded. "Yeah, come on. Mia? Come on. You next."

Together the four females walked over to the health and beauty aids section of the store, while Laiken's boys continued to run wild down other aisles.

"Thank you for seeing after my girls," Feenie offered without making eye contact. "I know it wasn't easy having to take them in, but I appreciate it."

"Oh," Laiken almost gasped.

"I can't say that I would have done the same so graciously, and I don't take what you've done for granted." This time Feenie's eyes met Laiken's; then she guffawed in shame. "It's a wonder you can even look at me."

Laiken wanted to agree that it was quite difficult to look at her, but she kept it to herself. "It was a big transition and a lot to swallow," she admitted. "But, umm, somehow we were able to work through it, I guess."

"Well, I sure appreciate it. These girls can be a handful," said Feenie.

"Actually the girls haven't been that bad. I mean other than . . . you know." Laiken let Feenie draw her own conclusion about what she meant.

Feenie didn't respond.

"But they're actually great around the house. They pick up behind themselves very well, unlike those rambunctious boys of mine," Laiken added.

Feenie turned down the aisle containing ethnic hair care and glanced over the products until she came across a bottle of African Pride Leave-in Conditioner. "This is pretty good right here."

She showed Laiken the bottle, then pooled some in her hand before massaging the locks of hair on Mia's head. Laiken watched as the child's hair was transformed from unmanageable to smooth, shiny strands, which were neatly plaited together in minutes.

"I know you don't think much of me." Feenie spun Mia around the other way and quickly groomed the other half of her head. "Y'all go to the toy section or something," she said to her daughters before continuing. The twins dashed off, leaving the two women to talk. "But I really do want to thank you for allowing the girls in your home and taking care of them."

"You're welcome," Laiken returned, more out of learned cordiality than sincerity.

"I did tell Rance that I wanted to get the girls back," Feenie mentioned.

"Yeah, he told me."

"I'm sure you wouldn't mind that, huh?"

"Well, you are their mother." Laiken laughed nervously, a bit uncomfortable with Feenie's question. "And they've said many times how much they've missed you."

"It's been hard without them."

"I can imagine, but sometimes I wish I could take a break from my two. At least your girls are respectful. My sons both have the sassiest mouths." She shook her head.

"You should be grateful."

Laiken let out a sarcastic chuckle. "Maybe if you keep those two, they would come back home with more manners." For a minute Laiken had forgotten that Feenie had been charged with child neglect and would be the last person she'd take parenting advice from.

"They wouldn't last a hot five minutes at my house," Feenie responded, rolling her eyes. "Anyway, I don't want to hold you. I know you didn't expect to meet me here."

"It's no problem," Laiken said, dismissing the issue. "You know, I still have some shopping to do. Umm, if you want, maybe you can have lunch with the girls in the McDonald's while I finish up. They haven't eaten yet."

"Oh! That would be great." Feenie beamed genuinely for the first time in a long time. "I guess I better go back there and find them."

"Yeah, yeah, go ahead." Laiken shooed Feenie away with her thin hand.

"Okay. We'll be right over there when you're ready." Feenie bobbed her head toward the fast-food establishment inside the store. Maybe if I have time, I can do a little more with their hair, something that will last for a couple days," she offered.

"That would be awesome." This time Laiken smiled. "I'll see you in . . . I don't know . . . an hour?"

"Sounds good."

The women parted ways. Laiken headed back toward the grocery department, where Jonathan and Michael were misbehaving, and Feenie toward the toy department, where Mia and Cara were having a hula hoop contest.

"I bet I can beat you," Feenie challenged. Pulling a hula hoop from the display, Feenie expertly swiveled the plastic ring around her neck, then lifted both her arms, forcing it to descend to her waist.

"I'ma win!" Mia squealed, wiggling her body and manipulating her hula hoop so that it circled her body faster.

Instead of competing, Cara slowed her motion and let her hula hoop fall to the floor.

"You out!" Feenie yelled, not noticing the sudden change in her daughter's disposition.

"I didn't wanna play anymore," Cara stated as she returned the toy to its rightful place. "It was making me tired." She moseyed away, uninterested in her mother and sister, and began looking at dolls.

It took only another two minutes for Mia to lose control of her hula hoop, although she tried to hold on to the rotation around her knees. "You win," she panted with a smile. "Whew!"

"And I was just about to give up, too!" Feenie exclaimed, pretending. She caught the hula hoop with her hands and returned it. "Y'all hungry? I want some McDonald's."

"Yes," the girls answered in unison. Mia draped Feenie's arm around her shoulders and leaned into her.

"We haven't ate there in a long time! Miss Laiken normally just cook," Cara added, coming around for a chance to dine at her favorite restaurant.

"Really?" Feenie asked rhetorically. "What does she cook?"

"She cooks stuff like tomatoes and onions in some kinda juice with some little white square things that's shaped like dice," said Cara.

"What?" Feenie crinkled her brows, unsure of what Cara was trying to describe.

"And she be cooking like spaghetti, but it don't be having no sauce on it. It be kinda plain with some cheese on it that you shake on it, like in this salt shaker, but the holes are bigger. Then it be having like some squash with some other stuff that look like squash, but it's green instead of yellow," Mia reported.

"Sounds good," said Feenie.

"It be nasty!" Mia replied, with her nose as crinkled as she could get it.

Feenie burst into a laugh.

"That's why I'm glad you're here!" Mia added.

The trio sat at a table with burgers, fries, and drinks, and Feenie just let the girls ramble on about whatever was on their minds. They talked about everything, from school to their half brothers, their favorite games, what was on TV the night before, and a plethora of other subjects. Feenie interjected something occasionally to acknowledge whatever it was they had shared with her, but for the most part she allowed them to speak freely. She felt it was the best way to hear what had happened in the past year and a half. Probing would have probably put the girls on the defensive. When she was ready, she put her own cards out on the table.

"So what do y'all think of moving back home with me?" Feenie asked casually as she pushed a few fries into her mouth, then sipped from her drink.

Mia answered right away, clapping her hands. "I can't wait!" She beamed.

Cara, on the other hand, had a different response. "I don't know, Mommy," she said. "I like living with you, and I like living with Daddy and Miss Laiken, too."

"Why is that?" Feenie asked, probing.

"Because it's fun over there. We get to play in the sprinklers, and our brothers live there," Cara explained. "And we go to a real nice school, and somebody is always home with us, so we don't have to worry about the police coming over and asking us where our parents are," she added.

"I see," Feenie commented, studying her daughter's face, feeling a piercing pain in her heart. "So if you got to bring all your toys and games home with you, and I was always there with you so you didn't have to worry about the police showing up, would that change your mind?"

Cara shook her head. "No, not really. I still think it's better for us to stay at Daddy and Miss Laiken's house."

"What about your hair? It's going to be a tangled mess all over the place every day," Feenie noted.

"Not anymore, because you showed Miss Laiken what stuff to buy, so she will be able to fix it now. And I am practicing on how to fix it myself, too. So I think we will be fine," Cara concluded.

"Sounds like you've given this a lot of thought, Cara," said Feenie.

"Not that much," Cara replied through a mouthful of food. "Daddy told us that we might be going back to live with you since you won't be in jail no more, so it did run across my mind one day."

"What do you know about something running across somebody's mind?" Feenie giggled a bit at her daughter's choice of words.

"Mommy, that means when you think about something for a few minutes," Cara informed her. "And Jill Scott sings this song that goes,

'You just run across my mind, you just run across my mind'!" Cara sang, turning Feenie's giggle into a laugh.

"So you'd rather live with your daddy, huh?" said Feenie.

"I think so." Cara felt that she'd made a good argument, and the decision of where she'd live was all hers, so she nodded with finality.

"I don't wanna stay there all the time, Mommy," Mia threw in. "I think we should live with both of y'all. So we could have a room at your house, Mommy, and keep our room at Daddy's house, 'cause our room is real pretty."

"Really?" replied Feenie.

"Yes!" Mia exclaimed. "It's all pink and white and stuff, and we have our own beds apart, instead of bunk beds, and we got a big closet and all that. And we be keeping our room clean, too!"

"For real?" said Feenie.

Mia nodded. "Yes, and sometimes I help Jonathan and Michael clean up, 'cause they be having stuff everywhere!"

"Well, maybe one day I will get a chance to see your room at your daddy's house, but I did get a new apartment, and it has a room for you girls, and I think you will like it a lot," Feenie said.

"Hmm. I don't know, because our new room is really awesome!" Cara interjected. "It's the best room ever."

"Even if it is, Cara, I really want you to come home with me because I miss you," Feenie shared. "You don't have to come today, because I'm not finish getting your room together yet."

"Maybe next week?" Mia asked.

"I don't know. I have to talk to your daddy first, but hopefully it won't be long," said Feenie.

"That would be great!" Mia chimed, but right away Feenie took note of Cara's withdrawal from the conversation and her light sulking.

"What's wrong with you, Cara?" asked Feenie.

"I don't wanna move," Cara answered honestly. "I like it at Daddy's house better."

"I'll talk to your daddy about you being able to visit then, but hopefully, in a few weeks y'all will be back living with me."

Cara responded only with a sigh, showing Feenie that she had a lot of work to do.

12

Dominique couldn't contain her tears as she dialed Tamara's number. "Please take a break from studying," she sobbed. "I'm on my way over there."

"What's wrong, Nique?" Tamara asked with sincere concern. "Everything okay with the baby?"

"Yeah. I just really need to talk. Do you mind if I drop by?"

"You know you can come over anytime. As long as *Grey's Anatomy* is not on," Tamara snickered. "Or *Scrubs*." When she heard Dominique's sniffling, she regretted trying to make a joke. "I'm just kidding," she threw in, trying to redeem herself.

"I know," Dominique squeaked out. "I'm on my way."

"Since you can't have wine, should I have ice cream ready?"

"Yeah. And maybe a pillow and a blanket. I'll see you in a few."

Dominique struggled to pull herself together on the fifteen-minute drive to her old town-home, which she had rented out to her sister. She could barely see the road in front of her as water pooled in her bottom eyelids every few seconds. Over and over again she pushed her fingers between her shades and her face to smear the tears away but it did no good.

"Girl, what happened!" Tamara exclaimed when she opened the door for her sister.

Dominique was silent for several minutes as she slumped on the couch and tried to stop sniveling enough to speak. She accepted a wad of tissue from Tamara, blew her nose hard, then drew her knees to her chest, resting her feet on the couch. "Marvin is seeing Feenie," she whispered.

"What? Please! No, he is not! Where did you get *that* from?"

"He is!" Dominique wailed, becoming a bit angry at her sister's disbelief.

"Okay, and again, where did you get that from?" Tamara asked a second time, with her eyebrows lifted practically to her hairline, while she watched Dominique dig through her purse and pull out Feenie's letter. "That man is crazy about you." Tamara leaned forward, taking the paper from her sister's hand. She quickly scanned the handwritten words, although the letter was a copy of the original, and furrowed her brows. "So what? This doesn't mean he's seeing her."

"Then why would he hide it from me?"

"Because it means nothing to him." Tamara shrugged. "Where did you find this?"

"In his gym bag. I made a copy of it on our scanner."

"Did you ask him about it?"

"No. Not yet. Where's the ice cream?" Dominique asked rhetorically as she pulled herself to her feet and headed toward the refrigerator.

"Why not?"

"I don't know. I just haven't yet. I mean, first of all, she sent this to his job. How does she know where he works?" She pressed her lips together pensively, giving Tamara something to think about. When there was no response in the next few seconds, Dominique continued. "Then, this is probably not her only time writing him; so how long have they been talking?"

"They can't be doing too much talking. Who writes letters these days? If they were seriously talking, they'd be e-mailing or texting."

Dominique pondered the thought for a few seconds. "They probably are, but those can be deleted. That can't be deleted," she said, pointing an ice cream scoop at the letter that Tamara still held. "It could have been trashed, but I guess he forgot to throw it out before he got home."

"You need to ask him, Dominique, before you jump to conclusions," Tamara coaxed.

"I'm not asking him anything! I'm not stupid." The bowl rattled against the counter as Dominique slung four scoops of butter pecan into it. "Why would he hide it from me all of a sudden?"

"Maybe he didn't want to upset you. I mean

look at you now. You dripping snot all in the bowl."

Dominique giggled a bit through her tears, then wiped her nose with her sleeve. "Shut up," she muttered.

"Seriously, Nique, I highly doubt Marvin is seeing that woman. After all that mess she put him through? He's not that crazy. He has a beautiful wife whom he adores."

"I'm not beautiful," Dominique wailed. "I'm fat and pregnant and covered with stretch marks! I'm ugly! Look at my belly!" She yanked her stretch T-shirt upward and exposed her stomach, which had developed a multitude of pink squiggly lines. She couldn't help but burst into tears all over again.

"You are not fat. You're beautifully, glowingly pregnant. There's a difference. Now, I don't know what's going on with his ex, but, Dominique, Marvin loves you. He loves you and he loves that baby. There's no doubt in my mind about that."

"Okay, but he's told me everything else about that woman. Everything! So why would he hide this, unless he had something to hide?"

"Look. You just need to ask him. I'm sure it's nothing."

"And then to make it so bad, they have a road game next month right up there, where she lives. Suppose they plan on meeting up?"

"You need to stop worrying yourself to death. Just go up there with him."

"And what is that going to do? He will just call his little date off if I announce that I'm going. Besides, I just can't jump up and get on the bus with the team," Dominique argued.

"So drive."

"Marvin's not going to go for me driving all the way to Maryland just to watch the game. I hardly go to the home games anymore, and I would have to miss a day of classes."

"It won't kill you to be out one day, and if you need me to, I'll drive. I'm sure if you drive up there, even if you don't let him know you're coming, you'll find him doing what he's supposed to be doing, which is coaching his team. Not meeting up with some crazy woman who tried to destroy him. Do you know what his ex-wife looks like?"

"No," Dominique sniffed. "I'm telling you, something's going on. I just know it."

"I think you're just getting yourself all upset for nothing. And neither you nor my niece slash goddaughter needs that right now."

"And what I don't need is to see Marvin's face right now. I'm crashing on your couch."

"Does Marvin even know you're over here?"

"Nope. And just like he didn't tell me he's talking to his ex, I'm not telling him."

"Dominique," Tamara said in reprimand.

"What? I'm serious! He didn't respect me enough to tell me she's writing him, so why should I tell him where I am?"

"Because two wrongs don't make a right, for starters," Tamara replied. "And secondly, that man's gonna be worried sick about you. You know that."

"Well, right now I don't care." Dominique

circled the now empty bowl with her spoon. "Anyway, I'm too sleepy to drive now."

"At least let me call him."

"No! He doesn't deserve a phone call."

"Yes, he does. Now, he might be wrong for not telling you about this letter, but you're pregnant and you need to tell your husband where you are," Tamara said in a motherly tone.

"All right, all right! Shucks!" Dominique huffed. "You can call him, but tell him I fell asleep watching a movie or something."

"Well, you best go to sleep, because you know I don't like to lie unless it's an extreme emergency, and this ain't one." Tamara pointed a remote at the television, tuned it to BET, and settled back in the couch.

"Thanks, Tee."

"Yeah, whatever. Now gimme your phone." Tamara searched through her sister's phone until she found Marvin's number and called. "Hey, brother-in-law," she began when he answered.

"What's going on, sis?"

"I just called to tell you your beautiful wife is over here, passed out on my couch, looking not so beautiful."

"What happened to her?" Marvin's first response was always concern.

"Nothing. She's been over here watching movies and eating ice cream. She dozed off on the couch. It was getting late and I didn't want you to worry about her. I know how you get."

"Do I need to come get her?"

"I don't know. She's sleeping. From what I

remember, waking her up can be ugly, but I guess you are used to that by now."

Dominique hid her giggle as she tossed a pillow at Tamara's head. Tamara ducked, making the playful assault a near miss, then stuck her tongue out.

"Yeah, I am." Marvin laughed. "I'll swing by there after the game."

"All right. She'll be here. Her big head ain't going nowhere." Tamara ended the call and tossed Dominique her phone. "He's coming to get you after the game. So much for staying away."

Just as he promised, Marvin showed up at Tamara's door at the end of his night. He tapped lightly, knowing that Tamara would be expecting him since he'd called first. She opened the door, let him in, and pointed him to the couch.

Marvin approached his wife with a half smile and dropped to one knee. "Baby," he drawled teasingly. "Baby, wake up. It's the man of your dreams," he sang, peeling a layer of covers down from her head. "I'm here to take you away."

Dominique groaned inside, knowing there was no way she'd be able to fake truly being asleep. She stretched a bit, then fluttered her eyes open.

"Hey, Sleeping Beauty."

"Hey."

"You ready to go home?" he asked, stroking, then kissing the side of her face.

"Hmm?" Faking sleep was harder than Dominique had thought.

"Come on, princess," he coaxed, pulling gently on her arm.

"I'm too tired, babe," she whined.

"Do you need me to carry you?" Marvin offered lovingly.

Tamara stood watching, trying to hold back a guffaw.

"You know I will," Marvin added.

"I really don't feel like moving at all," Dominique uttered. "I'll just stay here."

"Then how am I supposed to sleep tonight? You know I can't sleep without my momma bear beside me," said Marvin.

"Oh, Lawd! Give me a break!" Tamara rolled her eyes, then turned and left the room. "Lock the door on your way out," she hollered over her shoulder, knowing there was no way her brother-in-law was leaving his wife there for the night.

"Come on, sweetie." Marvin tugged on Dominique a bit more, until she finally gave up and complied, cringing inside all the while. It was hard for her to reveal what she knew to her husband, but she remembered something Lue Renay, her grandmother, had taught her: "Never let the cat know you see him comin' out the bag."

"Thanks for calling me, sis," Marvin hollered to Tamara since she was out of view. And with that, he took his wife home and slept silently through the night.

13

The sun was just making its morning entrance, and Feenie sat facing east on her mother's back patio, watching it rise, which was how she chose to spend each morning. She sipped on a cup of coffee, enjoyed the wonders of nature, and glanced down at the Bible in her lap, reflecting on a scripture in Psalms to keep her encouraged throughout the day: "The Lord will perfect that which concerneth me: thy mercy, O Lord, endureth for ever: forsake not the works of thine own hands."

It had become one of Feenie's favorite verses, reminding her that God had heard her cry for help and would help her to change. She realized she couldn't change the past, but she'd committed to allowing God to guide her future.

"Thank you, Lord, for a successful day," she whispered upward as she stood to go inside, having a full day ahead of her.

It would be a bit of a drive, but Feenie was determined to see her ex-husband. Not wanting to give Marvin the wrong impression, she chose her clothing carefully. Before, it had been nothing for her to slip into something backless and featuring an extreme cowl-neck to expose a wide strip of skin on her front, a pair of shorts that allowed her cheeks to more than peek out at the bottom, or a dress so short, her business would be in the wind if she bent over just a little. She'd grown out of that, however, and while she had maintained a perfect size six and still took pride in her figure, she had learned not to flaunt it as much as she had in the past and now rejected that style of dress.

It took her a while, but she finally decided on a sleeveless wrap dress in black with chic white piping on its borders. The johnny collar, the surplice neckline, and a hemline that fell well below her knees gave her a classic and mature look. Feenie actually looked her age, which was nearly forty-four, and liked the way she looked. It was far different from what she would have worn had it been two years before. She accessorized with white jewelry and a pair of heeled, gladiator-style sandals. With a dollop of gel and a brush, she smoothed her hair back into a neat bun and accented it with a white flowered ponytail holder. She smiled, satisfied with her look, thinking she favored a Sunday school teacher. Grabbing her purse and keys, Feenie headed for the door.

"Ma, I'll be back late," she called.

"Where you going?" Mary asked.

"I just need to take care of some business."

"Well, you look nice," Mary threw in. "Look like you got a breakfast date or an interview."

"Neither. It's nothing like that. Just got an important meeting. I'll be back." Feenie knew if she stayed longer, Mary would begin to pry harder and harder.

She slid behind the wheel of her Kia Rio5, backed out of the driveway, and headed for the Virginia state line.

As she coasted down I-95, she sang along to Israel Houghton's *A Deeper Level* CD and prayed that she would find the right words to say to Marvin when she saw him. She'd rehearsed the meeting in her mind ten times over, but she was still nervous about how things could go. Her plan was simple: she would see him, say what she needed to say, and leave.

While it was nearly a five-hour drive, the time seemed to pass quickly. Before she knew it, she was guiding the car onto the campus of Old Dominion University and finding her way to the gym. Her heart began to beat a little faster, but it didn't shake her confidence. She was ready.

Not knowing his schedule, she figured she'd find her ex-husband on the gym floor, surrounded by sweaty young men and the sound of screeching tennis shoes, coaching his team. The gym doors had been opened, allowing Feenie easy access inside the building. She was surprised to find it strangely silent. Feenie snickered to herself, realizing that she hadn't taken into consideration that the team's players actually went to class during the day and practiced in the evening hours. In her mind, that would make her visit less of an interruption. The sound of her heels clicking on the tiled floor filled the hallway, announcing her coming. She read the name tag outside of each door, then stopped when she found Marvin's. His door was closed, so Feenie took a few seconds to inhale, then slowly exhale, whispered a quick prayer, then knocked.

"Yeah?" Marvin answered.

In an instant Feenie felt a rush of emotions from just hearing his voice. If asked, she wouldn't be able to rightfully describe what she felt, but she would best sum it up as nervous fear, anxiousness, and anticipation. Taking one more deep breath, she opened the door. Marvin hadn't even looked up.

"Marvin."

He cut his eyes upward, barely looking, but immediately did a double take. "What the hell are you doing here?"

"I had to come see you, Marvin. I sent a couple more letters, but I wasn't sure if you received them, because I never heard back from you," Feenie stated. Right away she took note of the ring he wore on his left hand but made no mention of it.

"That's because I have nothing to say to you." Marvin leaned back in his chair and looked square into his ex-wife's eyes. It had been years since he'd seen her, but she clearly wasn't the woman he'd been formerly married to. *At least on the outside,* he thought. His physical side could appreciate how Feenie looked. He could even describe her look as sexy, but quickly the memories of their tumultuous past blacked out all that made her attractive. "Get out of my office," Marvin ordered without raising his voice.

"I will leave, but I need to talk to you first. I drove all the way down here from Baltimore. Please just give me five minutes."

"I don't care if you took a boat from Timbuktu. I don't want to hear anything you've got to say. Now leave."

"I think you want to hear this." Unshaken by Marvin's adamancy, instead of leaving, Feenie took a seat and crossed one leg over the other. She could see his face slightly contorting his expression of anger and disgust. "Just please listen."

"You've got two minutes to say whatever it is you came here to say. Then I don't ever want to see you again," he stated, keeping his tone even and low.

Feenie again took a deep breath and began. "Marvin, I lied to you about our baby."

Marvin looked on with no response, mildly confused.

"That night you pushed me over the table, there was no baby." She bit into her lower lip as tears escaped her eyes.

"What are you talking about?"

"I—I," she stammered. "There was a baby, but when you lost your contract with the NBA, I had an abortion," she confessed.

"You what?" Marvin winced and narrowed his eyes. "You what!"

"That's why I made you leave the hospital

before the doctor came back in the room." Feenie covered her mouth with her hand, unable for the moment to say anything else.

"For all these years, you had me thinking I'd killed my firstborn child?" he bellowed, slamming his fist on the desk, startling Feenie into a jump.

She kept silent, expecting and accepting his tirade.

"Do you have any idea what that did to me, Feenie? Any idea at all? Do you know how less of a man I felt?" His questions were rhetorical, although he paused between each one. "Why? Why did you do that?"

Feenie slowly and shamefully shook her head. "There's no justifying it. I was selfish. Beyond selfish," she admitted. "I'm sorry. I was just devastated that you weren't going to be able to pursue an NBA career."

"So you decided to destroy me? Don't you know I nearly lost my mind over what you said I'd done?"

"Yes," she whispered. "And I couldn't say this before, but, Marvin, I'm sorry."

"You damn near ruin my life and all you can say is you're sorry?"

"That's all I can say." She nodded, digging into her purse for tissues.

Marvin let out a sarcastic chuckle. "You killed my baby, but you're sorry? You let me believe that I did it, but you're sorry. You come waltzing in here, all cavalier and whatnot, to tell me this, and you're sorry." Then, other than Marvin letting out a few sighs as he digested what Feenie had just told him, there was silence.

A minute later he went on. "It wasn't enough that you ruined my life one time. Here you come twenty years later to do it all over again." If looks could kill, Marvin would have been arrested for murder. "What is it this time, Jerrafine? What is it that you want or can't have? What's your motive? Why are you really here? You're on a quest to see how much money you can get? That's always been your MO. Is that it?" His hands flew upward and fell back down to his lap. "You're getting too old to turn tricks and you need your rent paid, or you need some money, so here you come with some story?" he spat. "You haven't done enough?"

His words cut like a knife, but Feenie knew it was warranted. She swallowed hard before she spoke. "I don't want anything from you. All I wanted was to tell you about our baby. I didn't want to tell you on the phone, so I made the decision to make this trip to tell you face-to-face. I thought you deserved to know." Feenie gathered her things and stood. "You don't have to worry about me coming back or ever seeing me again. Take care, Marvin."

At that, Feenie sped out of his office and nearly bulldozed a woman just outside the door, standing in a pair of tennis shoes, yoga pants, and a loose-fitting T-shirt. Marvin's office door slammed hard behind her, scaring the daylights out of them both.

"Excuse me. I'm so sorry," Feenie mumbled through her tears as she quickly stepped around

Dominique, practically ran down the hall, and exited the building.

Dominique stood frozen in the hallway just outside of Marvin's office, holding a picnic basket with a lunch meal for two enclosed. She'd heard her husband bellowing as she walked up, but she hadn't gotten close enough to where there was clarity to his words. What she had managed to hear was this woman who'd just about knocked her down tell her husband that she was having his baby. She wanted to burst into his office and run the other way at the same time, but instead, her feet felt like cement blocks and refused to move one way or the other. She dropped the basket, leaned back against the wall, and stared up at the ceiling.

"This can't be happening . . . I don't need this right now," she said aloud to herself. "This can't be happening." Tears fell from her eyes as she thought about the woman who had just rushed out of her husband's office, and not knowing who she was, she couldn't help but compare herself to her. Although their encounter had lasted all of a half a second, Feenie's beauty could not be overlooked. She was tall and polished, her belly was flat, and her hair straight and neat. Shorter and rounder, with a mini Afro for a hairdo, and dressed in sweats, Dominique felt completely inferior. Marvin had told her a million times that he loved her and there was no one on earth more beautiful in his eyes, and those words usually made her feel like a goddess, but today his words meant nothing. Today she felt like a fat garden troll.

Dominique loved Marvin and had always believed he loved her too much to find comfort or pleasure in the arms of another woman. She never questioned his whereabouts when he went on the road with the team. He called often, and every night when he was away, he whispered that he missed her, loved her, and couldn't wait to see her again.

"And I believed it," she mumbled. "I actually believed it." She gasped. Dominique lifted the lunch basket from the floor and left without seeing her husband or leaving any sign that she'd been there.

Sitting with his head buried in his hands, Marvin was shocked and overwhelmed by the news Feenie had just given him, and myriad emotions ran through his body and flooded his mind. For nearly twenty years he'd believed that by his hands his first child had perished, and then he found out that it had all been a lie. He'd lived tortured by guilt and condemnation due to a selfish and cruel act of manipulation by a woman he'd once believed loved him. The nights he'd cried, the mental anguish he'd suffered, were all for nothing. Finally he felt like he understood why he'd survived his drinking-and-driving suicide attempt. His mind journeyed back again ten years, to that time in his life after he'd been pulled from his car.

In a total state of confusion, Marvin sat at a bar, ordering drink after drink, starting with a concoction of bourbon, sweet vermouth, and bitters, thinking over his life, although he hardly considered it that. He switched to chilled gin, with a splash of vermouth and a completely soaked olive. Next, he tried a caipirinhas, a Brazilian drink made with lime juice, sugar, and *cachaça*, which just about made new hairs sprout on his chest. Marvin coughed a few times but drank it all. "I just want answers," he said to the bartender.

"Me too," the bartender answered, which in his drunken state, Marvin found hilarious. He laughed uncontrollably, but then retreated to his dismal mood.

"I mean, just tell me who I pissed off?" Marvin added, then pointed to the menu. "Get me one of these right here." Marvin pointed to a drink featuring vodka, gin, tequila, rum, triple sec, and Chambord. "What the hell did I ever do to anybody?" he slurred. "I pay my taxes. I go da work every day. I don't botta nobody! So tell me why the hell *my* life is all jacked up." By the time he finished the sweet but highly potent drink, he was unable to stand up. "Call me a cab," he requested. "I'ma wait outside and get some air."

Marvin stumbled toward the door with no intentions of waiting for anyone to take him home. After a few minutes of muddled thought, he found his vehicle, just about collapsed inside, closed the door, then reached behind the passenger seat and grabbed a beer on the floor. In seconds he gulped half of it down, jammed the key into the ignition, and sped out of the parking lot and onto the streets of Norfolk. With the radio blasting, he zigzagged crazily for several yards, and at this point, Marvin couldn't see or think straight. He cursed at himself, regretting the day he ever put his hands on Feenie. Had he realized that one action would result in the rapid downward spiral he had experienced from that day on, he wouldn't have even come home that evening. "I shouldn't have ever married that girl!" he sneered.

In a drunken stupor, Marvin felt numb, hot, and nauseous, so he let all the windows down, allowing the wind to slap his face. It did nothing to sober him, though; he was too far gone and glad about it. His foot pressed heavier on the accelerator, and he sped to his fate. The truth was, Marvin had never intended to make it home, and just as he had planned, with his vision blurred, flashes of light moving around him, and horns blowing in the background, his car came to an abrupt halt when he slammed into a light post. His seat belt had never been fastened.

Several days passed before he opened his eyes, but when he did, he wondered why he was still there, still living. Slowly he recognized that he'd been confined within hospital walls, but he was unable to remember how he got there. He tried to sit up, but his range of motion was severely limited. An IV connected him to a pole, and an oxygen tube felt like a rope tying his head to the pillow. He couldn't discern all his injuries, but judging from the immense pain he felt, he figured he was banged up pretty badly. Cutting his eyes toward the window, he caught sight of a huge basketball-shaped balloon, flanked by others with GET WELL sentiments printed across each one. On the rolling table sat a large basket of fruit and an oversize card. He knew it would be impossible for him to reach the card, so he didn't even try. Instead, he closed his eyes and searched his memory for what had taken place to land him flat on his back. All he could remember was a crushing sense of anger, dread, remorse, and grief.

"Good morning."

Marvin opened his eyes and let them travel toward the voice he'd heard.

"You're awake. That's a good sign." The nurse went about her work, taking his blood pressure and temperature, then jotting her findings on his chart. "How are you feeling?"

"What happened to me?" he murmured almost inaudibly. He'd meant to speak louder, but his voice's volume control wouldn't cooperate.

"You don't remember? You had a bit too much to drink and ended up in a terrible accident," she informed him. "A lot of people have been worried about you."

He released a weak guffaw. "Like who? Don't nobody care about me."

"You had a whole group of young men in here a few days ago, all wanting to see you re-cover."

After a momentary silence one corner of Marvin's lips turned upward. "My team," he shared. "My boys." They'd not been considered in his equation to end his life, but he knew he'd let the members of his community basket-ball team down, first by drinking—something

he'd always discouraged them from doing—
and then by getting behind the wheel of a car.
As much as it made him feel good that they had
come to see about him, he wished they had
never found out about his accident at all.

"You must have had quite an impact on those
boys. We don't see a lot of that in our commu-
nities."

Marvin didn't comment.

"For their sake, I hope you recover and get
back to mentoring them. They need that. They
need men like you."

Her last sentence stuck in Marvin's mind
long after the nurse finished her shift that day
and he was released some days later. He spent
the next two weeks in his backyard from sunup
to sundown, tossing a basketball at a goal, playing an imaginary game with every personal
demon that challenged him. Each morning his
muscles would ache, not just from his injuries,
but also from the physical exertion from the
previous day, but he kept at it. He coached himself, he challenged himself, and he did to himself what he had done to every inner-city youth
that had ever stepped foot on his court—he
dared himself to live.

Now that dare stared him straight in the face.

14

Feenie's drive home seemed to take twice as long as it had taken her to get to Norfolk, but only because her mind was consumed with how her interaction with Marvin could have gone better. He had reacted in the way that she thought he would. With anger and disgust. She had hoped that she would see the slightest bit of relief on his face, but from her perspective, it had never appeared.

"He hates me. He has to," she concluded. "If only I could turn back the hands of time." Feenie sighed. She wished there was something more she could do, but knew there was nothing. Her apology was the only piece that had been missing, for certainly the pregnancy she had terminated could not be re-created. As she drove farther, she prayed, believing God could bring healing.

"Lord, I've done my dirt, and I can't undo any of my actions. The most I could ever give to Marvin at this point was the truth and my apology, and I've done that. So now I pray that you take over and bring peace to his mind, his soul, and his spirit. Release his spirit from the emotional prison that it's been in all these years. And again, I ask your forgiveness in creating this situation in the first place. Thank you for giving me the opportunity to right my terrible wrong. And restore to Marvin everything that I stole from him so many years ago. Amen."

She got back to Baltimore just in time to make it to her first parenting class. Though exhausted from her drive, Feenie entered the doors of a local elementary school right at 6:00 p.m. She was welcomed by a petite woman, who stood at the entrance to the school's library, handing out participant books to each parent as they walked through the door.

"Hi! Welcome to the Strengthening Families Program," she said, beaming. "Go ahead and take a seat at one of the tables."

There were a few other parents already seated at small tables, sized for children rather than adults. Feenie picked a table midway in the room, took a seat, and thumbed through the course material as she inconspicuously eyed the other participants. Her very presence in the class made her ashamed and uncomfortable. She wanted to judge the others there, wondering what had they done to their children, but realized that she was one of them, someone who society would label as a child abuser.

Denise, the course facilitator, introduced herself and opened with the class objectives.

"First, we're going to go around the room and just give a brief introduction, because we're going to be here one night a week for the next thirteen weeks, so we wanna get a little comfortable with each other, right?" She smiled.

Feenie cleared her throat, deciding to fully engage in whatever was necessary to get her girls back. "My name is Jerrafine Trotter, but everybody calls me Feenie. I have twin girls, Mia and Cara, and right now they live with their dad. I lost them a couple of years ago, being stupid, but I'm ready to get them back." She stopped there but felt a sense of accomplishment in having stated what she had done.

"Great. Welcome, Feenie," said Denise.

Over the next twenty minutes the other participants briefly stated their names and situations, ending with an interracial couple, Rhonda and Todd. Todd explained that he and Rhonda had four children but were not married, and their children were currently in the foster-care system.

"See, this what happened, right," he began. "I had dis stuff in my room that was something like poison, and I had tol' my kids, 'Don't go in there.'"

"Poison?" Denise exclaimed.

"Yeah, it was this stuff I had," Todd explained. "I had told my kids to stay out my room, right." He punched his hand with his fist. "But they went in there, anyway, and my son had my four-year-old daughter playing in it. So when I came home, I seen what they did, and I beat 'im wit a belt. Then he went to school and told his teacher and them. Next thing I know, Social Service was at my door, takin' my kids." He rubbed a hand over his fuzzy cornrows. "They should'na done that, you know what I'm sayin'? I mean, they just jumped to conclusions, like me and her crazy."

Another participant spoke up, stating that she'd intentionally served her daughter Ex-Lax-filled marshmallows, which had landed her a seat in the class as well as a court date. A part of Feenie wanted to comment, but she kept silent, again recognizing that by leaving her daughters home alone for long periods at a time, they could have easily gotten into "poison." *Probably drugs,* she thought. *Or medicine.*

"Well, in this course, we're going to talk about some other strategies that you can use to both discipline and nurture your children," said Denise. "We are going to look at how you can interact positively with your kids, such as being enthusiastic and giving them positive attention for good behavior, how to let your child take the lead in activities, and how to praise them when they do something great. Your family communication will improve, because you're going to use active listening. We'll show you how to set up family meetings so that you and your children can discuss things in a group. You're going to learn how to be more consistent with your discipline, including consequences and time-outs."

"Time-out?" Todd blurted. "What is that supposed to do? You know what? You put one of my kids in time out, as soon as it's over, they gone right back to what they was doing."

"Yup," the Ex-Lax marshmallow woman confirmed. "Kids don't pay that mess no attention. I make my daughter sit in the corner for 'bout two or three hours."

"It don't do no good, do it?" Todd asked.

"Shole don't," said the Ex-Lax marshmallow woman.

"And I mean, I did beat my son witta belt, and it lef' a li'l bruise, but I rather beat 'im than to have to put 'im in the ground, see what I'm sayin'?" said Todd, punching his hand with his fist again. "Social Service acted like I 'bout killed the boy. It won't nothing wrong with him. Now they got me sittin' up in here every week, wasting my time. I could be out working and bringing in more income to support my family. Social Service just don't be tryna help you out."

While others jumped on the bandwagon, Feenie had long come to terms with accepting responsibility for her actions, so she remained silent until she was called on.

"Feenie, did you want to share what brought you here?" asked Denise.

Feenie cleared her throat, then spoke. "Well, I just made some poor decisions when it came to the welfare of my children. I feel like I've paid for those mistakes, and I just want the opportunity to bring my girls back home with me again." That was enough of an explanation for a mixed crowd.

"Well, I'ma tell you this. If Social Service got

anything to do with it, good luck. You might not ever see them kids no more," Todd uttered.

Finding that he was unable to focus on any of his work tasks, Marvin wrapped up his day and left for a drive to nowhere. He had to be back by six for practice, but for now he just needed some time and space to think. With seemingly no help from him, his S-Class Mercedes eased onto 64 East, merged onto 264 East, and headed toward the beach. It wouldn't be so crowded in the middle of a workday, and even if it were, there could be a thousand people playing in the sand and on the shore, but he knew he'd still have a sense of seclusion. Within thirty minutes, he'd parked in the Hilton Hotel's parking garage at Thirty-first Street, taken the stairs down three flights, and meandered across the street to the sand. It was hot, and he had on a pair of wind pants and a white collared polo, with a T-shirt underneath, but he didn't mind it. He did stop to remove his tennis shoes and socks. He tied the shoelaces together and swung the tennis shoes around his neck, rolled the legs of his pants midway up his shins, and headed for the water.

Gentle waves covered his feet, then rolled backward as he walked, lost in his thoughts. *All this time. She was lying all this time. All my misery, all she put me through . . . And she killed my baby.* His thoughts trailed off. Marvin seated himself in the sand and just watched peaks of water chase each other until they rolled over against the shore. He thought about the child he had never held or known about until it was too late. To ensure no one saw him, he hung his arms over his knees and dropped his head. He bit into his lower lip as tears fell from his eyes one at a time and dropped to the sand below. He cried out of grief; he cried out of anger; he cried out of a sense of relief; he cried because there was no other way for the moment that he could express what he felt inside.

An hour passed, then two, before he rose to his feet in order to get back to the gym in time. He pushed his team extra hard and snapped at them for every error. The men did notice it but said nothing. It wasn't the first time they'd practiced with an angry coach.

"Good job, team," he mumbled as he dismissed them.

He drove home in complete silence, still consumed in a sea of thoughts, but he pushed it out of his head before he went inside. As far as Marvin was concerned, despite his run-amok emotions, Feenie's confession wasn't worth upsetting the peace in his home. *I have a beautiful wife, I'm having a beautiful baby, my life is perfect, and I refuse to let Jerrafine mess it up for me—for us.*

15

Marvin inserted his key into the lock and entered his home. "Babe," he called. He dropped his bag at the door and climbed the steps to the second floor, finding his wife in the room she was converting to a nursery. "Hey," he said, sincerely happy to see his wife.

Dominique did respond, but Marvin barely heard her. Nonetheless, he pulled her away from the changing table, where she stood looking at Onesies and other baby clothes, and wrapped his arms tightly around her. She couldn't even look at him, let alone stand his touch, but somehow endured.

"I love you so much, Dominique. You are the most beautiful, amazing, sexy, incredible woman I know." He pulled back to kiss her and noticed her grim facial expression. "What's wrong, babe?"

"Nothing," she said, feigning casualness.

"You sure?" He bent his neck to peck her lips, but Dominique turned her head and wriggled from his grasp.

"I just don't feel that well, that's all."

"Why? What's wrong?" Marvin furrowed his brows and studied his wife's eyes.

"Nothing," she replied, exiting the room and leaving Marvin standing there alone.

"Where're you going?"

"To the bathroom," she blurted over her shoulder, not slowing her stride.

"You sure you're all right?" he called behind her.

He got only the sound of a closing door in response. Marvin found his wife's behavior strange, but he wasn't too alarmed, thinking it was just some type of hormonal imbalance, which he'd heard pregnant women went through.

He left the nursery and went down to the kitchen for a light snack. Every evening he and Dominique would sit talking or watching TV and sharing a snack between them. Marvin looked forward to this intimate time with her; it had become one of his favorite times of the day. Grapes, strawberries, and cubes of extra sharp cheddar cheese went onto a plate, accompanied by a large wineglass filled with apple juice. A few Bordeaux cookies, his favorite by Pepperidge Farm, went onto a saucer before all the items were placed on a bed tray. Thoughts of Jerrafine's visit fought for time in his head, but he ignored the urges. He wanted to focus only on his wife.

"Babe," he called up the stairwell as he passed by on his way to the den. He sat the tray on the table, picked up the remote, and flicked through channels, stopping briefly on all sports-related programming. "Nique, you coming?" Marvin called a second time, but just a bit more preoccupied with the television set than with his wife's presence or lack thereof.

After ten or so minutes passed, he climbed the steps, curious about what was keeping her. "Dominique, I'm waiting on you, babe." Rather than finding her on her way downstairs, Marvin found Dominique in the nursery again, seated in her glider, reading a book. She wasn't reading aloud to her belly but seemed to be reading for her own personal pleasure. "Babe?"

"What?" she answered curtly, not bothering to look up.

"What's going on with you tonight?"

"Nothing."

"There's something going on," he emphasized. "What is it?"

"I just don't feel like it tonight." Dominique shrugged.

"What do you mean? We always spend this time together. What's going on with you tonight that you don't want to spend time with your husband?"

"I told you it's nothing," she said, becoming more snappy.

Marvin looked on silently for a minute or two before responding. "I'll tell you what. I'll be right back," he commented, making a quick exit.

Dominique rolled her eyes once he was out of view, brooding over what she'd found out earlier that day.

Too soon for her liking, Marvin was back,

toting the bed tray across his arm and holding the glass of apple juice in his opposite hand. "Since you don't want to come downstairs, I'll come up here." He sat the tray on Dominique's lap and took a seat on the floor beside her. "What are you reading?"

Dominique glanced at the book cover, as if she needed a reminder. "*The Perfect Shoe*," she mumbled against her will. What she really wanted was for Marvin to leave her alone.

"Oh. What is it about?"

"About this girl who likes shoes," she answered, truncating the story's plot.

"Sounds good. Read me some of it." Marvin popped a grape in his mouth and sipped some juice, then offered the glass to his wife.

"I don't feel like it," she brusquely replied.

"Go 'head babe. Let me engage myself in your interests. Plus, I want to hear your sexy voice," he said as he reached for a cookie, bit it in half, then offered her one of the halves.

Dominique cringed inside, then sighed, then began reading.

Terrance and I had been seeing each other again for nearly three months. I was still a little intimidated about letting him fully into my space, trying not to be the same fool twice, but at the same time, still seeking the fun, excitement, attention, and affection of a relationship. I guess I felt a little safe where Terrance was concerned because we had so much history. Not all of it was pleasant, of course, but there had been some good times.

I was still protective of my goodies but was feeling super frisky tonight. Terrance and I had planned on just staying in at his place and watching a few good DVDs or cable movies over some Chinese takeout, but I had something else in mind. On my bed I laid out the items that I'd bought from the store: a pair of long white gloves, some white thigh highs, and a two-inch-wide piece of white ribbon. I then dug through my panty drawer and found a white thong, a pair of boy leg briefs, and a matching strapless bra. I put all of those pieces on, then went to my closet and pulled on a tight-fitting all white jogging suit, covered it up with a looser-fitting black jogging suit, and then put on a crazy pair of white Baby Phat pumps.

I overdid my eyes and lips in white makeup and placed a white headband on my head to keep my hair out of my face. Tucking the black lightbulb I'd picked up at the mall into my bag, I headed for Terrance's, calling him on the way and expressing that I wanted to shoot a little pool tonight.

"Pool?" he asked. "You don't even like pool."

"I know, but tonight I thought I'd try it again and see how well I do. As a matter of fact, I just want to see you play."

"Let me see if I got this right." He chuckled. "You want to come over and spend the evening watching me play pool by myself."

"Yeah, pretty much. I mean, you look so sexy the way you lick your lips and slide the cue stick between your fingers. I just wanna watch."

"I don't know about all that, Deece. I really
don't feel like standing up at the table tonight."

"Deece?" Marvin commented, breaking Dominique's reading flow. "That's the girl's name?"

"Her name is December," Dominique huffed,
still irritated. She started again, repeating the
last sentence she'd read.

"I don't know about all that, Deece. I really
don't feel like standing up at the table tonight."
"Do it for me. I'll make it worth your while,"
I coaxed.
"We'll see when you get here."
I pulled up to his place ten minutes later and
rang the bell. He opened the door and burst into
laughter.
"What in the world do you have on?"
"You won't be laughing long."
I took him by the hand and led him upstairs
to his pool room. It was perfectly dark there. Oh
yeah, this was going to be fun! I flipped the
light on, quickly changed the bulb to the black
lightbulb, and pretty much disappeared from his
sight—other than the white that highlighted my
face, hair, hands, and feet.
"I'll tell you what we're gonna do," I said as
I grabbed a cue stick from the rack and handed
it to him. "For every ball you sink, a little bit of
this is gonna come off."

"Mmm! That sounds like fun," Marvin inter-
rupted again. He munched on another cookie,
then gulped more juice. "Here, babe."

Dominique took the glass, sipped, then handed it back to her husband.

"Those people are gonna mess around and make me buy a pool table. Keep going," said Marvin.

Dominique rolled her eyes again and continued.

Terrance nodded his head and chuckled. "Okay."
He wasted no time racking the balls. "Forget what I said about not wanting to shoot pool tonight."
"Mm-hmm," I moaned seductively. Right before he cracked the set of balls, I moved toward the stereo in the corner and fumbled my way through starting his CD player, not knowing what he had loaded. The room filled with the sounds of some romantic favorites from a Body & Soul *collection.*
I stood across the table from him as he began to call shots as best he could in the alternate lighting. When the first ball sank, I fully removed my black jacket, revealing the white one underneath. The second ball dropped, and I removed the dark pants. I was now glowing from head to toe like the Ghost of Christmas Past. Quickly, he sank the third ball, then waited for my response. I unzipped my jacket, exposing the contrast of my glowing bra against my skin, which was dramatically darkened by the black light. He let out a groan, which let me know he was pleased with what he saw. The next ball hit the pocket, and I fully removed my white jacket, better highlighting my figure in the bra, gloves, and pants. When the next ball dropped, I removed the white pants, and I thought he inhaled all the air in the room through his

teeth. Another ball hit. I removed the boy leg briefs slowly and seductively, revealing the skimpy thong beneath, while in the background Johnny Gill cried out, "My, my, my."

"Mmh!" Terrance exclaimed and called his next shot. By the time he'd pocketed all the balls, there was nothing left on me but the ribbon I had tied around my neck and the thong. I had been strategic in my positioning and had stayed my distance the entire game, but now, with all the balls cleared away, he approached me slowly and wrapped his arms around me, then let his hands explore my flesh.

Gently lifting me up, he sat me on the edge of the pool table, and I wrapped my legs around his back. He began kissing me all over, taking me to a familiar place that I'd not been to in a very long time. Together, we slid back onto the table. My eyes closed, and I began to give myself to the moment and to his kisses, which had become more and more passionate. My body trembled in anticipation of what I knew Terrance was going to put on me, but then he became Denzel Washington . . . in a way that I couldn't appreciate.

"Ssss, Tiffany girl . . ."

My eyes popped wide open, and I pushed him off of me. This was a scene right out of Spike Lee's Mo' Better Blues, when Denzel's character, in heated sexual confusion, mixed those two women's names up.

Suddenly Dominique was glad about the chapter she was reading to her cheating husband. At this point she eagerly continued.

"Tiffany!" I screeched.

"Deece, I'm . . . Deece . . ." He was taking slaps upside the head as I struggled with all my might to get off the pool table.

"December, wait a minute. I didn't mean that. I just—"

"You just called me someone else's name! That's what you just did!" I screamed. In a fit of tears, I collected whatever clothes I could find, which, of course, was all the white stuff, pulled the pants and jacket on as best I could, and ran out of the room and down the steps. Terrance was right behind me, trying to calm me down, but knew better than to try to grab me.

"December, just wait a minute! Please!" I spun around, angrier than a swarm of hornets whose nest had been disturbed.

"Wait for what, Terrance? Wait for you to tell me that you're sorry!" I spat. "Well, I don't want to hear it! And you know what the sad part is? If you were to say to me, right now, that you're sorry, that would be the most honest thing you've ever said to me."

"That's a shame." Dominique stopped in the middle of the chapter. "It's funny how men act one way in front of one person but really got some other mess going on. Like sleeping with other women and then thinking 'I'm sorry' is going to fix it."

"Yeah. That is jacked up," Marvin replied unsuspectingly. "Women do it, too, though. Trust me, I know." For a few seconds he thought about the many times he'd caught his ex-wife in the arms and bed of another man.

"Men are so stupid. They got everything they need right at home but can't even appreciate it. Or just are too greedy to appreciate it," she sneered.

"Yeah. It's pretty sad." Marvin bit down into a strawberry, then popped another grape in his mouth. "Always thinking there's something better out there." He paused momentarily to swallow. "Ain't nothing out there but trouble. I have seen it happen to a thousand guys." Marvin shook his head, then looked up at his wife. "But I got all I need right here, with my baby, and my baby." With a grunt, he lifted himself from the floor, along with the tray, which now held only empty dishes.

Dominique was tempted to kick the tray out of his hands, unable to stomach his hypocrisy, but then she'd have to let the cat out of the bag, and she wasn't quite ready to do that.

"How much longer are you going to be in here?" he asked, his voice trailing as he headed out of the room and back to the kitchen.

With him now gone, Dominique didn't bother to give a response, but to her dismay, he came back just moments later and repeated himself.

"I don't know," she answered.

"Well, don't be too long. You know I don't get a good night's sleep if you're not in my arms." He dipped his head downward to peck Dominique's cheek. "Love you," he said, then placed his hand on her belly and gave a light squeeze. "Love you too." At that Marvin retreated to their bedroom.

16

"Just sit that right there," Feenie instructed the movers. Three men heaved a plush sectional across the room and to the wall she had pointed out. They eased it to the floor, then went out to their truck to bring in other items. Feenie walked into what would be the girls' room and hung a few pictures on the wall. She'd been able to work out with Rance and Laiken that the girls would spend the weekend with her. She couldn't remember a time that she'd been so excited to see her children, and she wanted to make a good impression.

Instead of the bunk beds they'd had when they lived with her before, she'd gotten them separate twin beds and decorated the room in purple and turquoise, the two colors she'd designated for them to distinguish their possessions. She smiled at the room, satisfied with what she'd done with it. The walls were painted, the beds were made, the pictures were hung, and she hoped the girls would be pleased.

Hearing the movers come in again, she walked back to the living room, pointed out more placement spots, then thanked the men and saw them out. Not even a minute after she closed the door behind them, there was a knock. Thinking that one of them had forgot something, she pulled the door open without looking through the peephole.

"Forgot . . . oh. Hey, Bryan," she said, clearly not excited about seeing him.

"Hey." He grinned. "Thought I'd come by to welcome you to the neighborhood and see if you needed any help."

"Where were you when I was painting and hanging curtains?" she commented, rolling her eyes and turning away, leaving him standing alone.

"Well, can I come in?"

"I didn't slam the door in your face, did I?" she sneered.

That was enough of an invitation for Bryan. He came in and looked around, pointing the corners of his lips downward as he nodded his head. "Looks nice. Like you been living here for a couple of years."

"Thanks," she said dryly.

"Something smells good." He tilted his nose in the air like a puppy and sniffed. "What did you cook? Got an extra place at the table?"

"Actually, I don't. The girls have been staying with their dad for a good while now because I had to take care of some things, and they are coming over to spend the night for the first time, and we need that private family time, you know?"

Bryan nodded slowly.

"It will be their first night with me, and sharing that time with a man won't make the best impression for them and will only make them feel like I didn't want to spend time with them. Otherwise, I'd ask you to stay." She shrugged. "Maybe next time."

"What time will they be here?" Bryan took the liberty of following her into the kitchen.

"I'm picking them up in about thirty minutes."

"Oh, okay. I got a few minutes, then."

"Actually you don't. I still have some things I need to take care of before they get here, if you don't mind."

"Can we just have a quick glass of wine?" Bryan asked. "I'll respect your time and leave right after that."

Why is this man sweatin' me like this! "Really, Bryan. I can't tonight. Maybe some other time."

Bryan couldn't stop grinning; he'd been expecting Feenie to toy with him a bit, but Feenie wasn't budging.

"Seriously," she said, walking toward the door and opening it for him. "I'll call you later, okay?"

Bryan pressed his lips together in disappointment. "All right."

"I'll walk you out. I just remembered I need to pick up a few things before I get the girls." Feenie grabbed her bag and keys, followed Bryan out, then closed and locked her door. "I'll call you later, okay?"

"Yeah." Bryan bent a bit to kiss her cheek.

"Enjoy your evening with your daughters."

Feenie climbed into her Kia Rio and drove to the Alexanders'. She rang the bell, nervously uncomfortable with entering her former lover's marital home.

"Hi, Jerrafine," Laiken greeted in a cordial but less than welcoming tone.

Today Laiken could clearly see Feenie's physical qualities, which she guessed the average man would find attractive, but still, they didn't justify Rance's behavior. And while their interaction a few weeks prior had not been the worst, Laiken still had her reservations about Feenie. At the same time, after giving it some thought, she had decided it might be in the best interest of the girls to have their mother back in their lives, even if it was limited. Even more importantly, Laiken felt she'd served enough of a sentence for a crime she hadn't committed, and saw an opportunity to bring the whole thing to what she hoped would be an accelerated end.

"Come on in," Laiken urged.

"Thanks. You have a lovely home," Feenie complimented, quickly looking around. She wondered, but she dared not ask, where Rance was.

"Thanks. You can have a seat. I'll get the girls for you."

Laiken left Feenie seated in the living room, then walked down the hallway leading to the girls' room, and seconds later Feenie heard feet storming toward her.

"Mommy!" Mia yelled, running at her mother full speed. Feenie braced herself for a bit of a collision and wrapped her arms around her daughter. "I couldn't wait to see you!"

"And I couldn't wait to see you, either. Where is your sister?"

"She's coming," said Mia.

Just then Cara emerged from the hallway. "Hi, Mommy," she said plainly.

"Hey, baby. You ready to go?" Feenie asked, taking immediate note of her daughter's nonchalant attitude.

"I guess." Cara shrugged, eyeing her mother up and down, assessing her attire. Feenie looked far different than she had when Cara had seen her last. This time her mother was dressed in a pair of cuffed capri jeans, a stylish rhinestone-embellished T-shirt, and a pair of heeled leather sandals. Her hair fell in loose ringlets, framing her face, which displayed just a hint of lip gloss.

"What's wrong?" asked Feenie.

"Nothing." Cara hugged her mom purely out of obligation.

"You sure?" Feenie asked, hugging Cara while she floated her eyes to Laiken in question but read no response.

"I'm sure," Cara affirmed, pulling away.

"You hungry? I cooked your favorite," Feenie sang, trying to encourage some enthusiasm from the older twin.

"Not that much," Cara answered, hoisting her overnight bag up on her shoulder.

"I am," Mia chimed in. "I'm very hungry!"

"Well, good, because dinner is going to be delicious, and I can't wait for you to see your room. Say good-bye to Miss Laiken and the boys," said Feenie.

The girls said their good-byes, then walked out to the car with Feenie.

"Mommy, you got us new beds?" Cara asked.

"I got you a whole new room in a whole new house. I think you will like it a lot," Feenie replied.

"Is it far from here?" Mia asked, leaning up from the backseat.

"Put your seat belt on. It's not that far."

When Feenie pulled into the parking garage, the girls oohed and aahed, and once inside the apartment, they continued as they explored each room. They screamed when they got to their own bedroom.

Feenie let them enjoy themselves while she warmed up homemade lasagna and pulled a salad from the refrigerator and placed it on the table, along with a bottle of blue cheese dressing. She could hardly remember a time when the three of them sat together and ate like a family, but Feenie was all for new beginnings. She smiled as she sat their plates and forks on the table.

"Mia, Cara . . . come on and eat," she called.

The girls rushed to the bathroom, washed their hands, then raced down the hallway to the table.

"I'll say grace!" Mia offered, both surprising and impressing Jerrafine. "Let's hold hands, because it's our first dinner together as a family," she suggested.

"Okay," Feenie agreed, grabbing the extended hands of her daughters.

"Okay, close your eyes," Mia ordered, then began her prayer. "Thank you, Lord, for food we eat and fresh, clean water that we drink. Thank you, Lord, for rest and care and little children everywhere. ABC, one, two, three, thank you, Lord, for feeding me. Amen."

After dinner the trio collectively washed the dishes. Then the girls bathed, kissed Feenie good night, and dove into their new beds.

"I like the new house," Mia whispered from her new bed.

"Me too," Cara admitted. "It's almost just like being at Daddy's house."

"It'll be fun having two houses and two rooms and going to two schools."

"Yep! If we don't like our teachers, we can switch on the days that they're being mean."

"Or we could eat lunch at school two times," Mia suggested. "And if we forget to do our homework one day, we could just go to the other school."

"That would be fun. And we could go to recess twice."

"Let's ask Mommy about it tomorrow, okay?"

"I gotta think about it a little bit more first," Cara whispered.

"Why? This should be a no-brainer," Mia commented, using jargon she'd picked up from her brothers.

"'Cause."

"Because what?"

The old Jerrafine would have reprimanded

the girls for talking past their bedtime, but she let them carry on with no consequence. She happened to be passing their partially closed door with an armful of laundry and stopped to listen in on the girls' conversation.

"'Cause I still don't know if I wanna live here."

"But why not? I mean, it's our mom," Mia argued. "And the house is pretty!"

"'Cause."

"'Cause what?"

"'Cause she don't have a job," Cara replied, enlightening her sister.

Mia mulled over Cara's reason before speaking again. "But Mommy don't never have a job. She didn't have a job before."

"So how do you think she was paying bills, Mia?" Cara asked, as if Mia was unable to see the obvious.

"I don't know. Maybe she didn't have bills or something."

"All grown-ups got bills. That's why they have to have jobs in the first place."

"But she didn't have a job before, so she must not have had any bills to pay."

"But food and stuff is not free. And then she would always say, 'Y'all better stop running up my light bill!' Remember?" Cara asked.

"Yeah."

"So I know how she was getting money and why she used to leave us at home all the time," Cara said informatively.

"How then, since you know so much?"

"She be holding up a sign at all the Wal-Marts so people can give her money."

Feenie's eyes grew wide as she stood outside the door.

"Uh-uh!" Mia challenged.

"Yes, she do, 'cause one time when Miss Laiken took us to the store with her, I saw her."

"When?"

"You remember that time we had got those peanut butter cookies, but we couldn't have any until we got our room clean?"

"Yeah."

"It was that day," Cara pointed out. "All uh us was in the van, and it was my turn to ride up front with Miss Laiken, and when we was leaving, I saw her."

"I don't believe you," Mia responded, unable to imagine her mother as a beggar.

"For real! I can even tell you what she had on. She had on those jeans that's all raggedy on the bottom, and a pink, wrinkled up T-shirt, and them flip-flops that's in her room, in the closet. And remember how her hair was looking that day she took us to McDonald's and how it was all over the place, but she had a hat on? That how she was looking when I saw her. And she was holding a sign up that was made out of a box, but I couldn't see what it said 'cause the light was green and we was going too fast."

With Cara's description, Feenie knew she'd been spotted by her daughter.

"Did you say hi to her?" Mia asked.

"I tried to wave a little bit, but she wasn't looking."

"That still don't mean we can't live with her,

though," Mia said, bringing the conversation back around full circle.

"Yes, it do, because I don't wanna be all at school and somebody say, 'Where does your momma work?' Then I have to say that she be standing outside, tryna get people to give us money. Everybody would be laughing."

"Just don't tell them."

"Okay, but then when we have to go to PTA or something, suppose somebody see her and then be like, 'That's your momma?' And then when we say yeah, they gonna say she be beggin' at Wal-Mart all the time."

Feenie pulled herself away from the door, embarrassed that she'd been seen by one of the twins. It was easy money but could hardly be considered honest money. She couldn't blame Cara for being ashamed. Feenie already knew that she couldn't go on begging forever in the first place, but the conversation she'd overheard was definitely a wake-up call.

She stood at the end of her bed, folding clothes and putting them away as she replayed Cara's comments in her head. With the back of her hand, she smeared away a few random tears that escaped her eyelids and thought about what she should or could do. Denial was her first thought. *I'll just go in there and tell them that I heard them talking and just say that that wasn't me.* It seemed like a good idea only for two seconds, but beyond that, the lie only made her feel even more guilty and disgraceful.

"I'ma have to tell them the truth," she whispered aloud. "It's the only way I'll be able to get their respect later." She rejected the urge to think further about it, dropped what she was doing, and just about burst into the girls' room, where they were still chattering about something. Her quick entry startled them, and immediately their conversation ceased.

"Hey," Feenie said, careful to keep her tone light rather than reprimanding.

"We was 'bout to go to sleep," Cara answered without hesitation, remembering times past when she and her sister had been yelled at for talking rather than sleeping.

"No, it's okay. I wanted to talk to y'all for a minute."

Silence hung in the air for a few seconds while the girls questioned her with their eyes.

Feenie inhaled deeply, still unsure of what exactly she intended to say, then let the words spill out. "Y'all saw me at Wal-Mart?"

"Cara said she did, but I didn't," Mia offered.

"No, I didn't," Cara said, denying the truth. "I said that I thought I saw—"

"Yes, you did," Feenie gently interjected. "I heard y'all talking."

Both girls fell silent.

"Well, I wanted to come in here and say . . ." Feenie paused and blew out a long breath. "I wanted to say that you did see me," she admitted, "and I'm sorry that you saw me like that, and I'm sorry for embarrassing you."

"But why was you doing that, Mommy?" Cara asked.

Feenie leaned back on the edge of the dresser and decided to be honest with her children. "I was doing that because I didn't really want to get a job. I was being lazy." She paused and looked back and forth between the two girls. "I don't ever want you two to do that, because you are so smart and bright, and you won't ever need to."

"But you're smart, too, though," said Mia.

"You're right, Mia. I just needed some money really fast so I could try to get somewhere to live, and instead of working for it, I begged for it, which was completely wrong. I shouldn't have been doing that," Feenie said, shaking her head. "I should be giving you girls a better example of how grown-ups are supposed to act and live. And you're right, Cara. All grown-ups have bills and should have jobs. I have made you ashamed of me by not having a job, but I'm making the promise to both of you right now that I'm going to get a job and go to work every day, so you never have to worry about any of your friends seeing me ask for money."

"Okay," Cara responded in a gap of silence.

"I've not always been the best mother to you girls, but I'm going to prove to both of you that I can be the best mom ever," Feenie added.

"You already are the best mom ever," Mia replied.

Her words brought tears to Feenie's eyes, and she dropped her face in her palms and sobbed.

"Don't cry." Mia threw back her covers and flew to her mother's side, followed by Cara. "You'll find a job, Mommy. Want us to pray for you?"

Feenie sniffed hard, fanned at her eyes, then answered, "Yeah, that's a good idea."

Cara whispered a brief child's prayer, requesting help for her mother in securing employment, then hugged Feenie tight.

"I love you girls," Feenie murmured, then leaned down to kiss each girl's cheek.

"Love you too," the twins said in unison.

"All right. No more talking. You get some sleep." Feenie took the time to tuck her daughters into their separate beds, then left the room, turning off the light on the way. "Good night, sleep tight, and don't let the bedbugs bite!" she teased, getting a giggle from the kids.

After pulling the door closed, Feenie walked to her living room, collapsed on the couch, and cried for the next several minutes, feeling sorry for herself and wishing she could turn back the hands of time and do a few things differently. Actually, there were several things she wished she could do differently. "But I'd settle for a few," she mumbled to herself.

She sat silently as her eyes circled the room, looking at the various furnishings in her home. The pride she had felt when her social worker and even Laiken had come by and complimented her on her decor and style was now diminished by shame over the means she'd used to secure and furnish the apartment.

"Your home is beautiful," Laiken had to admit during a quick visit before allowing Feenie to pick up the girls. "Did you decorate it yourself?"

"Yeah, I did," Feenie had responded smugly.

"It's something I've always enjoyed and been kinda good at."

"This looks like something out of a magazine. The colors, the textures . . ." Laiken's expression had suggested she was impressed with Feenie's eye for design and ability to put together an incredibly warming and inviting living space. "Things look like they are really coming together for you."

"Thanks, Laiken. I'm working really hard at it." Feenie had smiled and let her eyes travel around the room in feigned modesty.

And at that time and all the way up until this evening, Feenie had thought her home was beautiful. But now every item in the room was an eyesore to her, because she knew she had not put in a single day's work to obtain anything she laid her eyes on.

Feenie now realized she wasn't fooling anyone but herself. Cara had helped her to see an image of herself that she hadn't quite paid any attention to before. She felt like an undeserving, begging whore, living a complete lie but trying to make others believe that she had it all together.

"I can change," she whispered to herself, wiping her nose against the sleeve of her shirt. "It's not too late for me." She dialed Bryan's number; he answered after two rings.

"I thought you were just putting me on when you said you'd call me later," he said.

"I try to keep my word," Feenie replied humbly. "You busy?"

"Not really. Why? What's going on?"

"I just wanted to talk to you about something

you mentioned before," she stated. "I need to be real with you."

"You want me to come over?" Bryan asked suggestively.

"It's nothing like that, Bryan. Seriously, I need to talk to you. I mean, you can come over, but the girls are here, and I don't need to mess up my chances of getting them back by compromising."

"Right," he replied, changing his tone. "What's going on?"

"I really need to find a job, and I know you said that there might be a few down at city hall that you might be able to refer me for."

"Oh. Yeah, I can do that. What kind of work are you looking for? Any particular department or field?"

"I'm actually open to anything, to be honest with you. I mean, I still have some money, but I won't be able to get custody of my girls unless I'm gainfully employed."

"I see."

"I know beggars can't be choosers, but I'd like to find something that pays more than minimum wage, you know?"

"Oh yeah, I know all about starting from the bottom and working my way up. I'll tell you what. Let me get in the office tomorrow and see what we have posted and then get back to you."

"Okay. Thanks."

"How soon you looking to start?" Bryan asked.

"The sooner the better."

"Gotcha. Let me see what I can find out. You can look online and see what's there, too."

"I'll do that. Can I call if I see something?"

"Sure."

"I wanna talk to you about something else, too," Feenie said.

"What's that?"

"I like you a lot, Bryan, but the truth is I can't keep seeing you the way I am right now. Don't get me wrong. You're good company and everything, but with the girls coming back, I have to be careful how I manage my personal life."

"So you don't want to see me anymore? That's what you're saying?" Bryan asked.

"I'm not saying that as much as I'm saying I need to clean my life up and get myself together."

"Right, right."

"I mean, you know me and how I usually am, down for whatever, but I can't keep living my life like that. I gotta make some changes. I've made some big mistakes in my life, and I'm just ready to get it all cleaned up. I need to do right for my girls' sake." Feenie sniffed and brushed away a fallen tear.

"You gotta do what you gotta do," Bryan commented.

"Yeah. I hope you understand," she answered.

"Of course I do. I'll get with you tomorrow and let you know what's available. We can hook up some other time."

"Thanks, Bryan."

"No problem."

Feenie hung up the phone, then retreated to her bedroom and said a short prayer.

"Lord, I know I've been asking for a whole lot lately, but if you don't help me, I won't be able to do anything. Please have mercy on me and extend your hand to me at least one more time. I'm trying to get my life together, and I need a few more things to work out for my good, like your word says in Romans eight, twenty-eight—all things work together for good to them that love you—and I do love you, so I will wait with great expectation for you to come through for me with a job. Lord, I can't keep on standing on the corner, asking for money. I promise if you bless me with a job, I will go to work every day and perform at my best. Even if Bryan decides not to help me, I know that you are my source and can easily provide for me, so I thank you for it right now. Thank you for your faithfulness and your mercy and your grace. Amen."

17

"It's worse than I thought," Dominique told Tamara. She hid under a large sun hat and shades out on the deck at Jillian's. She picked at her appetizer of four mini cheeseburgers topped with Thousand Island dressing and onions.

"What do you mean? I know that he's not seeing his ex," Tamara said, scooping some salsa onto a tortilla chip.

"He got somebody pregnant." Dominique was able to hold back the tears because she'd spent the last week crying every day, while Marvin was at work, and every night, after he went to sleep.

"Dominique, uh-uh! You are seriously trippin'. There is no way on this earth that Marvin is cheating. And then to get somebody pregnant? Who?"

"I don't know who she is!" Dominique exclaimed. "But I heard her tell him that she was pregnant."

"What? Wait." Tamara lifted her hands, motioning for Dominique to pause for a moment. "Tell me the whole story."

Dominique pinched the bridge of her nose, feeling both the onset of tears and a headache at the same time, took a deep breath, then began. "Okay. Although I was feeling some type of way about the whole ex-wife letter and all that, I thought maybe I was just overreacting and I should just let it go. After all, like you said, it is only a letter. Who knows what that crazy woman wanted. So I decided to surprise Marvin at work with lunch. I get there, go in the gym, and I'm on my way to his office, and I hear him yelling about something."

"About what?"

"I don't know, because I couldn't make out what he was saying, except something like, 'You need some money, so you come in here with a story?' By then I was standing right outside his office, at the door. Then the woman was like, 'I just wanted to tell you about your baby. I don't want nothing from you.' Then she walked out and almost knocked me down and left the building. Marvin slammed the door as soon as she walked out, so he never knew that I was standing there."

Tamara could find no words, and she mulled over what Dominique had just spilled. "There's got to be some explanation, Dominique."

"Yeah! I'm sure there is! He done got somebody pregnant!" Dominique blurted. "I think she was there asking for abortion money or something." Sniffles followed her sentence. "And he wouldn't give it to her."

"So you hear this woman tell your husband that she's pregnant with his baby, she walks out of his office, runs smack-dab into you, and you don't say anything to either one of them?"

"No."

"Why not? Why didn't you at least ask her who she was? Did she seem surprised to see you?"

"No. She just bumped into me, said excuse me, and left."

"And you let her get away?"

"What was I supposed to do?"

"Beat her ass!" Tamara yelled loud enough for everyone dining on the deck to hear. "Ooh, sorry."

"I can't be fighting in my condition."

"You definitely should have slapped Marvin. Why didn't you at least do that?"

"I was too shocked and devastated."

"So what did you say to him when he got home?"

"Nothing." Dominique shrugged.

"Why?"

"I couldn't. I mean, what was it going to do, anyway? I already know what he did, so what was bringing it up to him gonna do? Besides make me cry after he tried to feed me a bowl of lies? Do you honestly think that he was gonna sit up there and just admit to me that number one, he's been messing around, and number two, he knocked some girl up?"

"What did she look like? Did you at least look at the girl, since you didn't do anything else?"

"Don't fuss at me, Tamara. I feel bad enough as it is without you trying to have me caught up in assault charges."

"I'm sorry. Girl, you know I've always been the fighter. Anyway, how did she look?"

Dominique sighed. "Tall, pretty." She shrugged. "Hair pulled back in a ball. Nice figure." For a moment, the inside of Dominique's lip took the place of her meal, as she bit gently into it. "I just can't believe Marvin would do this to me. I can't believe it."

"I'm sorry, girl," Tamara sighed.

"I'll tell you this. He thought his ex-wife put him through the wringer. He ain't seen nothing yet."

"Don't mess around and go to jail, because I'm in school, and I can't take that baby for you," Tamara joked, trying to lighten the mood.

"Then he came home talking about, 'Oh, I love you so much. You're so beautiful.' Yeah, whatever!" Dominique smudged her tears into her skin. "I just gotta think of ways to get back at him without damaging myself."

"And I'll help you," Tamara promised.

Marvin was infuriated when he walked into the parking lot after practice and found that his S-Class had been terribly keyed.

"What in the world!" he exclaimed, circling his car two full times. Instantly he suspected his ex-wife. With pressed lips, he shook his head, remembering her antics from years before. He hadn't talked to Jerrafine long enough to find out if she had relocated to the city, or if she was in town, visiting, or had simply made a special trip, like she'd told him. All he knew was that this was exactly like her. Whenever she didn't get her way, she retaliated. "She hasn't changed one bit," he commented aloud.

He was tempted to scroll through his phone and find her number, which he'd called weeks ago. He was sure that it was still stored in his BlackBerry's history. The more he looked at the deep scratches in his car, the more infuriated he became, and the more he struggled not to call Feenie and give her a piece of his mind. Instead he called Dominique.

"Hello," she answered without feeling.

"Baby, someone keyed my Benz!" he blurted in fury.

"Really?" Her tone was nonchalant, but Marvin was too angry to notice.

"I cannot believe this!"

"Why would someone key your car, Marvin?" she asked innocently.

"That is what I'm trying to figure out!" he exclaimed, really not knowing why Feenie would do such a thing. "I haven't done anything to anyone, so who in the devil would have done this?"

"I don't know," she answered smugly. "Did you call the cops?"

"What are they going to do? I didn't see anything. I can't prove anything. All I can do is fill out a report. Look at this mess!" With the phone still pressed to his ear, he circled the car another time.

"You don't have any idea who could have done it?" Dominique taunted. Marvin would never guess or believe that it had been her.

"If I think long and hard enough, maybe I could come up with somebody, but not really," he answered, covering his suspicions. "This doesn't make sense."

"Is it repairable?"

"I'll have to get the whole thing painted," he sighed as he climbed into the driver's seat. "Anyway, I'm on my way home."

"Okay."

"Did you cook? I'm famished."

"No. I was going to, but the baby wouldn't let me," Dominique lied. She actually had felt fine all day but was not interested in cooking for her husband. *Maybe that wench will fix you something,* she thought.

Marvin sighed but accepted that he'd have to stop off somewhere to pick up something to eat. Quickly he thought about what he'd pass on his way home. "I'm just going to stop at Hooters and pick up some wings and shrimp. You want anything?"

"No, I'm not hungry," she commented but made a mental note to stop by Hooters over the next few days to see if Marvin's lover worked there. She had captured enough of Feenie's image in their two-second meeting to recognize her again.

"Did you feed my baby today?"

"Yes," she answered without feeling. "I'm pretty tired. I'm going to bed."

Truth be told, she didn't want to deal with Marvin at all. It was becoming more and more difficult for her to hide her feelings and pretend that nothing was wrong. She cringed every night when he crawled into bed beside her, scooting over as far as she could on her side of the mattress. If he touched her, it was easy to complain about her discomfort to make him stop. Disappointed, Marvin would always recoil, but just the fact that he lay beside her was too much to deal with. Secretly, Dominique had started making plans to leave her husband—baby or no baby.

"I'll see you when you get home, okay?" she said, ending the call.

Marvin started his drive home, feeling like a spectacle with the new markings carved into the sides of his vehicle. It seemed like every car he passed, the driver—male or female—fixed his or her eyes first on him, then on the body of his car, then on him again. Brothas seemed to snicker, chuckle, or just burst out in full-blown laughter.

"Man, she tore your jonk up!" snorted a saggy-pants teenager who stood on a corner with a few of his friends. The young men gawked and elbowed each other, pointing out the damage. "Hope it was worth it, yo!"

Marvin was embarrassed, and that made him angry. In his growing fury, his fingers couldn't dial Jerrafine's number quickly enough. Without thinking, he skipped the sequence of digits that would mask his number under a private label. Only a few seconds passed before his ex-wife's voice calmly came across the line.

"Feenie, what the hell!" he thundered before she could even finish the word *hello*.

"Excuse me?"

"Are you crazy?" he asked, beginning his tirade, which was heavily seasoned with his choice of four-letter words.

"Who is this, first of all?" Feenie asked for confirmation, although she thought the irate caller sounded like her ex.

"It's Marvin," he bellowed. "Don't play stupid now!"

"Why are you calling me, yelling in my ear, Marvin?"

"Are you crazy? Have you lost your little ghetto mind!"

"What are you talking about?"

"What do you mean, what am I talking about? You know exactly what I'm talking about!"

"My business with you was done weeks ago, Marvin. I don't know what you're ranting and raving about, but I don't appreciate you calling here with some bull that I don't know nothing about."

"You are a trifling somebody, you know that? You always were and always will be."

"That was the old me, Marvin, and I'll admit that. I have already admitted it as well as apologized."

"So this is how you're gonna act? Like you're just so innocent, huh?"

"Why don't you just tell me what you're talking about? If you're gonna call here and accuse me of something, you could at least tell me what I did."

"You jacked up my Benz!" he yelled.

"No, I did not!" Feenie retorted, further fueling his anger and frustration.

"And you actually expect me to believe that? You come whisking into town, show up at my job with some story that you should have told me twenty years ago, and then my car gets keyed, and you expect me to believe you when you say you didn't do it?"

"Why would I do that? I told you, I only came to tell you the truth and assure you that you would never have to worry about me again. I meant that. Now, I don't know what crazy woman you got around there, stalking you, keying your car up, but it ain't me."

"The only crazy person I know is you! When are you just gonna leave me alone, Feenie? When are you gonna stop it? You don't love me. You never did. You never wanted me or cared about me. What is it with you? What is it about me that makes you hate me so much that you are just hell bent on destroying my life?"

"Marvin, you need to stop wasting your time cussin' and spittin' at me and start looking for the chick that messed up your car, because it wasn't me."

"Yeah, right. You got me a thousand times before, but you won't get me again. I'm going to let the police deal with you," Marvin threatened. "I'ma see what you gonna be saying then!" He pressed the end key on his phone, wishing he could slam it against a cradle like an old-fashioned house phone just to release a tiny bit of tension. Instead, he hammered his steering wheel with his fist.

Marvin pulled into a gas-station parking lot, got out, and again took a painful look at his car and cursed. "Look at this," he said out loud to himself. He glanced around, hoping that no one was paying him any attention, but he could have sworn that every set of eyes that passed him studied his car. Not only were the scratches ugly, but they implied indiscretions, which he was not guilty of. He hadn't cheated on his wife, gotten caught in any compromising positions, or done anything that was worthy of the damage done to his car.

18

Sans résumé, Feenie was nervous sitting in the human resources office of the city hall building. She hadn't been on a job interview since she was sixteen years old, and now in her midforties, she felt like a teenager trying to get his or her first job. She'd looked online for sample interview questions in order to prepare herself, but there was hardly a question that didn't concern previous work experience, and Feenie hadn't had a job in over fifteen years.

"All I can do is my best," she reminded herself.

"Jerrafine Trotter," the human resources assistant called.

Feenie immediately stood, tugged at her short hemline, and walked forward.

"First, we're going to need you to complete a typing test. Then we'll get you over to an interviewer," announced the assistant.

"Okay. How many words do I need to be able to type again?"

"What job are you applying for?" the assistant

asked, glancing at Feenie's online application results. "Oh, I see it here. Desk clerk. That position requires a typing speed of thirty-five words per minute."

"Oh, okay. No problem." In all actuality, Feenie was terrified of what her two-finger typing speed might be.

"You can warm up for about three minutes, and you can do the warm-up twice. Then you will take the actual test, which will also be for three minutes." The woman got Feenie settled at a computer station, left her alone to practice, then returned to start her on the actual test.

Concentrating and bouncing her eyes between the computer screen and the keyboard, Feenie pushed lettered keys using only her index fingers and prayed for a passing score. The three minutes went by quickly, and she nearly broke into praise when the result popped up on the computer screen, putting her at thirty-seven words.

She next met with her interviewer, Kerra Butler, a heavyset white woman who looked to be in her midthirties. Kerra was dressed in what Feenie would consider a muumuu, a large colorful smock of a dress that did nothing more than drape her body. Her feet looked jammed into a pair of red flats, which seemed to be stretched by the wideness of her feet. Kerra's hair hung limply around her shoulders in a frizzy mess, like she had gotten hold of a bad perm. Her hair was kept out of her face by a wide red headband. Her face was plain and, by Feenie's assessment, had never seen the likes of a make-up brush, an eyeliner pencil, or a tube of lipstick. The sad part to Feenie was Kerra could look a whole lot better with just a little effort. The only thing Kerra had going for her at that moment was her straight white teeth.

"So, I just have a few questions for you here," Kerra stated.

Like Feenie had anticipated, she could hardly speak about her past job experience but did her best. Each time she answered a question, she noted Kerra's slight frown, which was an indication to her that her interview was not going as well as she needed it to. Although Bryan had given Feenie the okay to do so, she had failed to utilize his name on her application, not wanting to be in his eternal debt. But now that she sat in front of Kerra, struggling for answers, she wished she'd accepted his favor.

She took her chance when Kerra asked, "So how did you find out about this job?"

"I was actually doing some networking." Feenie carefully chose her words. "With the city manager, Bryan West. I'd mentioned to him that I was trying to get a job, and he told me to check online to see what positions were available. I did just that, so now I'm here." She smiled.

"I see. Well, Ms. Trotter, while the position available is an entry-level position, we typically look for candidates with more work experience that what you have here—"

"I know," Feenie cut in, "but I promise you, I'm a hard worker, and I'll put my very best foot forward. I'm sure Mr. West can give you a good recommendation on me."

"Did you list him as a reference?" Kerra asked, flipping through a couple of pages of Feenie's application profile, looking for Bryan's name.

"No, I didn't, because I wanted to try to get the job on my own." Now Feenie wasn't sure if that had been the best decision.

"I see," Kerra responded, then paused, still glancing over the limited information she had before her. "I look to hire the best candidates, Jerrafine, and with your lack of experience, I'm just not sure that you'd be a good fit for this role."

"I know I don't have much work experience to speak of, but it's only because I was fortunate enough to not have to work," Feenie explained. "You see, I'm a single parent with twin daughters, but their father has always provided for the three of us, which gave me the privilege of staying at home to raise my girls. I know a lot of parents don't get the opportunity to do that, or maybe even value working outside their home more than being a mom, but I can honestly say, I'm grateful that I was able to do it."

"So how did you decide that this particular department was a good fit for you?"

"I looked at the qualifications and thought that I could meet most of them. I have cash-handling experience, even though I haven't had to use it since my girls were born, but I do work well with little to no supervision. I know what quality customer service looks like because I expect it everywhere I shop or go. I have good computer skills, although I've never had to use them in an office setting. I'm sure the other skills you are looking for, I can quickly develop with a little bit of training. All I need is a chance to prove myself, because I am a very determined person."

Kerra studied Feenie's face for several seconds. "I just feel like there's something else there that I haven't quite tapped into yet."

Feenie's heart skipped a beat, unsure if Kerra was trying to let on that she knew more than what Feenie had shared. She couldn't discern if Kerra was digging for more information from something she sensed, or if she had already done some type of background investigation. "What, umm, what makes you say that?" she stammered.

Kerra shrugged, but her eyes were piercing. "Just a gut feeling."

In two seconds' time, Feenie thought about every bad decision she'd made that put her in a far less than favorable light. "I have nothing to hide . . . ," Feenie replied, crossing her fingers underneath the table, where her hands rested on her lap. "But I do have something to share."

"Mmm." Kerra folded her fingers beneath her chin and gave Feenie her full attention.

"Miss Butler, I really need this job. Like I said, I really don't have much of a work history, because I was able to stay home with my girls. That's the God's honest truth." After heavily exhaling, Feenie continued. "But I got in a little bit of trouble and ended up having to serve some time, and I'm not very proud of that, which is why I didn't mention it."

"I see. Tell me about it," Kerra said, probing.

"Well, it wasn't a felony or violent crime or anything like that. Honestly, I left my girls at home alone, which was so stupid of me. They were only eight at the time, so I ended up having to go to jail for child neglect," Feenie said, spilling the words out. "While I was gone, they stayed with their dad, but I really would like to have my children back home with me, and me getting a job is a big piece of that," she added, her voice starting to quiver a bit. "I need to erase this negative example that I set for my girls, and I'm willing to do anything—any job that you have, even if it's nothing more than scrubbing toilets." She paused, indicating that she'd finished her spiel. "I'm just asking that you give me a chance."

When Feenie left that day, she didn't know what to think. Kerra had made it clear that she wasn't the best interview candidate, but Feenie hoped that her honesty and eagerness would net her at least a callback. That same day, with a fluctuating amount of faith, she stopped at Burlington Coat Factory in Security Square Mall to pick up a few work separates to mix and match, knowing that most of the clothing in her closet would hardly be acceptable to wear in a professional work environment. She shopped carefully, trying on every piece she chose, making sure nothing grabbed her hips or her bust too tightly. Each time she slid into a new outfit and looked in the mirror, she felt a new sense of pride and self-worth. She felt respectable, which was something she'd never before been able to say, as much as she played the part of the in-control, take-charge diva.

After two days passed without a callback, Feenie dialed Bryan's number. "Hey," she said once he answered.

"Hey, Jerrafine. How's it going?" he asked casually.

"Good. I was calling to see if you could help me out or check on something for me. I applied down at city hall, like we talked about, and I had an interview the other day, but I've not heard anything back. Can you talk to the lady and let me know what she says? Like if she is going to hire me or not?"

"I probably can't get to it today, but give me until the end of the week. I have a lot of meetings and things going on all week, so I will have to work it in during my free time. I'll do my best," Bryan said, making no promises.

Feenie was disappointed, semi-expecting him to drop what he was doing to find out the information she'd requested. She knew he could probably hear it in her tone of voice, but she tried not to let it be obvious. "Okay, well, I will call you later then, if that's all right with you."

"Sure. Maybe we can get together for dinner or something."

"Ummm." Feenie paused, not wanting to commit to anything. "Maybe so. I just really need to focus all my efforts on finding a job, though, to be honest with you, Bryan."

"I understand, but you do have to eat, though, right?"

"Actually, I've been fasting here lately," she answered, hoping he'd find that a turnoff.

"Fasting? That's what you're into?"

"What do you mean?"

"I mean, you done got all religious and sanctified and stuff?"

"If you want to call it that. I told you I was trying to get my life together. How can I do that without God?" Feenie questioned.

"What is it that they say? Old things have passed away and everything is new, or something like that," Bryan mocked with a snicker, but Feenie did not laugh with him. "Man, you really have changed, huh?"

"I'm trying to."

"All right, well, I'll let you know what I find out, if anything."

"Thanks. I appreciate it," she quipped, although the conversation made her not just regret calling Bryan in the first place, but wish that she'd not used his name to try to get the job at all.

Feenie hadn't been off the phone for even thirty seconds before it rang in her hand. After recognizing the number as that of city hall's human resources office, she wasted no time in answering.

"Hi, Jerrafine. This is Kerra Butler calling about the job you applied and interviewed for earlier this week?" she said as a question.

"Yes," Jerrafine said excitedly. "How are you?"

"I'm great. Thanks for asking. I wanted to

give you a call to let you know I've decided to make you a job offer for the clerk position."

"That's so awesome!" Feenie beamed.

"Now, because you don't have any recent job experience, you'll start off with a ninety-day probation period. How do you feel about that?"

"That's perfectly fine with me. I don't mind at all. I promise you, you will not regret it."

19

Over the next couple of months, Laiken and Feenie formed an unlikely friendship. They could hardly be thought of as best friends, but Laiken would have never thought that there could be any kind of peaceable relationship between her and a woman who'd slept with her husband. Nonetheless, as Feenie came around more and more to get the girls, the two women found themselves engaging in conversations that even Laiken had to admit were pleasant. Feenie had made the first step toward their camaraderie one evening after dropping the girls off.

Laiken had allowed her the privilege of tucking Mia and Cara into bed, which Feenie did quickly. Rance wasn't home, as he tried his best to stay away when he knew Feenie was coming over to avoid serious potential conflict, and Feenie didn't want to give the perception that she was waiting around to see him. As she headed for the door to let herself out, she found her feet seemingly stuck to the floor of the foyer of the Alexanders' home, wrestling with herself over a conversation she knew she needed to have with Laiken. It would have been easier for Feenie to simply say good night and leave, but a gentle pressing on her heart wouldn't let her cross the threshold without getting a few things off her chest. Glancing down at her watch, she knew she'd have to make it quick.

"Laiken, can I talk to you for a few minutes?"

Laiken, seated in the living room, looked up from the magazine she'd been reading. "Okay." Her tone expressed that she was a bit puzzled, but she thought that Feenie was about to tell her she was ready to take the girls home permanently.

"It won't take me long to say what I've got to say."

"Should we sit?" Laiken offered.

"Thanks." Feenie took a seat on the couch, folded her hands in her lap, and cleared her throat. "I don't know exactly how to say this or where to start, so forgive me if it doesn't come out quite right," she began as Laiken took a seat in an armchair adjacent to her. "Laiken, I just want to tell you that I am so sorry. I have jacked your whole life up," she said, shaking her head sorrowfully. "Because I wanted to be selfish and conniving. I had no right doing what I did, getting involved with Rance, then purposely trapping him." She sighed. "And I knew that he was married and you two had children, but I didn't care about nobody but myself. I never thought of the impact it would make on other undeserving people. I look at the way you have looked after my twins, and I can honestly say, if I were in your shoes, I don't think I would have taken it quite as well, and I sure wouldn't have let them in my home. I probably would have put my husband out and sent the kids with him and let them all live in the streets."

Laiken didn't comment but just listened intently.

"I so admire you for your strength, Laiken. I know it had to be real hard. I can't even imagine. And then to deal with me personally is a whole nother story. I mean, what wife wants to openly deal with her husband's . . ." She paused for a moment, trying to find a word that wouldn't sound too bad but found none. "Well, you know. If it were me, I would have gone to throwing blows, but you didn't. It takes a special type of woman to deal with all that and then not put a bullet in somebody." She chuckled nervously.

"It has been a struggle," Laiken admitted. "It still is."

"I know." Feenie paused. "And I'm so sorry for putting you through this. I know that an apology is not much, but it's all I can offer you. I can't undo anything, but I can let you know how sorry I am for ruining your family. Please forgive me."

Laiken nodded quickly, wiping away a tear that had escaped her right eyelid.

Feenie stood to her feet, smudging away tears

of her own. "I guess I better go, but thank you for everything you've done for my girls and for me." She extended her arms toward Laiken, and Laiken quickly stood to her feet and accepted. The two women held the embrace for several seconds, both releasing tears.

"Thanks for the apology, Jerrafine," Laiken whispered. "I appreciate you saying that."

They loosened their holds on each other, and Laiken walked Feenie to the door.

"Drive safely," Laiken said.

"Thanks. Enjoy the rest of your evening. Good night."

Laiken closed the door and played the conversation back in her head. She believed Feenie's apology was sincere and heartfelt. She'd definitely been right in what she'd said about things being hard. She sat back on the couch and did some soul-searching about what had made her stay with Rance in spite of what he'd done.

Initially, she'd felt hopeless, confused, and stupid. Not to mention ugly and unattractive. She believed she'd always been a great wife to Rance. She felt she was perfectly domesticated, cooking, doing laundry and dishes, keeping the house tidy, and managing the kids. She worked out religiously, so she easily maintained her size four figure and was never more than five pounds away from the weight she'd been at when she and Rance met, pregnancy not included. She'd engaged in sex at Rance's every request for the most part, rarely using a headache as an excuse, and found creative ways to work around her monthly period. She had even gotten her breasts done when she noticed a bit of sagging and loose skin. In her mind, she still looked hot in a bikini, and she had always given attention to her appearance, especially ten years ago, when Rance obviously had gotten involved with Jerrafine. At that point, they'd been married only a few years and hadn't had any major battles. So why would he cheat on me? It was the question she'd asked herself a million times over, but she never was able to come to any conclusion.

As she sat lost in thought again, her anger slowly building, Rance came through the door.

"Hey," he said casually, not expecting much of a response. "Are the girls back?"

"Why did you do it, Rance?" she shot at him, catching him off guard.

"Huh?"

"Why did you do it? Why did you cheat on me?"

Rance stood silent, knowing that no reason he gave would be justifiable. "Where is this coming from?" It was his poor attempt at a stall.

"I want to know what it was that made you violate our vows and your commitment to me and sleep with another woman. Was I not pretty enough?"

"You know you've always been beautiful to me, Laiken. You're the most beautiful woman I've ever laid eyes on."

"Right, but not beautiful enough for you to remain faithful," she snapped.

"It wasn't because you weren't beautiful. It was because I was stupid. I've told you that. I was foolish and greedy and an inconsiderate, selfish jerk that didn't even think about the consequences until it was too late."

At this point the words came easily. The topic had already been visited and revisited in counseling sessions. Similar conversations had been had multiple times behind the closed doors of their bedroom. Fights and arguments had brought forth Laiken's question a few times before. So his response was pretty much programmed in his head and poured from his mouth almost naturally and with little effort.

"Laiken, 'I'm sorry' is never going to be enough. Any answer I ever give you is never going to make it right or make you feel any better about it." He headed toward the kitchen.

"So you're going to walk away from me just like that?" She furrowed her brows, following her husband.

"I'm not walking away, Laiken, but really, where is this conversation headed? What are we going to accomplish? I've been apologizing for damn near two years now, and what has it accomplished? Has it helped things?"

"How dare you!" Laiken gasped. "You go out here and have a couple of kids and then get mad at me when I call you on it?" she said through clenched teeth. "You've got a lot of nerve!"

"No, it's not nerve," Rance said, pulling the refrigerator door open. "It's going in circles. It's trying to reach a compromise and never getting to one. Now, don't get me wrong. I'm not saying that what I did is easy to forgive or is excusable, but what I am saying is you are going to have to reach a point where you decide what it is that you really want to do. Do you want to continue to fight about this, or do you want to really work together to get past this? I can't do it by myself."

Completely shocked, Laiken just stood with her arms folded across her chest and her face twisted in an angry scowl.

"You just let me know what you want to do. I love you, always have, always will, but we've got to reach a point of moving on." He paused, bringing his hands together in a point. "Or move on." He then pulled his hands away and pointed them in two different directions. "Now I've done all I know how to do. The ball is in your court."

With that said, Rance left the kitchen, leaving Laiken standing there speechless, went to the guest bedroom, and closed the door behind him. He sighed as he sat on the bed and removed his shoes. He'd reached his end with putting forth the effort of being faithful but making no progress, so he'd accepted the reality that the marriage was not going to make it. He just didn't want to be the one to pull the plug. He'd done enough damage, he reasoned. Without removing his clothes, he lay back on the bed and was asleep in minutes.

"Rance, I can't keep doing this." It was just past two in the morning when Laiken stormed into the guest bedroom and woke her husband up. Her arms were again folded across her chest, and her expression displayed a mixture of anger, hurt, and torment.

In slight confusion he sat up, glanced at the clock, and forced himself to pay attention. "What's going on, honey?" he mumbled.

"I can't do it anymore. At one point, you made me happy, but now . . ." She shook her head. "I hate this life. I hate this house. I hate this crappy situation you have me living in."

Rance scratched his head, knowing he really couldn't ask more of his wife. He'd done her wrong.

"Every day it's a struggle for me to stay here and for me to do for those girls. Every day it's a struggle for me to even know that you're in this house. I hate it!"

"So what are we going to do?"

"We? There is no *we* anymore, Rance. You threw we out of the window for some tramp named Jerrafine ten years ago. The day you started sleeping with her was the day that we ended. I just didn't know about it. But now that I do, I refuse to do to you what you did to me."

"Okay, so what are you going to do?"

"I'm leaving. As a matter of fact, I've already found a place, and I'll be moving there this week."

"What?" Disbelief crossed his face.

"You heard me. I'm done with this lie of a marriage." Laiken didn't so much as raise her voice, having well thought out her plan.

"Okay. What about the kids?"

"What about the kids? Didn't you say that Jerrafine wanted her girls back? Give them back. She's been coming to get them every weekend, anyway."

"What about the boys?"

"You were paying someone all this time to take care of your daughters. Get a nanny. I'm tired of the way you let the boys disrespect me. They talk back and you say nothing. They don't do anything I say, Rance, and you never step in to correct them. Well, you know what? I've finally realized that I'm nobody's doormat."

"So you're just going to walk out on us?"

"You can't be serious, Rance," Laiken said incredulously. "At least I respect you enough to let you know first. You better start making plans for what you're going to do with your four kids." At that Laiken spun on her heels and exited the room, leaving Rance speechless.

Feenie had just slipped into a chocolate pantsuit, with a crisp white blouse beneath the jacket, and a pair of brown and white pumps. By the grace of God, she'd been able to land a job at the commissioner of the revenue office, despite her criminal conviction, and each morning she looked forward to putting on a suit, going down to city hall, and sitting at a desk that was actually labeled with her name. She felt good about trading an honest day's work for an honest day's pay.

She could look at herself and truly smile, feeling that for once she'd made a right decision, one that she would not regret or have to apologize for down the road. She was sitting at her dining-room table, sipping on a cup of coffee, enjoying a few of her favorite passages of scripture when her phone rang.

"Good morning," she sang into the mouthpiece.

"Good morning, Jerrafine. It's Rance."

"Oh. Good morning," she repeated.

"Listen, I am giving you a call about the girls and their living arrangements," he stated. "I know you are interested in having them come back to live with you, and I wanted to talk to you about that."

"Okay," Feenie easily agreed. "You asked me if I was working with a counselor or anyone on getting them back, and I'm not, but I have been taking parenting classes for about three months now and will turn my parenting certificate in to my social worker. If you want, I can have her send you a copy of the certificate when I finish."

"That will be fine, although it's not entirely necessary. I just think at this point the girls really need their real mother. I've been keeping up with you a little and heard that you have quite a few things going for yourself now, like a solid job, a church home, and a new apartment sufficient for the girls."

"Yeah, I've been able to make some positive strides." Feenie smiled at the fact that her accomplishments had been recognized. "I think I've been on quite a journey in the past two years. I still have some work to do, though."

"If you keep moving forward at the rate you're going, it won't take you long," Rance encouraged. "So, how soon do you think you'd like to get the girls back?"

"I'm ready whenever you'd like to release them to me. I mean, I would need to set up some appropriate day care for them. I'm not going to make the same mistake twice."

"Glad to know that you've been able to learn from your experiences," he replied. "What were you thinking in terms of child care?"

"There are a couple of after-school programs that I could look into. The girls could go once school lets out, and I'd be able to pick them up after work," she suggested. "And then the city offers a couple of programs right at the school. That could be an option as well."

"What does it cost?"

"I don't know off the top of my head, but I can take a look at it and get back to you sometime today."

"Sounds good. And, of course, with you taking the girls back, I'm willing to support them," he threw in. "But it has to be a fair and reasonable amount."

Feenie didn't comment, slightly embarrassed by her previous attempt at extortion.

"Now what do you feel is fair?" Rance asked.

"Ummm . . ." Feenie paused momentarily while she considered the cost of raising two girls who would soon be teenagers. She quoted him the cost of her monthly rent, which was less than what Rance had paid her in times past. Rance readily agreed.

"I'd suggest you file a petition for custody so that we can do things right," Rance stated.

"Of course, I won't fight you on it as long as you have a place to keep the girls, you keep your job, and you include me on their school registrations and those kinds of things."

"I can do that," she agreed.

"Great. So I'll give you a call in a couple of days to see where you are with things and then see where we go from there."

"Thanks, Rance," Feenie said, ending the call. She returned the phone to its cradle, then grinned up at the ceiling. "Thank you, Lord," she whispered. "Thank you for bringing my girls home. Help me to be not just a better mother to them, but the best mother to them. Restore to me the time I wasted and lost being foolish. Help me to be wiser this time. Amen."

She gulped down the rest of her now cooled coffee, picked up her keys, and headed for her favorite place to spend the day—work.

20

"Tamara, where's Dominique?" Marvin leaned one arm against the door frame and rested a hand on his hip. He'd spent the entire night calling Dominique's phone over and over again and driving randomly around the city, hoping to see her car. He was exhausted in both mind and body.

"I don't know," Tamara lied. "What did she tell you?"

"She didn't tell me anything." His tone was calm, but Marvin was clearly frustrated. "She just left, and I know you know where she is."

"No, I don't. Dominique hasn't said anything to me."

"I don't believe you, Tamara. I don't. And I don't appreciate you not telling me. You know I love that girl, and she's pregnant with my baby, and you're acting like she's throwing me a surprise party that I'm not supposed to know about or something."

"Well, I can't tell you what I don't know," she answered, rolling her eyes.

"You're lying," Marvin accused, pointing a finger toward her face.

"And you don't know where your wife is," Tamara snapped.

Marvin studied her face silently with pressed lips. "Tell my wife I love her and to call me and let me know what's going on." He turned and in defeat walked to his car, got inside, and pulled off.

"Girl, he looks so sad." Tamara closed the door and slunk back to her couch.

"I don't care." Dominique had been standing in the kitchen, holding her breath, her heart, and her stomach. The baby seemed to know that something was going on and started doing what felt to Dominique like backflips. "He done messed around and started seeing some tramp, and now she's pregnant, and I'm supposed to feel sorry for him because he looks sad?"

"You should at least call him and let him know where you are. He's miserable."

"And what am I? Do you think I'm having the time of my life? I don't owe him any explanation. If anything, he should have been explaining himself to me!" she exclaimed, joining her sister in the living room.

"So let me ask you this, Nique. Is this it for your marriage?"

"What do you mean?"

"I mean, do you plan on not ever going home again? You're carrying this man's baby, and you know how he feels about that. You can't ignore him forever."

"Why can't I? He is keeping a secret from me and obviously has been for some time."

"Oh, trust me, I'm not suggesting that he's in any way innocent, but what I am saying to you is you really need to think about how you want this thing to end. You hiding from him, or attempting to hide from him, is not going to last forever. As a matter of fact, it's not going to last very long."

Dominique knew her sister was right, but she still hadn't been able to filter her feelings and get to the place where she knew what it was she wanted to do.

"You're going to have to face him sooner or later," Tamara declared.

"Well, right now it's going to be later, because I don't feel like dealing with him." Dominique stood from where she sat and tiptoed to the window, as if Marvin would hear her footsteps. Barely moving the curtains and blinds that hung there, she peeked out, looking for his car.

"I don't know what you're peeping for. He knows you're here."

"No, he doesn't."

"Nique, come on. How many places could you be? Number one, he knows you still have a key to this place, since it technically is still your house."

"Technically?"

"You know what I mean." Tamara winced. "Anyway, he knows your car's probably in the garage, since I'm parked in the driveway. That doesn't take a rocket scientist to figure out."

"He could be thinking I went home to see Grandma," Dominique argued.

"Oh, please, like you're going to jump up and go all the way to California on a whim. Yeah, right."

"I wonder what Grandma would do if she were me."

"Girl, you know Grandma didn't play!" Tamara giggled. "She probably would resort to slinging grits. Let's call her and ask." Tamara reached for her cell phone to dial the number of the woman that had raised both her and Dominique after their mother passed away from breast cancer.

"No!" Dominique pulled away from the window and dashed over to snatch the phone from her sister's hand. "I can't have her all up in my business. It's bad enough that you know everything."

"We won't tell her it's you. I'll say it's me," Tamara squealed, dialing the number, then pushing the key to engage the speakerphone.

"Hello," Lue Renay answered after a few rings.

"Hey, Grandma," both women sang at once.

"Who is dis? Is dis my suga babies?"

"Yes, ma'am," Tamara and Dominique said in unison.

"Hey, babies," Lue Renay gleefully greeted.

"Grandma, we got a question. Well, really it's me," Tamara said.

"What is it, baby?" Lue Renay asked.

"What would you do to get back at somebody who cheated on you?" Tamara asked.

"Cheatin'! Oh, Lawd. Who gettin' cheated on?"

"I think my boyfriend is doing some tippin', Grandma." Tamara chuckled.

"That ain't good. How much trouble you wanna get in?" Lue Renay asked, forcing laughter from her two granddaughters.

"Not a whole lot," Dominique quipped. "We just want to give him something to think about."

"Well, you could take you some bacon grease and you rub it in his shoes real good."

"Bacon grease?" said Dominique.

"Yeah. After you fry you up some bacon, you save the grease in a big can, and you get you some uh dat and work it in real good in his shoes. When he go to wear them, he'll have every dog in town chasin' him down the street. He wanna be a dog, let him play wit the dogs."

"Grandma, what in the world?" Dominique laughed.

"Chile, you ain't seen a man run until you seen a dog tryna get at his feet."

"What else, Grandma?" Tamara asked, egging her grandmother on.

"Is he a dancin' man, or do he go ta church?" asked Lue Renay.

"Umm . . . we go dancing every now and then," Tamara replied.

"Then cut the linin' in his suits and fix it with some hem tape. You know what dat is?"

"Yes, ma'am," said Tamara.

"Yeah, you get you some of dat and hafway

fix 'em back. Then when he go to move, dem seams gonna bus' wide open."

Dominique found herself giggling again.

"Now, if you don't wanna go to jail, you can do dat right there," Lue Renay added.

"Suppose we wanna get in trouble, Grandma. Then what?" asked Dominique.

"Chile, take you some bologna and slap it all over his car. Now, you gotta do it when it's hot outside. Do it while he at work so the bologna can sit all day. When he come outside and pull dat sandwich meat offa his car, he gonna have circles everywhere. The paint will be clean gone."

"What? You've tried that?" Dominique lifted her brows, pondering the idea. It sounded childish and juvenile, but it would make her feel a little bit better. She tapped Tamara on the shoulder and nodded with a grin.

"Oh yes, I have. This was 'fore I met your granddaddy. I caught that slickster tippin' out with somebody else, and he had to drive around with a polka dot car for about a year."

Tamara howled with laughter. "No, you didn't, Grandma."

"Who didn't? Yes, I did too! Now, I ain't never done nothing to hurt nobody, 'cause somebody that don't care enough about you to be faithful, they shole ain't worf going to jail for. You don't want to be sittin' behind bars over that mess."

"Yeah, you're right. I'm going to try the bologna one." Tamara giggled.

"Send me some pictures when you do, baby.

I can put it up on my Facebook page," Lue Renay said, referencing the social networking site.

"Your Facebook page?" Dominique burst with laughter. "What are you doing on Facebook?"

"I done told you girls, you cain't sit back and just let life pass you by. You gotta keep up."

"You're right about that, Grandma," said Dominique.

"You girls call me later. I'm 'bout to miss my show," Lue Renay said.

"All right. Love you," Tamara and Dominique chimed together.

"Love you, too, now," replied Lue Renay before hanging up.

"Let's go." Dominique grabbed her purse. "You drive. I don't want him to see my car, just in case he's driving around town."

"You're actually going to paste lunch meat on his car?"

"No. I've got another idea. We're going to Home Depot."

Tamara slipped into her shoes while they talked. "What's at Home Depot?"

"Paint," Dominique announced.

"Umm . . . what are you going to do with that?"

"Hold on. Look out there again and see if you see Marvin."

"Girl, he been gone. Come on here." Tamara grabbed her sister's arm and pulled, but Dominique cautiously resisted.

"Wait!" Dominique peeked out the front

door and looked both ways, as if she were crossing the street. Seeing no signs of her husband, she blurted, "All right. Let's go."

The women hopped in Tamara's Altima and headed toward the home improvement store.

"So seriously, sister, what are you planning on doing about your marriage?" Tamara asked.

"I don't know. I'm too angry to even think straight right now. All I want to do is hurt him like he hurt me." Dominique paused a moment. "Except I'm not a cheater."

"Well, just go out with one of his friends."

"Nah." Dominique shook her head. "That's not my style. Plus, he'd never believe that I wasn't sleeping with the friend if he found out."

"Just because you go out with somebody doesn't mean you're sleeping with them," Tamara remarked. "And why would you care, anyway? He didn't care about you."

Dominique still found that point hard to believe. "I don't know. Maybe I'm just hoping she was lying or something," she sighed.

"Well, even if she's not pregnant, or if it's someone else's baby, he had to be sleeping with her for her to even make that accusation."

"Right."

"If you care about your marriage, you should at least ask him about it. You owe that much to yourself. You can't just act like you don't know what you know."

"I'll ask questions later, but for right now, I'm going to buy some paint."

"What are you buying paint for?" Tamara asked again.

"You'll see."

Minutes later the sisters pulled into Home Depot's parking lot and walked through the entrance.

"Which way is your paint?" Dominique asked a young lady at the customer service desk.

"Right on aisle eight." The clerk beamed. "Getting your nursery ready?" she asked, noticing Dominique's baby bump.

"Yeah. At least trying to." Dominique laughed nervously, knowing that it was not her intent for the paint.

"Boy or girl?" asked the clerk.

You sure are nosy, Dominique thought. The last thing she needed was for someone to be able to identify her, considering what she planned to do with the paint. "I find out next week." She smiled and walked quickly toward the paint aisle. "She tryna find out my whole life story!" she remarked to Tamara.

"She's just trying to be friendly. You're just paranoid." Tamara chuckled. "Because you're about to do something you ain't got no business doing."

"Anyway!" Dominique laughed, sucking her teeth. "You're my accomplice and my alibi, so you can't say too much."

"Oh yeah. I forgot that part."

Dominique didn't know which paint to buy to give her the best results for her project. "Should I get glossy, flat, or semigloss?" She crinkled her brow, staring at several cans.

"I don't know what it is you're trying to do, so I couldn't tell you."

"I'm 'bout to help Marvin repair those scratches somebody put on his truck."

"Uh-oh! Girl, no, you ain't!"

"Think I ain't when I am?" Dominique pulled a can of semigloss off the shelf and took it to the mixing counter. She'd originally planned on doing lime green, but when she got to the counter, "Black, please," tumbled from her lips.

"Sure. Whatcha painting?" asked the clerk at the counter.

What is it with everybody being all up in my business? "My husband is painting our garage floor," Dominique lied a second time.

"Nice," he commented.

A few minutes later Dominique was headed back to the car with her purchase. "All right, let's go get something to eat, and then we can head to Marvin's house. It will be nice and dark by then."

"How you plan on getting over there? You not about to have my tags identified!"

"Just park around the corner then, scaredy-cat!" Dominique said.

"You better be glad I love you, but I'll tell you this. You better make this paint job quick."

"It won't take but a second." Dominique tucked the paint-can opener in her purse. "The less you know, the less you can be accountable." She smirked. "But right now this baby needs some steak. Let's go to Outback."

"You 'bout to stop ordering me around like you somebody's momma?"

Right on cue, Dominique turned up the

radio as Rihanna crooned the line "Shut up and drive, drive, drive."

Both ladies laughed at the timing and headed for Water Street. Once they reached Outback Steakhouse, the ladies took a booth in the middle of the restaurant, and Tamara immediately ordered a drink.

"Sorry, sis. I probably need this for what you're about to get me roped into."

"Well, what you don't need is a DUI, so you'd better watch it," Dominique warned.

"Like you don't know how to drive," Tamara snorted as the server approached with a blueberry martini for her and a sweet tea for Dominique. "We'll have this for starters," she said, pointing to the Alice Springs Chicken Quesadilla, quesadillas stuffed with grilled chicken, sautéed mushrooms, crispy bacon, and melted cheese, and served with a honey mustard sauce.

Dominique's mouth watered at the photo of a New York strip encrusted with cracked black pepper, topped with a savory brandy sauce, and served with potato wedges. "I'd like to have the Savory Pepper Mill NY Strip please, well done, with a blue cheese salad on the side."

"No problem. I will go ahead and put this in for you and will be back shortly," said the server.

Tamara dug back into her sister about her plans to damage more of Marvin's property. "Are you sure you don't want to ask him about what's going on before you munk up the man's ride . . . again?"

"There's nothing to ask," Dominique replied,

taking a sip from her tea. "I heard it with my own two ears."

"Yeah, but that just don't sound like Marvin."

"What woman ever wants to believe that her man is cheating? Nobody. But how can I deny it? I heard what that skank said. I was standing right there," Dominique explained for what seemed like the one hundredth time. "How could he not be when she plain as day said, 'I just wanted you to know about your baby.' How else could that be interpreted?"

"Ain't too many ways you could read that wrong," Tamara admitted. "I just can't believe, given the way he slobbers all over you, that he would do something like that."

"Well, it is what it is, and I'd be a fool to think it ain't what it is."

Later, with full bellies and under a dark sky, the ladies cruised I-64 and took the exit to get to Marvin and Dominique's home, which sat at the end of a cul-de-sac. Dominique could see from several feet away that Marvin's truck was parked in its normal spot in the driveway; she supposed the Mercedes was tucked safely away in the garage. There were no lights shining through the windows, and Dominique knew Marvin well enough to assume that he was already in bed, sleeping.

"Turn your lights off and slow down," she instructed.

Keeping the can of paint inside the plastic bag, she pried the lid off. Tamara pulled up in front of the house and watched her sister climb out of the passenger seat, then lift the gallon can. Dominique walked to the front of Marvin's truck on the driver's side and doused the windshield with the paint. The dense liquid rolled down the glass and seeped through the vents leading to the engine. Quickly, she walked to the other side and slung the remaining paint on the part of the windshield that had not yet been covered, then sat the empty can on the truck's hood.

"Let's go," Dominique huffed, heart pounding and out of breath.

With widened eyes, Tamara jammed her foot on the gas pedal but avoided any screeching as she sped away.

"Girlll! Marvin is gonna kill you!"

"Marvin is not gonna know I did it," Dominique responded, leaning and crouching, trying to see her house through the side-view mirror. "I should have left a note on it that said 'Sorry for scratching your car. Here's a paint job on me!'"

"Like he wouldn't be able to identify your handwriting," Tamara scoffed. "You're a pretty stupid criminal, you know."

"You can say that if and when he catches me."

21

"Ms. Trotter, you've filed a petition for full custody of two minor children, Mirance Alexander and Carance Alexander?" the judge asked, looking over the documents before him.

"Yes, sir," said Feenie.

"And, Mr. Alexander, these children are currently in your custody?" the judge asked.

"That's right, Your Honor," replied Rance.

"You're the biological father. Is that right?" said the judge.

"Yes, I am."

"Have these children always been in your care?" the judge asked Rance.

"No, they were in their mother, Jerrafine Trotter's custody up until about two years ago," said Rance.

The judge turned his attention back to Feenie. "What happened that you had to turn custody over to Mr. Alexander?"

Feenie was nervous, but she'd practiced what she would say when given the chance.

"Your Honor, I made some stupid mistakes as a parent and didn't use good judgment. I compromised the children's safety by leaving them home alone, which I take full responsibility for. Because of that, I was charged with child neglect and had to serve a sixteen-month sentence. I finished serving my time and took parenting classes to better my parenting skills and learn some new strategies in raising my children."

"Where did you take the classes?" asked the judge.

"They were offered by Social Services. I have my certificate of completion if you'd like to see it," she offered.

The judge motioned with his hand, and the bailiff approached Feenie to pass the document on to the judge. He looked it over quickly, then handed it back to Feenie, again through the bailiff.

"Mr. Alexander, what concerns do you have with Ms. Trotter regaining custody of the two children you and she share?" asked the judge.

"I have no concerns, Your Honor," Rance stated in his lawyer's tone of voice. "Since Ms. Trotter's release, she has established suitable housing for the girls, secured solid employment, and as she stated, completed parenting classes. I'm confident that she is able to take on the responsibility of our children with no incidents similar to what took place in the past."

"Where are your working, Ms. Trotter?" the judge asked.

"I work in the commissioner of the revenue

office in city hall as a desk clerk, and I'm working on starting my own interior design company," Feenie answered proudly.

The judge nodded. "And how long have you been doing that?"

"I just passed my ninety-day probation last week, and I brought a letter of recommendation from my manager to show that I'm exceeding expectations at work. I'm still working on building up my business, so I haven't quite started that." She offered the document to the bailiff to present to the judge, which he looked over, then handed back.

"Will you be able to secure appropriate child care outside of school hours while you're working?" asked the judge.

"Yes, sir. I plan to enroll them in the city's after-school care program at the school they will be attending. They have hours both before my work shift starts and after it ends, so they will be properly cared for."

"I don't see any reason why custody cannot be granted, so I'm entering the custody order as of today for the minor children Mirance Alexander and Carance Alexander to return to their biological mother, Jerrafine Trotter." The judge slammed the gavel against his desk.

"Thank you, Your Honor," Feenie blurted with a smile as she picked up her manila folder, which held her check stubs, apartment lease, letter of recommendation and parenting class certificate, items she thought that she might need for her case.

Both Feenie and Rance exited the courtroom at the same time.

"Thank you, Rance," Feenie said, lightly touching his arm as they walked.

"You're welcome," he uttered.

"Listen. I'm sorry for all this trouble I caused between you and your wife."

"It's not your fault," Rance replied. "You didn't have a family that you were committed to. I did. Whatever has happened between Laiken and me could have been avoided had I been the husband I should have been. I can't blame anyone but myself."

They both stopped and looked at each other for a few seconds.

"Well, take care of yourself. You'll hear from me next weekend to get the girls." At that Rance turned on his heels and walked off.

Feenie let out a sigh and headed to her car. The girls would be home shortly, and they would be taking a beading class together, one of many activities Feenie had gotten the three of them enrolled in to bring them closer together.

"Things are going to be just fine," she whispered to herself. "Thank you, God."

22

"So do you think you can do something with this place?" Laiken asked Jerrafine as they toured the three-bedroom rancher, Laiken with a smile on her face. The hardwood floor echoed her steps as she moved from room to room, picturing herself dwelling in a home free of a cheating spouse. "You've done such a great job with your place. I'm sure you can help me figure out what to do with this. I'd love your insight."

"I'd be honored to help you. After all you've done for me, this is the least I could do." Feenie looked around the empty house and saw a blank canvas for her artistic interior-design talents. She dared not ask Laiken about her decision to leave Rance, knowing that she was a big factor in her coming to that conclusion. Instead, she kept her mouth shut and spoke only about what she'd been asked to do.

"I can't wait to move in," Laiken mentioned with an exhale. "And it's kind of weird talking to you about it, since . . . well, you know. But I just feel so much animosity toward Rance right now. It's not fair to continue to put him, myself, or the children through what I know they have to see."

"I'm sure you've given it a lot of thought."

Regardless of the hours they'd invested in giving reconciliation a whirl, it just hadn't been worth it as far as Laiken was concerned. As much as she'd tried, or maybe hadn't tried, she knew there was no way that she'd ever be able to trust Rance again. Not in a million years. She believed in forgiveness, but forgetting was something that was impossible in her eyes. And now that Jerrafine had been reintroduced into the girls' lives, Laiken wouldn't have to feel so bad about her inevitable decision.

"I really have, Feenie, and I just can't do it anymore. I'm just so ready to enjoy some peace, quiet, and time to myself."

"Forgive me if I'm overstepping my boundaries here, but what about your boys?" Feenie asked, concentrating her eyes on Laiken.

"Those disrespectful brats will be just fine with their dad," she answered. Laiken tried to hide it, but Feenie recognized the look of anger mixed with pain. It was the same look she'd seen when staring into her mirrored image while she'd been incarcerated.

Feenie let silence hang in the air while she decided on her next words. "Don't turn your back on your boys, Laiken," she said softly.

"Are you judging me?" Offense was taken immediately.

"How could I possibly do that? You know my story. I don't have the room to judge anybody. I just don't want to see you take your pain and frustration out on your boys. They haven't done anything. Right? Take it out on me. Take it out on Rance, but not your boys."

"I'm just tired, Feenie. Right now I need to think about myself."

"I understand. We all need an escape from reality sometimes. Just try not to do any long-term damage in the process. It will be hard enough on the boys with just their mom and dad splitting. Don't make them feel like they are completely losing you."

Laiken wanted to ask Feenie just who she thought she was, trying to give advice, but her words made too much sense.

"Have you already told them that you guys are splitting up?" Feenie asked.

Laiken nodded. "We talked to them a couple of weeks ago."

"How'd it go, if you don't mind me asking?" Feenie leaned a shoulder against a wall and fumbled with the top to the water bottle she carried in her hand, twisting the top off, then on again.

"It went okay. They had a couple of questions." Laiken shrugged. "Lashed out a bit, like they always do."

"So . . ." Feenie bit into her bottom lip, calculating her next words. "Did you let them know that they'd be staying with their dad?" Both ladies strolled into an empty bedroom where the walls were covered in pink paint. "They sure wouldn't want to stay in this room, huh?"

"We're still trying to work that out," Laiken answered, ignoring the comment about the paint. "I mean, they're my kids, so I'll always make room for them . . . I guess."

"Laiken, listen to you. What do you mean, you guess? Take it from me, you will enjoy the free time starting out, and that's okay for a little while, but your heart is going to ache for your children. After a while, it's going to feel like you have a great big hole right here." Feenie stabbed a finger in her own chest. "And by the time you feel that hole, the hole in your kids' hearts will be ten times that."

Laiken turned her head from Feenie in an effort to hide a few tears.

"I didn't mean to make you cry. I guess I just don't want to see you do the same kind of damage I did to my girls. It's a lot to try to undo," Feenie confessed.

Laiken nodded. "Thanks for sharing," she murmured, then cleared her throat. "Right now I just need a peaceful home to come home to."

"I understand." Feenie paused to allow Laiken a moment to pull herself together. "And with just a little bit of paint, some lighting tricks, a couple of bolts of fabric, and a hot glue gun, I can help you with that," Feenie said with a smile.

That entire weekend she and Laiken discussed ideas and themes. By the end of their consultation, Laiken had given Feenie free reign to do what she thought would be best.

"You won't be sorry!" Feenie promised.

With the budget Laiken had laid out, to include payment for Feenie's services, Feenie and her daughters shopped almost daily for bargains in a variety of places, and like an expert, Feenie painted the living-room walls of Laiken's home a buttery taupe and highlighted the crown molding in antique white. She put together black-and-white photos matted in black and framed in white on an accent wall, then picked out black faux suede chair covers to drape over the gently used couch and love seat, which she'd found at a hotel liquidation sale. Rolling up her sleeves, Feenie created some designer lighting pieces, used soft, low-wattage bulbs to create ambiance, and placed large potted plants strategically around the room to give it life.

Every evening for two weeks she continued her craft in each room in the house, including the bedrooms designated for Laiken's sons, using vivid colors and interesting accents to create a look that could easily be found on any decorating show.

"Feenie, this is incredible!" Laiken exclaimed. It doesn't even look like the same house!" Laiken was completely amazed when she saw the finished product. Although she'd seen it come together little by little every day, the finishing details seemed to make all the difference. "You really need to pursue your business, because this is indeed talent."

"Thanks Laiken."

Feenie was prouder than a peacock, walking through Laiken's home, admiring the work of her hands. "Now, this is something that I can be proud of," she told herself as she snapped several "after" images, which she would add to the photos she'd taken before she'd started the project. She also had before and after photos she'd taken when she'd moved into her own home. She planned to enlarge the images professionally to create her own portfolio for her business and start to gain clients.

23

"Good morning, Kerra," Feenie said as she passed by her manager's desk.

Kerra gave a solemn response, barely looking up.

"Everything okay?"

"Oh, yeah, yeah. Everything's fine," Kerra answered, trying to put a smile on her face.

Feenie paused, eyeing Kerra suspiciously for several seconds. "I don't believe you, but I'm going to leave you alone," she said but didn't move away from Kerra's desk just yet. "Are you sure you're okay? Can I get you anything?"

"I'm sure. I'm fine."

Not that Feenie believed her boss, but she stepped away respectfully. "Well, if you need to talk, I sit right over there." She pointed to her right.

"Thanks." Kerra nodded. "And thanks for finishing that auditing project for me last week."

"My pleasure. Anything special you need me to tackle today?"

"Not at this time." Kerra sniffed.

"You sure you're all right? You know if you need anything, I got you."

"Thanks, Feenie."

Putting her purse inside her desk drawer, Feenie logged on to her computer, verified the cash in her drawer, and followed other opening procedures while she sipped on a cup of coffee. She loved getting to work early; it seemed to allow the rest of her day to run smoothly. Most mornings it allowed her and Kerra a chance to talk. Some days their conversations were work related; Kerra would share business insights and give Feenie tips on how to improve her job performance. Other times the conversation took on a more personal tone, and Feenie would share how her daughters were doing in school and otherwise, and how grateful she was that they were back in her care. Kerra had even bought Feenie a congratulatory card when the custody decision was made and Rance officially released the twins back to her. Feenie kept the card on her desk and looked at it just about every morning.

"Hey." Celina Showers, a twenty-five-year-old, self-proclaimed diva rushed past Feenie in a blur. "You here early again?" She had hated Jerrafine from the day she was hired, because with something to prove, Feenie had an exceptional work ethic.

"Always," Feenie replied with a smile.

"I'ma have to find a way to get rid of you. You be making me look bad!" Celina chuckled. "I got five minutes to get myself together before we unlock that door. Whew!" She plopped in a seat, punched in a combination to open a small safe beneath her desk, and verified her cash. "What's going on with Kerra today," she asked, fitting her chin in her palm. "Looked like she'd been crying when I came in."

Feenie shrugged quickly. "I have no clue. I asked her if everything was okay."

"What did she say? When I walked past her office, she was on the phone with her husband, fussing about something," Celina shared.

"How do you know it was her husband? You need to stop being so nosy."

"Because I know his name is John, and I heard her say, 'That's not fair, John! I'm over-worked just like you are, and I never complain about what you do or don't do at home.' I just kept on walking like I didn't hear it, but it sounded like she was getting blasted."

"I'm sorry to hear that," Feenie responded, fighting the temptation to engage in gossiping.

"Go see if she's all right," Celina coaxed.

"Nope. If she wanted me in her business, she would have invited me. Besides, I have enough drama going on in my own life. I don't need to be meddling in hers."

"But she likes you, though. She probably would tell you if you asked her again. She talks to you all the time like you've been knowing each other since the first grade."

"Don't hate." Feenie smirked. "And if she told me anything, I wouldn't be stupid enough to tell anybody."

Feenie's jail experience had taught her to

listen but to keep her responses short and unbiased, as well as to engage in the art of confidentiality and loyalty. And loyalty was what she felt when she thought about Kerra, knowing that Kerra hadn't had to take a chance on her and offer her a job. Since her first day of employment, Feenie had been the model employee. She arrived to work early every day, stayed late as needed, although it wasn't generally necessary, and went the extra mile on every task, and for that Celina despised her.

"You two make me sick. You're just like the teacher's pet."

"And I guess you're like the redheaded stepchild, huh?"

"Whatever," Celina replied, squeezing in a fake giggle. "At least my nose is not brown. All you do is run behind her all day."

"No. What I do is my job all day. Which I love, so I don't mind."

Feenie turned her attention away from her peer to greet a customer who'd just walked in the door, kicking off the morning. Feenie then waited on a few customers who had come in to renew their business licenses or pay taxes, but it was midweek and the lobby stayed close to empty, with an occasional customer straggling in every twenty minutes or so.

"Jerrafine, once you wrap up there, please come to my office," Kerra said as she passed Feenie's desk.

"Yes, ma'am," Feenie beamed.

Ten minutes passed before Feenie was able to leave her desk in response to Kerra's beckoning. "You needed me?" she asked, standing in the doorway of her manager's office.

"Come on in and close the door." Kerra waved, then waited for Feenie to take a seat.

"What's going on?"

"Feenie," Kerra stated nervously, "I need your advice."

"Advice from me?" Feenie chuckled. "I'm not sure what you could do with that!"

"I'm sure you can help me. This is going to sound crazy, but . . ." Blood rushed to Kerra's face from embarrassment. "Can you teach me how to be sexy?"

"What?" Feenie contorted her face in disbelief. "What do you mean?"

"I mean, look at you, Feenie!" Kerra answered in a whine. "You look beautiful every day. I see the way men look at you and how they are naturally attracted to you, and I don't know . . . I guess I need to learn how to do that."

"Kerra, every woman naturally has some sexy in her." The words rolled off Feenie's tongue.

"Well, mine is lost, because I haven't seen it and neither has John," Kerra confessed; then swiftly covered her face with her hands.

Feenie held back her response until Kerra could say more, and handed her a tissue in the interim.

"The other morning, I got out of the shower and was doing my normal routine of getting dressed. It's no secret that I'm carrying some extra weight," Kerra commented, crossing her arms over her belly, trying to camouflage its size. "But I would have never thought John would look at me the way he did." She sniffed. "I was standing at my dresser, in front of the mirror, digging through the drawer for my bra, and my back was to John. He was across the room, putting on his tie or something, but I happened to catch a glimpse of his face in the mirror. He didn't know that I saw him, but, Feenie, he was looking just like this." Kerra crinkled her nose and furrowed her brows as much as she could, then eyed Feenie up and down in disgust as a demonstration.

Feenie shook her head, instantly feeling sorry for her boss. "I'm sorry that happened to you," she replied, thinking back on some responses she'd learned from her parenting class that seemed to be fitting.

"I never felt so hurt and ashamed before in my life," Kerra mumbled through a new wave of tears. "I mean, I know that I'm not shaped like a model, and I could stand to lose a few pounds, but . . ." Kerra couldn't find the words to end her sentence. "I have to do something," she whispered, emotionally desperate. "Anyway, I look at you and see the way you carry and keep yourself. You just always look so well put together and not like me—some frumpy, little old fat woman whose husband doesn't want her anymore."

"Kerra, you are not fat," Feenie interjected. "I'm sure that John loves you unconditionally. After all, you are the mother of his children, and you two are still married."

"Yeah, for now."

"Maybe John wasn't looking at you at all. Maybe he'd pulled his tie a little too tight or something and—"

"Oh, please," Kerra said, stopping her. "Don't try to sugarcoat something we can both see. I'm too fat. I appreciate you trying to help me feel better about it, but I know what I saw," she insisted, referring to her husband's reflected expression. "I need to do something about it, and crying is not going to get me the results I need."

This time Feenie nodded in understanding.

"So will you help me? Maybe help me to pick out some clothes that look better than this old-fashioned garbage that my closet is full of." Kerra looked down at her conservative, flower printed frock, thick panty hose, and worn-out pumps. Then her eyes floated over to Feenie's patent leather pumps stylishly accented with a bow. Her French-pedicured toes peeked out from the open toes. Kerra absorbed the style of Feenie's suit, assessed her jewelry, hair style, and make-up.

"You do dress like a little old lady sometimes," Feenie acknowledged, with a slight nod and raising her brows. "But we can fix that," she added with assurance.

"I'm desperate for help. I've been trying to diet for over a month now, but nothing's working. I look at you and wonder how you do it."

"Some of it is just in my genes, because I can eat like me and Miss Piggy are twin sisters."

Kerra giggled a bit for the first time since they'd started talking.

"I'll help you, boss lady," Feenie promised.

"There's a fitness center right in the building where I live. We can go there every day after work if you'd like."

"You'd do that for me?"

"After what you've done for me? Please! It's the least I can do. When do you want to start?"

"As soon as you're ready," Kerra answered with wide, grateful eyes. "I don't have any work-out clothes, though."

"So let's go get some at lunch today. We can go to Wal-Mart, Target, wherever."

"Okay." Kerra smiled. "Thanks, Feenie."

"Don't mention it. You will be sexy in no time and will be mocking Patti LaBelle singing Ooh, ooh, ooh, ooh, ooh." She winked, standing up from her chair. "Let me know when you're ready."

Feenie served customers for another hour and a half before Kerra emerged from her office with her purse on her shoulder. "You ready?" she asked, standing just behind Feenie.

"Yep!"

"Where are you two going?" Celina asked, always in search of something to talk about.

"We're on our way to mind our business. How about you hold the office down while we're gone?" Feenie curtly remarked.

Celina sucked her teeth. "You make me sick, Feenie." Her tone was teasing, but Celina's feelings were real.

"You told me. I'll bring you some Pepto-Bismol. That will probably make you feel better."

Feenie turned her head to Kerra. "Who's driving? Me or you?"

"I'll drive," Kerra offered. "We'll be back," she said, looking over her shoulder at Celina with a wink and a smile.

24

"What the hell!" Marvin bellowed when he walked out of his home the day after his unsolicited paint job. "That crazy heifer!" He dropped his gym bag and walked to his truck, ruined by his wife's artistic handiwork. Other obscenities flew from his lips as he stood with his hands planted on his hips, completely flabbergasted by what he saw. Marvin wanted to punch something, anything. There was nothing nearby that he could hit without having to pay for it later besides the large green trash bin he dragged to the curb every Monday morning. With three mighty pounds of his fist, he dented the top of the receptacle and then kicked it when he found that the pounding did nothing to release his anger and frustration.

He yanked his phone out of his pocket, punched in the sequence of numbers that would connect him to his ex-wife, and waited for her to answer. And as soon as she did, he let her have it.

"Your ass is going to jail!" he roared, loud enough for the whole neighborhood to hear.

"Why are you calling me, yelling in my ear, Marvin?"

"I'm sick of you and these shenanigans you keep pulling, but I've got a trick for that!"

"Marvin, I'm at work, and I don't know what you're talking about. Whatever it is, you need to hang up with me and call someone else," Feenie stated calmly.

"No, I got the right one! You ain't changed in twenty damn years, Feenie—but this is going to come to an end. Today!"

"Okay," she commented, unmoved by Marvin's infuriated discourse.

"Where the hell are you?"

"I told you, I'm at work, in Maryland."

"You need to send me a picture of you holding today's Maryland newspaper, then," he ordered.

"What?"

"Prove it, Feenie! If you're at work in Maryland, send me a picture with you holding today's paper, or I'm calling the cops on your ass in five minutes!"

"You can't call the cops over something I've not done, Marvin."

Feenie's nonchalant attitude angered him even more.

"I'm not about to engage myself in whatever you have going on there. I hope you find out whoever did whatever to you. Have a good day." Feenie pressed the off button on her phone and dropped it into her purse before heading out her front door for work.

As promised, Marvin did call the police but was both disappointed and confused when they reported back to him before the day was out that they'd verified Feenie's whereabouts, which placed her nowhere near his truck or home. It was bad enough that his wife was missing, and now he had some kind of crazy stalker on his hands.

By the time Monday rolled around, Marvin was sleep deprived and frantic. His eyes popped open at 5:30 a.m., after only an hour and twenty minutes of sleep. He jerked his head to the right in hopes that at some point Dominique had snuck into bed without waking him, but he had no such luck. He sighed miserably and studied the ceiling, wondering where his wife was. The multiple calls to her cell phone produced no results, and although Marvin was convinced that she knew every detail, Tamara wouldn't spill the beans.

"She can't hide forever," he mumbled as he pulled himself from their bed and unenthusiastically dressed in sweats and a T-shirt for a morning run, hoping it would relieve some of his stress and anxiety. It was still a bit chilly when he stepped outside his front door, but he shook it off knowing he'd soon work up a sweat. With his mind inundated with a thousand thoughts, Marvin started out at a slow trot and gradually increased his speed to a full run, then challenged himself to sprint short distances along his five-mile course. Along the way, he thoroughly explored and measured any reason that presented itself for why his wife would leave him. He believed her to be faithful, so in his thinking, another man was out of the question. He hadn't put his hands on her, stolen money, damaged her clothes, become too controlling, stayed out too late, or come home drunk. He paid the bills on time, showered her with affection, and felt he balanced his work and home life well. Marvin was just clueless as to what could have happened.

Now fully winded, and even more tired, he had just under an hour to shower and get to the university's campus. He rushed his shower, and with a towel wrapped at his waist, he spit out a mouthful of Listerine and finished his morning hygiene routine, thinking he would try calling his wife again, even though it felt foolish. He dialed her number for the umpteenth time, to no avail; just like before she didn't answer. He pushed a slow stream of air through his puckered lips and tossed the phone on the bed, then slid into his work athletic wear, grabbed his gym bag and keys, and headed straight for ODU's English hall.

Dominique's classroom was going to be his first stop. He whisked his rental car into the lot, parked, and took easy steps toward the building where he expected to find his wife teaching her class. He didn't care that her class would soon be in session; he had to talk to her and find out what was going on. When he peered into her room, much to his surprise, he didn't find her there. Instead, there was only a note stating that she'd be out and a posted assignment for her students.

"'Sup, Coach Temple?" one of the students said.

"Good morning," Marvin replied with forced cordiality.

"I coulda slept a little later," the student joked, but Marvin had turned away too soon to entertain the young man's comment.

Marvin next trekked to Dominique's office. He knew she probably wouldn't be there, but he hoped the dean of English could give him some information without him seeming too out of the loop.

As he anticipated, Dominique's office door was closed and locked. He had a key, so he opened the door himself just long enough to confirm that she indeed was not there.

His feet led him to Suzanne Mercadante's office. "Good morning, Suzanne," he said, popping his head just inside the door.

"Oh, hi, Marvin." Suzanne smiled. "Everything okay?"

"Yeah," he began, trying to figure out his next words. "Have you seen my lovely wife this morning?"

"Not today," she sang. "Usually when someone goes on leave, they don't come back to work until later," she said with arched brows.

Leave? Marvin thought. "Right, right. I know she had mentioned leaving something here in her office. I thought she may have swung by to pick it up," Marvin said, fabricating a story, not wanting anyone to know that he suspected his wife had left him. "I was so out of it this morning, I didn't hear her when she left."

Marvin's disappointment began to transition into fury as he walked to the gym. When he got inside, he unlocked the equipment closet, grabbed a ball, and took to the court, trying to figure out his next steps.

Maybe I should call the police, he thought as he chased the ball in different directions. *They'd at least be able to locate her and tell me if she's okay.* He shot the ball from the free-throw line, made the basket, then ran forward to get it. The more he pondered that idea, the better he thought of it. Before he could talk himself out of his reasoning, he jogged off the court, leaving the ball bouncing after a missed shot, and headed for his office. Before he dialed the number, he decided to just go down to the precinct with photos in hand to expedite the process.

After waiting for longer than he felt he should have, Marvin was finally escorted to a detective's desk. "My wife is missing," he said, practically collapsing in the chair.

"What's your wife's name, sir?" the female detective asked.

"Dominique Andrayah Temple." He slapped three photos on the desk. "I need for you all to find her ASAP," he instructed.

"Well, sir, first, we need to determine if she truly can be considered as missing."

"What do you mean? I haven't seen her in two, three days! She's missing!" His arms flailed upward and fell back into his lap with a thud.

"I'm going to have to ask you some questions sir."

"Okay, go 'head," Marvin huffed, frustrated with the detective's lack of empathy.

"What's the name again, sir?"

"Dominique Andrayah Temple."

"And you say she's your wife?" The detective scribbled notes on a form, hardly making eye contact with Marvin.

"Yeah."

"When's the last time you saw Mrs. Temple?"

"Last Friday morning, when I went to work."

"Where did you last see her?"

"She was home, in the bed, still asleep. I kissed her good-bye before I went to work," Marvin explained.

"Do you suspect any criminal activity?"

"I don't know what to think." He shook his head. "I don't think anyone broke into the house or anything. It just looks like she left me or something."

"And why would she do that, sir?"

"I have no idea," he answered honestly. The detective's expression suggested that he knew exactly why Dominique was gone. Marvin noticed and answered again. "I don't know. I came home, and she was just gone."

"How old is she?"

"Thirty-four."

"When is her birthday?"

"September ninth, nineteen seventy-six."

"Race?"

"African American."

"Describe her for me please, sir."

"Her pictures are right there." He nodded with his head.

"Mr. Temple, I need you to describe your wife, please."

"She's about five-seven. She's pregnant. She's about the color of a walnut shell, with short, short hair."

"Did you say she was expecting?"

"Yeah." Marvin dropped his head to his palms. "She's about six months."

"Any particular or unusual characteristics, like tattoos, scars, or birthmarks?"

"Not really," he answered, thinking a bit.

"Any medical problems other than the pregnancy, like asthma, depression, glasses, hearing aids, heart problems, medications, disabilities, or psychological problems?"

Marvin simply shook his head.

"Do you have her doctor's name and number?"

"Not off the top of my head. I have it at home, though. I can bring it back."

The detective picked up Dominique's photos, studied them momentarily, then paper clipped them to her report. "And where does your wife work, Mr. Temple?"

"She's an English professor at Old Dominion University."

"Did you check there today?"

"Yeah. She had called in."

"Give me her exact work address and phone numbers please."

Marvin shared the requested info and sighed.

"All right, well, we'll look into it, but I have

to tell you that in most of these cases, the person is not missing. They just don't want to be found by whoever is looking for them. And to be honest with you, that's what this sounds like to me."

"Excuse me? My wife is somewhere out there, pregnant, and you want to tell me what it sounds like?"

"Sir, I'm just saying that unless some criminal activity is involved, it seems that your wife left by her own free will, which doesn't exactly make her a missing person."

"Then what is she? I'm her husband, we live together, and she hasn't been home in two days. To me, that makes her missing."

"We'll look into it, sir," the detective repeated in a tone that gave Marvin no assurance.

He stood to his feet. "Thank you," he sighed, feeling like he was no closer to locating his wife than he'd been before he'd come.

"So he called, asking you to send a picture?" Kerra asked as she and Feenie breezed back into the building at the end of their lunch hour, passing by Bryan and Celina, who were casually talking in the hallway.

"Yeah! I don't know what that was about," Feenie said, then turned to Bryan. "Hello, Mr. West," she said with a smile. She hadn't heard anything from Bryan since the day she'd called him to try to get information about her interview. Even when she'd tried reaching him to let him know of her good news, he hadn't answered or returned the call.

"Hey, Feenie," he replied, almost as if it were a bother. His words for her had become few, as if they'd never known each other outside of work.

Feenie didn't take offense. In fact, she preferred it that way. The last thing she needed was personal drama interfering with her job. She appreciated the help that Bryan did extend to her and understood now that he wanted more than what she was willing to give.

"How was lunch?" Celina asked as they passed by.

"It was great. Salads, of course," Kerra shared without stopping.

"Nosy behind," Feenie commented under her breath, sure that she was out of Celina's hearing range.

"Yeah, she is quite inquisitive, isn't she?" said Kerra.

"She needs a life so she can stay out of mine," Feenie replied. "I forgot to tell you that one of the teachers at the girls' school is letting me redo her bedroom."

"Feenie, that's great news," Kerra said encouragingly. "After a while, we're going to have to watch you on TV!"

"Wouldn't that be nice?" Feenie chuckled. "Me, a TV star." She paused and imagined herself again on a design reality show. "That would really be something."

"It could happen, you know."

"I don't think so." Feenie shook her head.

"Why not? You're very talented."

Feenie shrugged her shoulders. "I don't know. I guess I've never given much thought to really jumping out there like that," she commented.

"I don't know why you won't. You might not be able to make it onto a TV show, but I'm sure you could make a living at it with the right contacts." Kerra turned into her office, and Feenie stopped just inside the doorway. "You should think about it. After all, you're doing it on the side."

"Yeah, I am, aren't I?"

"All you need to do is get a business license. Well, there's a little more to it than that, but that would get you started in the right direction. And look where you work." Kerra swept a hand around the room. "In the very office where business licenses are bought and recorded. Talk about leading the horse to water," she said with a laugh.

Feenie nodded as a smile crossed her face. "You know what? You're right. I'm right here at the river. I may as well take a drink."

"Oh, you two are drinking now?" Celina cut in, walking up behind Feenie. "I'm going to have to join you two on these lunch outings."

"I'll talk to you later, Kerra," Feenie sighed, ending their conversation and heading for her desk.

"You didn't have to stop on account of me," Celina joked.

"We didn't." With a few keystrokes, Feenie was logged back on to her computer and ready to serve her next customer, but the lobby was empty.

"I thought you were going home early today," Feenie commented, tired of her coworker's not-so-subtle prying.

"I'm about to leave right now. I just forgot my sunglasses." Celina picked up a pair of shades and perched them atop her head. "So I heard you were being considered for a promotion."

That bit of news caught Jerrafine by complete surprise. "A promotion? I don't know what you're talking about," she responded, although the topic piqued her curiosity.

"That's what I heard, but I don't know why they would pick you over me. You haven't been here long enough to get it, and I have been here two years and got a degree," Celina said, rolling her eyes.

"First of all, I don't know anything about a promotion, and secondly, maybe it's talent over tenure," Feenie remarked.

"Mmm-hmm. Anyway, I wanted to ask you. How's your back?" Celina smirked, pulling her purse up on her shoulder.

Feenie looked puzzled. "My back?"

"Yeah, your back. Doesn't it hurt?"

"No. What are you talking about? Why would my back be hurting?"

Celina dug through her purse for her ringing cell phone, but before she answered it, she blurted her response. "I was wondering how in the world you got hired here with no degree, but word on the street is you got this job by lying on your back." With a loud cackle, Celina clicked away in her stilettos, leaving Feenie with feelings of shame and humiliation.

25

Dominique sipped on a strawberry smoothie and nibbled on a turkey sandwich as she waited for Tamara to arrive for their lunch date. Panera Bread had become one of their favorite hangout spots due to their free Wi-Fi. She pulled her laptop from her messenger bag and waited for it to boot up. As usual, her sister was late, leaving Dominique to entertain herself until she arrived.

She moseyed around on MySpace, Facebook, and Twitter for a few minutes. Then, when a thought popped into her head, in a flash, her fingers led her to Google, where she typed in her husband's ex-wife's name. After a few seconds of waiting, results populated her screen, providing her with links to Jerrafine's place of employment and e-mail address, along with the names of others in her department. She quickly clicked a link, hoping to get a visual image of the woman she believed her husband to be sleeping with, but the only photo posted was one of Kerra Butler, Feenie's boss, who held the position of commissioner. Dominique clicked around a bit more, hoping she could find at least a staff photo, then try to pick Jerrafine out of the lineup, but had no such luck.

"What are you working on?" Tamara asked, dropping her schoolbag onto an empty chair, startling her sister.

"You scared me," Dominique commented, grabbing her chest. "Look what I found." She turned her laptop around so that it faced Tamara. "I found out where that wench works."

"What wench?"

"You know who. Jerrafine," Dominique answered, rolling her eyes. "She works for the city of Baltimore, in the commissioner of the revenue office."

Tamara took a look at the screen, studying the listed names and the organization chart. "You can find out anything on anybody online."

"Tell me about it."

"So what are you going to do with this information you found? Go to Baltimore and whup up on her?"

"I've already told you, I can't be fighting in my condition," Dominique answered. "I gotta think of something else. Help me think."

"You could send her a rat in a box," Tamara suggested. "That would probably scare the living daylights out of her."

"And where am I going to find a dead rat? Let's not even talk about touching it to put it in the box."

"I think you can order one online some-where. I'm sure some creepy place sells them."

"I'm not about to sit up here and waste my money sending rodent grams. She wouldn't do anything but throw it out."

"E-mail her boss and tell them she's stealing money."

"How is that gonna work? First of all, it would be coming from my e-mail address and—"

"Create a new, anonymous one just to get her in trouble," Tamara recommended. "Let me have some," she said, picking up the half of Dominique's sandwich that didn't have teeth marks in it already.

"I guess I could do that, but as soon as they investigate, they would know the e-mail was bogus. I want her to get fired."

"Have her car towed."

"I don't know what she drives."

Tamara swallowed a mouthful of sandwich. "You can easily find out, girl."

"How?"

"Watch this." Tamara pulled her phone out, looked at the information posted on the orga-nization's Web site, then keyed in the phone number. She winked at Dominique when her call was answered.

"Commissioner of the revenue. This is Jer-rafine speaking. How can I help you?"

"Yes, uh, Ms. Trotter, this is Tanya at Steve's Auto Glass. How are you?"

"Great. Thank you," Feenie answered, sus-pecting nothing, although she was curious about the nature of the call.

"I was calling because my technician is there, ready to replace your windshield, but he doesn't see your car in the lot."

"Excuse me?"

"We can't find your car in the lot, and we're really puzzled," Tamara said. "You have the oh-seven Dodge Intrepid, right?"

"No, I drive a Toyota Camry," Feenie freely volunteered. "I didn't order a windshield."

"Hmmm, that's strange. I have an order here for Trotter, windshield replacement, tan oh-seven Dodge Intrepid. Is it your husband's car?"

Feenie, humored by the thought of a husband, chuckled a bit. "No, I'm very much single."

"What color and year is your vehicle? Maybe I just have the wrong color or something." Tamara made random keystrokes on Dominique's laptop simply for sound effects, hoping Feenie would overhear. "Let me see what I can pull up in my system."

"It's a blue two thousand five."

"Oh, oh! I see what I did." Tamara pretended to laugh. "This order is for Jeremy Trotter. That's why nothing is matching up. I just assumed when I heard a female voice that you were his wife. That explains why we can't find the car!" Tamara laughed again. "I'm so sorry to bother you."

"No problem," Feenie answered. "But listen, how did you get—"

Tamara ended the call before she could be questioned about Feenie's work number.

"She drives a blue two thousand five Toyota

Camry," she repeated for Dominique with a smug look on her face. "Let me see something."

Tamara did a search of towing companies in the vicinity of Feenie's job. Within two minutes, she had an establishment on the line. "Yes, I need to have an illegally parked vehicle towed at the owner's expense please." After providing all the information, she snapped her phone closed, then turned and looked at her sister. "Done."

Marvin hammered Tamara's front door as if he had the intention of knocking it off its hinges. "Open the door, Tamara," he ordered. "I'll be out here all day if you don't," he warned.

It had taken the police about two days to locate Dominique's whereabouts and follow up with Marvin. He pounded for two more minutes before Tamara swung the door open, madder than a disturbed hornet's nest.

"What, Marvin? Why are you banging on my door like a madman! What!" she hollered as he pushed past her but stopped just inside the door.

"Where's my wife?" he demanded.

"She's not here right now." Tamara put one hand on her hip and kept the other on the doorknob. "I don't know who you think you are to just come barging in my house like this. I told you the first time you came, Dominique wasn't over here. Ain't nothing changed."

"Yeah, and you were lying then," he snarled

as he began to move toward the hallway to search the house.

"Oh no, you are not just gonna start walking around my house like you live here!" Tamara tried to block Marvin, but he easily pushed her out of the way. "I'm 'bout to call the police!" she idly threatened.

"Go ahead. I already did that. That's how I know she's here."

"No, she ain't," she said, chasing behind him.

"Oh please, Tamara. They came here and talked to both of you. Who do you think you are dealing with? A dummy?"

Marvin quickly looked in every bedroom, bathroom, and closet, with Tamara stopping in each doorway, but didn't find his wife, although he did take note of her personal belongings occupying space in the spare bedroom. For a moment he thought to look under the bed, but with her pregnancy, it was asinine for him to think she'd be there, so he dismissed the notion but checked the closet a second time, thinking that maybe, just maybe, he'd overlooked her crouching in a back corner. He went back to both bathrooms and jerked back the shower curtains, only to be further disappointed, then checked the kitchen, the only room he hadn't been in.

He slammed his hand on the kitchen counter and cursed. "I know she's been staying here. I do know that much." Marvin bit down on his lower lip and studied the pattern of the tiles on the kitchen floor, trying to sort out and diffuse his negative emotions.

Tamara simply watched him with folded arms, waiting for him to either speak or make his next move.

"What's going on with her, Tamara?" he finally asked, looking up at her. "What the hell did I do to deserve this?"

"You and Dominique have to work that out," she said, not wanting to get involved any more than she already was. "I don't think it's my place to say anything about it. Besides, you know I'ma be biased. That's my sister."

"Just tell me where she is right now," he begged. "I'm miserable without that woman."

You shoulda thought about that before you went skinny-dippin' in somebody else's pool, Tamara thought to herself. "I don't know. She went out." She shrugged.

Marvin sighed. "All right," he said, crushed. "I'm sorry for busting in your place like this. I just don't know what to do. Dominique is my whole world." He ran a hand across his head, inhaled deeply, then let out that same breath. "Well, if you see her—I mean, when you see her—tell her I love her very much and to please call me. Obviously, she doesn't want to see me." He pressed his lips together pensively. "I'll be waiting on her call."

"I'll let her know." Tamara closed the door, then rushed to the phone to call her sister's cell. "Girl, why your husband just come tearing through here like a madman, looking for you!"

"What? When?"

"Just now! He just left," said Tamara. "He said the police told him you were staying here. . . ."

"The police!"

"Yep. That's what he said."

"What in the world?"

"He must have filed a missing-person report or something. Then he went storming through here, looking all over the place for you."

"He saw my stuff?"

"Yeah, but I don't know if he knew it was yours. He didn't say anything about it."

"How did he look?" Dominique asked, probing.

"Girl, that man looked so pitiful, it didn't make sense. Face all long, looking like he was about to cry."

"For real?"

"Yeah. I almost felt sorry for him, but he don't deserve that."

"What all did he say?"

"He just asked where you were, said that he had talked to the police, so he knew you were staying here, and said to tell you that he loves you and for you to call him."

"Yeah, whatever," Dominique commented, although she did miss him some.

"He was like, 'Oh, I'm so miserable without her. What did I do? I don't know what to do.' And all that jazz. Buster!"

Dominique only sighed.

"Girl, I wouldn't be surprised if he started sitting out in front of the house, waiting on you to come in."

"I hope he doesn't do that," Dominique gasped.

"Well, you better call him then, because he was pretty desperate. But he did say he knew you didn't want to see him, so he wasn't gonna come back, but still. He was all to pieces."

"Is he still there? Because I was just about to come back home. I have done enough baby shopping for the day."

"Let me look." Tamara jetted to the window and peered through the blinds. "I don't see him, but that doesn't mean he's not down the street somewhere. You just better call him. You're gonna have to do that eventually, anyway," she advised. "You carrying that man's baby. You know you can't run forever."

"I know. I'm just not ready," Dominique responded.

"Well, you best get ready. Even if you decide not to get back with him, you're gonna have to talk to him to let him know that."

"All right, all right, Dr. Phil! I'll call him, but I'm just not ready to do it today. I don't feel like stressing myself or this baby out."

"Just send him a text message then. Shoot! He can't come busting up over here no more like he's on some kind of a drug raid. I'ma have something for his hips next time."

Dominique burst out laughing. "Girl, ain't nobody scared of your little four-eleven tail."

"Keep laughing," Tamara joked. "What I got for him next time is bigger than that. You forgot I'm a forensics major. I know how to take him up outta here and not leave no clues."

"Don't do nothing to my baby daddy. If somebody is gonna take him out, let it be me."

"Well, you better do it before he tries to break bad over here again!"

26

Kerra walked into her office, put her things down, and got settled at her desk. It was her routine to turn her computer on, then grab a cup of coffee while her e-mail loaded. Her heels tapped against the tiled floor on her way to the break room, where she met Jerrafine coming out of the ladies' room.

"You're looking mighty good there, Kerra," Feenie commented with a wink.

Every evening for four weeks straight, Kerra had spent with Jerrafine, exercising, shopping, eating, or having a drink. And now both she and Feenie were beginning to see the fruit of her labor. Kerra was dressed in a red pencil skirt that stopped just above her knees, paired with a white blouse with layered ruffles down its front. She had accented her neck, wrists, and ears with black and white jewelry, and had finished the look with a pair of stylish Steve Madden pumps.

"I'm going to have to start calling you hot lady instead of boss lady," Feenie teased.

Kerra giggled. "I'm just applying the lessons I was taught."

"Looks like you're passing." Feenie winked. "What is John saying?"

"Nothing," Kerra shook her head, wishing Feenie had not even mentioned her husband's name. "Nothing at all."

"Get outta here! Is the man blind? I know you've lost at least ten pounds. Things have got to be back to bumpin' in the bedroom," Feenie stated more than asked.

"Believe it or not, no," Kerra shared in a whisper. "He hardly even looks at me. It's still been forever since . . ." Her voice trailed off, allowing Feenie to draw her own conclusion about what came next.

"Don't worry about it, Kerra. He'll come around. You're getting sexier and sexier as the days go by. He will notice. If not, we're going to have to launch phase two of our plan."

"Yeah, we just may have to do that. What does that consist of?"

"I don't know yet. I haven't had a chance to think about it. I'm mean, I'm good, but I'm not that good!"

Both ladies poured themselves coffee, added creamer and sugar, then headed back to their desks.

"Maybe you can find a way to make him jealous or something. You know men can't stand the thought of someone else getting what they got." Feenie laughed. "And you're working with some junk in your trunk right about now," she added, leaning back to glance at Kerra's behind. "Hot mamma!"

Kerra giggled as she swished her hips, rounding the corner to her office. "I'll talk to you later."

"Ciao."

Kerra began her morning scroll through her e-mail. She worked diligently on her messages, responding to those requiring her attention, then paused pensively when she came across one sent from Jerrafine's personal e-mail account.

Dear Kerra,

Maybe I shouldn't be sharing this with you, but I can't help myself. Every day that I get to see you, my heart skips a beat. I desperately want to kiss you, touch you, and make love to you. Each night I dream about you, and how great it would be to just be able to wake up next to you each morning. I picture our bodies melding together, and I imagine the sound of your mellow, soothing voice escaping in a moan from your lips. I long to feel the silkiness of your hair between my fingers, and your breath on my skin. I lick my lips, imagining the taste of your sweet skin and whispering words of passion in your ear. I hope someday I'll be able to open up to you to show you what I feel. I know you're married, but I can't help but wish that one day I can experience and enjoy you. But even if this wish never comes true, I'll still dream about you each night and look forward to seeing you each day.

JT

Kerra sat at her desk, shocked by what she'd just read. Although she and Feenie had spent several hours each day in each other's company outside of work, she'd never gotten the feeling that there was any level of romantic interest. She pondered the typed words over and over in her mind and thought about the comments that Feenie had made just that morning. The words *sexy hot mamma* replayed a few times. Then she thought about the way Feenie had glanced at her behind.

"This woman likes me," she said out loud. Kerra had always been a heterosexual woman and had never entertained the thought of sharing herself intimately with a female, but because of Feenie's compliments and e-mail, she found herself disgusted, but strangely intrigued, at the thought. For another two minutes, her thoughts on the situation floated randomly through her head. She had a couple of friends who preferred women over men, but they had honored her marriage and had never tried to sway her. Nonetheless, she thought about the time she heard it said that no one could please a woman like a woman.

With that thought leading the way, followed by the lack of affection and satisfaction from her husband, she couldn't help but wonder if it were true. Kerra winced at the thought of being caressed by Feenie but at the same time found herself slightly aroused. "Stop it!" she commanded in reprimand. "Stop it right now." Her mind disobeyed her will as she thought about how long it had been since she'd had any type of sexual pleasure, outside of the times that she had felt forced to be intimate with herself.

Her fingers lightly rattled her keyboard but entered no strokes as she contemplated deleting Feenie's e-mail. A secret side of her wanted to save it, but the married woman in her screamed for the e-mail to be sent to the recycling bin. Not wanting a simple struggle to consume any more of her time, she quickly hit the delete key, then confirmed her choice.

Even with the e-mail gone, the thought of it lingered in Kerra's mind all day. She had to admit, she did feel sexy and attractive. She stood and smoothed her skirt, then ran her hands across her backside as she attempted to look behind her, trying to imagine what Feenie had seen that morning. Having her own bathroom in her office, she walked there, wanting to assess her appearance in the full-view mirror that hung on the inside of the door. She turned slowly, absorbing her curves and reshaped features. Per Feenie's recommendation, a few trips to Victoria's Secret had put Kerra in a bra that lifted and puckered her breasts, as well as gave the illusion of a cup-size increase. While her waistline wasn't exactly where she wanted it to be just yet, Feenie had helped her to pick blouses that stylishly hid her extra layers, rather than bringing attention to them, and the shorter-length pencil skirt was flattering to her calves. Kerra had done away with her standard wide-heeled, one-inch pumps and had bought a couple pairs of stiletto heels with features that were appropriate for work but added sex appeal.

She deemed that Feenie was right. She did look good. And forget John if he didn't see it, or no longer cared to. "One man's trash," she uttered, still turning and admiring herself. Heading back to her desk, she thought about how she should handle the situation. Should she address Feenie? Reprimand her and put her on some kind of disciplinary action? *Maybe I can just be straightforward and honest, and let her know I'm not interested. Then again, it's so nice to be flattered.*

Before she could finish her thoughts, there was a quick tap on her door, although the door was open. Kerra looked up to find both Celina and Feenie coming in the doorway with an arrangement of mixed flowers. Her heart skipped a beat from an uncomfortable nervousness when she saw Feenie. Their eyes met, and while there was a smile on her face, Feenie had no additional facial expression and gave no look that asked what Kerra thought of her e-mail. In mixed company, Kerra chose to say nothing about it and wasn't quite sure how she should approach it in the first place.

"Either you've been really good or Mr. Butler's been really bad." Celina walked forward with fresh carnations, lilies, roses, button poms, heather, and salal, artistically and professionally arranged in a clear glass vase.

"Those are for me?" Kerra asked, completely surprised. Her eyes bounced back and forth between her two employees.

"Looks like something's working," Feenie commented with a huge smile and a wink.

"Ummm . . . duh! I sure wouldn't be giving you *my* flowers." Celina set the arrangement down on her boss's desk.

"Where's the card?" Kerra asked rhetorically, searching the top of the bouquet. Her fingers quickly broke the seal of the small envelope and pulled out the piece of rectangular card stock.

"If those are not from Mr. Butler, me and Celina are gonna hold you hostage until you spill the beans!" Feenie threatened with a laugh.

The card read: *You're beautiful. You're sexy. Wish you were mine.*

Kerra had started reading the card with a smile and managed to keep it on her face, although she was completely bewildered. There was no signature from the sender.

"Well? What did John do that he had to send flowers?" Celina asked.

"I don't know that they're from John," Kerra stated, looking up at Jerrafine first, immediately thinking they were from her.

"Mmm!" Feenie hummed. "Let me find out you got you a secret admirer!"

Kerra bit down on her bottom lip and smiled slyly. "I think I do."

"Your husband better watch out!" Celina screamed. "Who do you think it is?"

"I don't know," Kerra lied, suspecting Feenie all the while.

"One thing about a secret admirer, they don't stay a secret for too long. Before you know it, they will come forward," Feenie noted.

"You don't recognize the handwriting?" Celina asked, reaching for the card.

"No. It was typed, so it probably was a phone order," replied Kerra.

"Are you going to see if your husband sent them?" Feenie asked.

She wants to see if I'm going to tell John, Kerra reasoned. "I don't know," she answered honestly, unsure how Feenie would interpret her response. "If I ask him about it and he didn't send them, that's only going to make him jealous and untrusting."

"And that's a bad thing?" Feenie smirked with raised brows.

With that comment, Kerra was sure the flowers were from Feenie. She didn't respond; she only smiled slightly.

"Really, it's no surprise that you've started turning a few heads. Look at you! You're not the same woman you were last month," Feenie added.

"Yeah, but I don't want to go home and start a fight, either. I'll just wait to see if he brings them up," Kerra replied. "Who's watching the front counter?"

"Jovan is still out there," Celina answered. "I better check and make sure there is not a line backup."

"So who do you really think sent you these sentiments?" Feenie quizzed, with a sly smile, as soon as Celina's footsteps could no longer be heard.

Kerra wasn't sure at this point how to act in Feenie's presence. She was a bit uncomfortable and even intimidated about showing any indication that she'd read Feenie's e-mail. She felt like Feenie was testing the waters, and Kerra didn't quite know how to respond to that. She struggled with just being forward and direct by blurting "I'm not gay," but on the other hand, her starvation and longing for sexual attention forced her to hold off.

"I'm not sure." Kerra felt that it was a safe response. "I don't want to waste my time playing guessing games."

"I know that's right."

"Here's how I see it. If you're going to spend the money on it, you might as well get the credit for it, right?"

"You got that right. No sense in letting someone else benefit from your efforts." Feenie laughed. "Well, I guess you will find out soon enough. Whoever it is will reveal themselves soon. They always do."

27

Every Monday afternoon like clockwork, Kerra received flowers with Feenie's initials on every card. Intrigued by the thought of the affair, and enjoying the daily flirting, Kerra never revealed to anyone who the arrangements were from. Jerrafine's smiles and compliments were all Kerra needed as motivation to continue to make healthy eating choices. Like magic, Kerra's weight dropped and her clothes size decreased. She found herself purchasing and wearing garment styles that she would have never considered before meeting Feenie, and Feenie never disappointed her by not noticing whenever she wore something new.

What Kerra did not see taking place was any changes in her marriage relationship. She still felt incredibly ignored by her husband, and he had said very little if anything at all about Kerra's renewed spirit and attitude. Nonetheless, Kerra was less bothered by it, as she was getting plenty of attention from Feenie.

The more time she spent in Feenie's presence outside of work, the more emotionally attached she became. She spent many evenings helping Feenie with marketing tips to land her a few more decorating jobs on the side, and helping her to think through a workable business plan, and at the same time Feenie helped her build her self-esteem with complimenting and affirming words. As Feenie landed a job here or there, and Kerra dropped a pound or two, they celebrated their successes over dinner, an occasional glass of wine, or a simple high five or hug. It was the hugs that Kerra enjoyed most.

Each morning she spent at least ten minutes reading what now had become a collection of steamy e-mails from the woman she was close to making her lover. To get her rise for the day, she opened up previously sent e-mails and brooded over snippets from each one.

Kerra,

From the day we met, I've been in love with you. I can't help but think about you every night when I slip naked between my satin sheets. I imagine the feel of your skin is as smooth and luxurious as my sheets.

As she read, she felt a familiar warming between her thighs. A feeling she looked forward to each day and she revisited throughout the day via e-mails. No longer was Kerra so concerned about regaining John's lustful eye. Now

everything she bought and wore was inspired by
Feenie. Kerra had transitioned from wearing
large briefs to the skimpiest, laciest thongs.
She'd traded out every Playtex 18 Hour bra for
a variety of bras that made her feel like a sex
kitten more than a grandma. She'd invested in
a few pairs of thigh-high stockings, which she
wore daily, in place of her old, bland nude hose.
She ran a hand up her thigh as she clicked on
another e-mail.

> When I think about you and how you compare
> to other men and women I have met, I can
> honestly say, no one seems to match all the
> qualities you possess.

Kerra's self-esteem had been boosted a mile
high over the past few weeks, and she felt like
a new woman. A woman who was ready to give
herself to another woman. At least once.

She didn't think it too strange that Feenie
had never made a physical pass at her, because
the girls would always be home. By helping
with homework, playing games, and talking
with them, Kerra had come to know the girls a
bit and thought they were delightful, and
knowing that Feenie was striving to make a
better impression on them than she had in the
past, Kerra could respect her level of discre-
tion. But tonight there would be no girls. It was
a Friday, and Feenie had already shared that
her girls would be spending the weekend with
their father, so Kerra decided that this would
be the night that she'd give in to Feenie's se-

duction. As usual, she'd be working out at the facility in Feenie's building. Then she planned to shower in Feenie's apartment and slip into something she thought Feenie would appreciate seeing her in.

Kerra had a bag packed in her vehicle that included a red baby doll with matching panties, along with a pair of red and black, open-toed, platform Mary Janes. She'd been careful to shave her private area and to make sure it was baby's bottom smooth, and she planned to cover her legs with black fishnets. She giggled at the thought of getting dressed for a rendezvous, something she hadn't done in a long time. John had made her feel so fat and ashamed, when she was at home, she slipped into her full-coverage pajamas or gown in the bathroom. Especially after the day of her epiphany, when she'd caught his reflection in the mirror. She swore that even if she lost a hundred pounds and went down to a size four, with a perfectly flat stomach and restructured breasts, John would never see her naked again.

What Kerra had planned for the evening caused her day to fly by effortlessly, although she was swamped with work. Right at five o'-clock, she flashed Jerrafine a smile and wink.

"Ready to hit the gym?"

"Oh yeah," Feenie answered, tidying her work space, then reaching for her purse. "Let's go."

Once at the gym, Kerra stepped on the treadmill and ran like she never had before, and grunted through strength-training repetitions with a new motivation. Within ninety minutes she was in Feenie's shower, primping for her new experience.

She viewed herself in the mirror with a smile, dressed in practically nothing. Slowly, she pulled the bathroom door open and listened to figure out where Feenie was in the house. Hearing her stirring around in the kitchen, Kerra tiptoed the opposite way to Feenie's bedroom and sprawled across her bed. She was a bit nervous but worked past her jitters by remembering Feenie's compliments, e-mails, and flowers. She took a deep breath, then called for Jerrafine.

"Yeah?" Feenie hollered from the front of the apartment.

"Can you come help me with something?" Kerra's heart skipped a beat when she heard Feenie approach the bedroom.

"What's up?" Feenie asked, glancing toward the bathroom first. "Where are you?"

"Here," Kerra called.

Feenie looked into her bedroom and gasped. "Kerra, what in the world? What are you doing?"

"I'm here for you," Kerra whispered. "I'm ready."

"You're ready for what?" Feenie asked with crinkled brows. "Are you crazy?"

"What do you mean?" Kerra asked, becoming confused. "What about your e-mails and flowers and stuff?"

"First of all, you need to get off my bed. Second of all, I don't know what e-mails and flowers you're talking about."

Kerra sat up slowly, now becoming embarrassed. "Feenie, you've sent me several e-mails telling me how you couldn't wait to be with me and how you thought I was sexy. Now you don't know what I'm talking about?"

"I haven't sent you any e-mails," Feenie stated, shaking her head.

"You've been calling me sexy and hot almost every day. But you were just leading me on." Suddenly Kerra wished she had something to cover herself up with. Frantically, her eyes searched the room, and when they came across a throw resting on the back of a chair, she jumped up and reached for it.

"I don't know who's been sending you e-mails or flowers—"

"All of them have your name on them, Jerrafine," Kerra blurted, cutting her off. "Well, your initials, anyway."

"Kerra, I promise you, I have sent you nothing. I'm not gay," Feenie stated flatly. "Now, I have complimented you," she admitted, "but that doesn't mean anything. I compliment everybody." She shrugged. "That doesn't mean that I want to have sex with you or anybody else."

"So all those e-mails were just a game?"

"I told you I haven't e-mailed you. You know what? I think you better leave, Kerra," Feenie stated, placing her hands on her hips. "I know you need to get dressed and all that, but as soon as you have your clothes on, you need to get out of here." Feenie turned and headed back to the living room.

A few minutes later Kerra stormed from

the back. She said nothing as she whizzed by Feenie and through the front door, slamming it behind her.

The next day at work was highly uncomfortable for both women. Feenie thought it best not to speak at all, although she walked by Kerra's office several times. Kerra did the same and didn't utter a single word to Feenie. It was about midday when Feenie's extension rang.

"Jerrafine, I need you to come to the HR office as soon as you're finished with the customer you're serving right now," Randolph Wilson, the HR manager directed.

"Sure," Feenie agreed. She had no worries about why she was being called, knowing that she'd be able to defend her innocence. She'd done nothing.

When she got to the HR office, Randolph, along with Synthia Dupree, his assistant, were waiting for her.

"Come on in, Jerrafine," Randolph said, although his tone was far from welcoming. "Do you know why you're here?"

"Not really." Feenie didn't want to make assumptions.

"I have a sexual harassment claim here, filed by Kerra Butler," Randolph informed her.

Feenie blinked. "Excuse me?"

"Can you tell me what your general interaction with Mrs. Butler is on a daily basis?"

"I mean, we work together like normal. We work out together in the evenings and have been out shopping and stuff like that, but I never did anything sexual," Feenie claimed.

"Mrs. Butler has printed off several e-mails that were sent from an account with your name on it. Are you familiar with these?" Randolph slid several sheets of paper across the table to Jerrafine for her review.

Feenie read a few and thumbed through the others, with her eyes stretched wide. "I didn't send these!" she exclaimed, reading the compilation of seductive and explicit words. "I don't know who sent these, but it wasn't me!"

"Do you recognize the e-mail address?" Synthia asked.

Feenie glanced over the address, Jerrafine.Trotter@ymail.com, and commented. "There must be two of me around here, 'cause that is not my e-mail address."

"Do you know why another woman with the same name as yours would be e-mailing your boss?" asked Randolph.

"No." Feenie shrugged.

"Have you been sending her flowers?" Randolph asked.

"No! I told her that," said Feenie.

Synthia laid out several cards that Kerra had saved. "Do these look familiar to you?"

"Not at all," Feenie answered.

"What if I told you we called the florist, who stated that they got weekly calls from you, requesting bouquets be sent to Mrs. Butler?" Randolph asked.

"I would still say I don't know what you're talking about," Feenie replied.

Randolph went on. "Mrs. Butler also states that you almost daily made comments to her about her body. Can you share with me what some of those comments were?"

"I would tell her she looks nice and stuff. She had come to me, asking me if I could help her be more sexy because her husband wasn't paying her any attention," Feenie explained. "I told her that I'd help her pick out some new clothes, and we could start working out together, but that was it."

"Did you ever mention to her that she had, and I quote, 'junk in her trunk', then call her hot mamma?" asked Randolph.

Feenie nodded. "Yes, but I only said that because she was losing weight and I was trying to help her self-esteem."

"I see. So you did make the comments, but you know nothing about the e-mails and flowers," Randolph confirmed.

"Right. I don't be sending no woman flowers or no sexy e-mail," Feenie stated, completely offended at the thought.

"Well, we're going to have to investigate the situation, and while we're doing so, we're going to have to suspend your employment," Randolph said firmly.

"What? I didn't even do anything!" Feenie retorted.

"And if not, that will be uncovered in the investigation," Randolph replied.

"Is she being suspended, too? She was the one that took it upon herself to get in my bed just about buck-balled naked," Feenie shot back.

Randolph frowned. "We're not here to discuss her employment. We're here to discuss yours."

Feenie sighed. "All right. Well, I haven't done anything so I'm not going to worry about it."

"Is there anything at your desk that we need to get? A purse or your keys or anything?" asked Synthia.

"No, I brought my pocketbook with me," Feenie answered, pulling it up on her shoulder.

"Well, we will give you a call in a few days to let you know the results of the investigation and if and when you can report back to work," said Randolph.

Feenie nodded.

"Before you go, I'll need you to write me a statement about the situation from your point of view, and make sure you include a phone number where you can be reached during your normal business hours," Randolph added.

"Okay," Feenie commented. She was handed a legal pad and a pen. She wrote her side, signed her name, and handed the pad back to Randolph.

"Synthia is going to escort you out, and we will be in touch."

"All right. Thanks," Feenie said, leaving the office feeling confused and betrayed.

She walked through the parking lot, trying not to become depressed about her situation. She couldn't believe the allegations that had been brought against her, knowing that she had never done anything to Kerra other than be a friend and that she had tried to be a model employee.

"She gonna scream harassment after she jumped in my bed, half naked?" she asked out loud in disbelief as she scanned the lot for her vehicle. She knew without a doubt where she'd left it parked, but it wasn't there. In her frustration, Feenie blurted a four-letter word. "Who the hell keeps towing my car!" It was the second time she'd come outside to find her vehicle gone.

Yanking her phone out of her pocketbook, she scrolled through her call history, hoping that the number of the company that had been responsible for the tow a few weeks back was still there. When she identified it, she quickly pressed the keys and waited to be connected, ready to give the owner a piece of her mind.

"Big Joe's Tow and Stow," a man bellowed across the line.

"Do y'all have my car down there again? 'Cause if you do, I'm coming down there and beating somebody's ass!" she screamed. She would repent for cussing later.

"What kinda car you got?" he asked, paying her ranting no attention. Feenie described her car, and the tow driver answered, "We ain't got that one."

"Y'all came out here and got it before."

"Well, we ain't got it today," he said, sounding like he had a cigarette dangling from his lips. "You need to check with somebody else."

Feenie just snapped the phone closed, wanting to toss it to the ground.

"Where the hell is my car?" She stood in the lot, turning in a circle and looking every which way, making sure she just hadn't overlooked it, but indeed it was not there. At that point, Feenie couldn't hold back the tears. Immobilized for two full minutes, she dropped her head and held one hand to her face, pressing on her closed eyelids, and let her tears plop to the asphalt beneath her feet. Once she pulled herself together, she called for a taxi, then walked to a nearby sidewalk bench and waited.

"God help the person who's munking with my stuff when I find them."

It was then that she saw Celina slowly drive by her, looking and laughing.

"Bet your ass won't be at work early tomorrow, will you!" she cackled before speeding off.

28

"How are you feeling today, Dominique?" Dr. Brophy entered the room where Dominique was sitting on the table, with a *Parents* magazine, waiting for her exam.

"Okay, I guess." Dominique shrugged, closing the magazine.

"You guess? Tell me what's going on." She flipped through Dominique's file.

"Nothing really, other than I can see only the tips of my big toes now."

"And considering your condition, that's a good thing, right? We do want to know that the baby is growing and developing. Lots of kicking going on?"

A snicker escaped Dominique's lips. "Yes, especially at night." She nodded. "If it's not my husband rolling over on me, it's the baby kicking me."

"Finding it a bit hard to sleep, huh?"

"For sure."

"And where is Mr. Temple today? He was

doing so well making the appointments with you," Dr. Brophy said as she motioned Dominique to lie back.

"He couldn't get away from work," Dominique lied.

It didn't matter what Marvin had going on in his day, he would adjust his schedule to attend appointments with his wife. Dominique just hadn't reminded him. She knew if she had, even though she'd left him, he would be by her side.

"He has to be really disappointed that he's missing the ultrasound. He was so excited about coming a few weeks back."

"Yeah, he was pretty bummed about it." Had he known, a team of wild horses wouldn't have been able to keep him away, Dominique thought to herself. "He will just have to see the pictures," she added.

"Let's go ahead and get you to the ultrasound room and take a look at your bundle of joy."

A few minutes later Dominique lay back on another table, with her blouse gathered just beneath her breasts. Dr. Brophy moved the transducer over her patient's belly and turned the monitor toward Dominique. In an instant a tiny face appeared on the screen, eyes closed and lips tightened in a ball.

"Oh my goodness," Dominique gasped. Dominique hadn't prepared herself for the image that she saw. She'd seen plenty of ultrasound pictures in the past, which were generally black-and-white blurry images that were hard to make out if the proud mom was not standing by to point out features. "I can see his face, or is it her? Oh my God!" Instantly her eyes began to water.

"He's beautiful," Dr. Brophy commented, pointing out the baby's sex organs. "Yes, it's a boy!" she sang.

Dominique looked on in awe, completely speechless, with her hand covering her mouth. In that moment it didn't matter that Marvin had cheated and was expecting another baby in another part of town. Realizing how much she loved him, she longed for her husband to be by her side as her eyes filled with, then spilled tears. She needed him to wrap his arms around her and rest his hands against her, to tell her that he loved nothing in the world more than he loved her.

"You can go shopping now. There're lots of cute things out there for little boys, you know."

Dominique could only nod, still overwhelmed by and teary eyed from the image of her baby boy. She took printed images from her doctor's hand and tried to pull herself together.

"Are you okay?"

"Yeah, I just need a minute." Dominique smiled weakly, staring at her son's first photographs.

"Well, when you're ready, you can go ahead to the front desk and set up your next appointment. You're coming along just fine," Dr. Brophy announced before leaving the room.

Alone, Dominique cried for the next several minutes, then finally felt she'd be able to stop her tears long enough to make it home. She tucked the photos in her wallet, waddled to the bathroom, blew her nose and washed her face, then leaned against the bathroom wall, thinking myriad thoughts. When she was ready, Dominique eased the bathroom door open and headed for the front desk, completely unprepared for and startled by whom she saw.

Marvin leapt to his feet in desperation and came toward her. "Babe! Thank God I found you."

In an instant Dominique's eyes became flooded with tears again.

"Where have you been? What's going on?"

"Move, Marvin," Dominique ordered, completely forgetting about how she had felt just minutes before.

"Not until you tell me what's going on."

Dominique's eyes darted around the waiting room nervously; she was concerned and embarrassed about the attention Marvin drew. "Not here," she said through clenched teeth.

"Then where? I haven't seen or heard from you in two weeks!" he exclaimed, his voice getting louder.

"Lower your voice. You're embarrassing me," she said in a loud whisper.

"I don't care about that. Do you know how miserable I've been? How are you just going to walk away from me like that, Dominique? And then with my baby, too? And you want me to calm down?"

"Let me at least check out. Then we can

talk," Dominique said, negotiating but just wishing Marvin would go away.

"Okay," he agreed, "but I'm not letting you out of my sight until you tell me what's going on."

Dominique rolled her eyes, turned to the receptionist, set up her next appointment, then unsuccessfully tried to outwalk Marvin. He easily kept pace with her and moved ahead of her to open the door to let her out. As soon as they were on the other side of the door, he nearly exploded.

"Now, what in the world is going on with you? You just leave and don't say anything? Where have you been?"

"I don't even want to talk to you, Marvin," Dominique spat, trying to lengthen her stride.

"You can at least tell me why." Marvin grabbed her arm to slow her down.

"You know why!" she insisted.

"No, I don't! I love you, and I'm frustrated that you are walking around here, not talking to me. You need to tell me something. You owe me at least that much."

"I don't owe you anything."

"How do you figure you can just walk out of my life, with my baby with you, and not say anything? What is it? You don't love me anymore? You're seeing someone else? What is it?"

Dominique whipped her head toward her husband and looked him square in the eyes. "Why are you acting like you don't know what I'm talking about, Marvin? You know as well as I do what you've done. Then you want to stand in my face and demand answers? Seems to me, you need to be the one explaining and telling *me* what's going on!"

"You really want to know, Dominique? I've been sitting at home, about to lose my mind, worried to death about you and my baby. That's what's going on. I been holding on to a thread of hope every day that you were going to come home or at least call and talk to me. Racking my brain every night, wondering what ungodly awful thing I did that would make you up and leave me!" he bellowed.

"I know about the witch you slept with and knocked up!" Dominique finally screamed.

"What? Who?" Marvin's face expressed complete and utter confusion.

"Don't play stupid, Marvin," Dominique scoffed, not caring who was looking at them as they stood in the parking lot, having a public dispute.

Marvin tilted his head upward toward a sky of blue and let out an exasperated sigh. "Dominique, I have no clue what you are referring to." His tone was now much calmer. "You are my wife, I love you, and I haven't as much as looked at a woman, let alone got somebody pregnant."

"You're a liar!" she accused.

"I don't know where you got this information from or who you've been listening to. But you are so wrong."

"So you just think I'm stupid?"

"No, I don't think you're stupid, but I do know that whatever you think you know, you have never been more wrong about anything in your life."

Dominique searched Marvin's eyes for truth and sincerity and could almost swear she found it, but she also knew what she'd overheard.

"Now, you need to tell me where you got this foolish notion from," Marvin insisted.

"Not out here in this parking lot. We have to go somewhere else."

"Where?"

"I don't know." She shrugged.

"Pick a place, because I'm not leaving your side until we squash this whole thing. I need a ride home, anyway."

"Why is that?" she questioned, as if she didn't know.

"Because both the car and truck are in the shop. Somebody poured black paint all over the windshield of the truck," he snarled, still not fully convinced that it had not been his ex-wife. "And as soon as I find out who it was, they're going straight to jail."

"Who do you think it is?"

"I don't even want to speculate," Marvin replied. Had he said who he thought it was, it would have brought on a multitude of questions right in the middle of the unpleasant conversation they were already having. The last thing he needed his wife to think was that he was seeing or even talking to his ex-wife. "I don't have any enemies that I know about, so it's impossible for me to even guess."

"Mmm-hmmm." Dominique feigned sarcasm.

"So where are you taking me?" He opened

the driver's side of his wife's Lexus ES sedan, letting her in.

"I'll figure that out on the way."

Marvin seated himself beside her, feeling a mixture of emotions. First and foremost, relief that she was alive and well, then anger that he hadn't seen or heard from her in two weeks, then complete love and yearning for her.

"So what did the doctor say?" he asked, trying to fill the silence in the car with words.

"She said we're having a boy."

"Oh! Today was the ultrasound, wasn't it! Babe, why didn't you call and remind me? You knew I wanted to be there."

"Thought you'd be tied up with your other baby momma," she snarled.

"That was low," Marvin huffed. "I already told you there is no one else. But I got cheated out of a once-in-a-lifetime moment because you want to believe whatever you want to believe."

"I know what I know, and I believe what I know."

"You know what, Dominique? You're going to have to stop this car right now and tell me what it is you think you know. Here. Pull over right here," he directed, pointing her to a shopping center parking lot. "This is just as good a place as any."

Dominique wheeled the car into the parking lot of a small shopping center, put the car in park, and then just sat there.

"Now, what is it?" Marvin demanded.

Dominique let tears trickle freely down her

face as she stared straight ahead, focusing on nothing in particular, until Marvin gently turned her head toward him.

"What is it, babe?" he said with love.

Dominique took a deep breath before she started. "I was bringing you lunch one day to your office, thinking that you were probably hungry and would appreciate something from your wife. And I was standing right in the hallway when that woman told you that she was having your baby," she said, spilling the words out.

"What woman? Babe, nobody came to my office, telling me they are having my baby."

"Yes, she did!" Dominique argued. "I heard her!"

"When was this, Dominique?"

"About two months ago. Why are you playing stupid, Marvin? I told you I was right there."

"Tell me the whole story, babe."

"I just told you. I heard her tell you. I came to your office and was right outside the door when she told you. She just about knocked me down running out of there."

"How'd she look?" Marvin asked, putting two and two together. "Was she tall, brown skinned, with her hair straight back in a ball or bun, or whatever it's called?"

"Yes."

Marvin dropped his head, letting out a cynical chuckle, and shook his head.

"So that's funny to you?" Dominique snapped, becoming angry.

"Not at all," he answered, thinking back on the day Feenie had paid him a visit. "Not funny at all."

"Well?" Due to her rising anger, Dominique's tears had slowed a bit.

"I need you to listen to me, babe." Marvin paused momentarily, then began again. "I love you, and I would never intentionally do anything to jeopardize our marriage—"

"So you're gonna tell me that you didn't mean it and it just happened," Dominique said, cutting him off.

"Dominique, just hear me out."

She tucked her lips inside her mouth in silence.

"The woman that you saw was my ex-wife." Marvin watched the expression on his wife's face change. "I hadn't seen her in about ten years until that day."

"So why was she telling you about your baby?" she mocked with a shake of her head.

"Do you remember me telling you how she miscarried our baby?"

"Yeah."

"Well, the part I didn't tell you was that I caused the miscarriage . . . Well, I thought I did."

"What do you mean?"

"Jerrafine came to tell me that she had an abortion before she told me she was pregnant. We got in a fight." He quickly rethought his words. "Well, not a *fight* fight, but anyway, I pushed her and she fell. That's when she told me that she was pregnant. I took her to the hospital, and when the doctor listened for the baby's heartbeat, there wasn't one." Marvin paused pensively. "All this time she had me believing that I was the reason the baby didn't make it."

"So how does she know where you work, to just show up at your job?"

"I have no idea. I told you I hadn't seen or talked to her for ten years. Maybe she Googled me or something. I don't know." He shrugged his shoulders, revealing a bit of exasperation.

"So this woman shows up at your office unannounced, you have no clue how she found you, and you didn't think to ask her?"

"No, I did not. For what? First of all, I was shocked to see her there, period, and secondly, I wanted her gone. I wasn't trying to hold a conversation with the woman. I told you before, she's crazy!"

"Then why didn't you just tell me, Marvin? Tell me that she came by and what she said?" Dominique asked, wanting to believe her husband but not quite sure that she could.

"I didn't want to bring that home. That woman caused me so much hurt and pain, and for her to pop up ten years later with more drama?" He shook his head again in disdain. "Naw. I'd just much rather forget about her. Right when my life couldn't get any better, here she comes with more of the same. I didn't tell you, only because I didn't want to even worry you with it at all. And the very thing I was trying to protect you from, I led you right to."

Dominique listened silently, studying Marvin's face and digesting his words.

"But you know what? Nothing has ever hurt me as much as you walking out on me and not speaking to me." He looked at her, baring his soul through his eyes. "That crushed me."

Dominique broke down again, beginning to feel guilty. "I'm sorry. I should have just asked you, instead of jumping to wild conclusions." She thought about the damage she had done to their vehicles, especially the paint job, and concluded there was no way she could ever come clean about it. *That has to go with me to my grave,* she thought. *Or at least to our fifty-year anniversary.*

"It's not your fault. I should have said something to you. I'm sorry, babe. He smudged her tears with his thumb. "This won't happen again, Dominique. From now on I'm not keeping anything from you, okay?" he promised.

Dominique could only nod.

"So let me go ahead and tell you this . . . I think she knows where we live," Marvin revealed.

"What do you mean, you think? Has she shown up at the house?"

"I'm not sure, but I think so. I think she's the one that messed the cars up."

"What's wrong with the cars?" Dominique asked, pretending to be none the wiser.

"Well, you know the Mercedes was keyed pretty bad, and the truck got a paint job, with a gallon of house paint all over the windshield.

The car got keyed while I was at work, but I woke up one morning to find the truck covered in paint. That's why I think she knows where we live."

"Did you file a police report?" She hid her nervousness about what his answer could be.

"Yeah. I had to make a vandalism claim."

"Have they come up with anything?" Dominique asked, her heart now beating twice as fast.

"Not yet. They claimed that my ex didn't do it, but I don't know if I fully believe that. They don't know her like I know her. I was hoping they'd at least be able to get some fingerprints off the paint can, but they couldn't."

"Why not?"

"After she or whoever covered the windshield, they sat the can in a pool of paint on the hood, which covered the prints."

"Oh," she commented but hid her relief.

"I did call Feenie and cuss her behind out, though."

"How'd you get her number?" This time Dominique didn't hide her concerns. "You've been talking to her?"

"No, she wrote me a letter—"

"What!" she exclaimed, cutting him off.

"Calm down and let me finish. A couple of months ago she wrote me a letter, apologizing for all the stuff she did and saying that she needed to talk to me. Her phone number was in the letter, and she asked me to call her so we could meet up."

"And you saved her number?" Dominique eyed her husband incredulously.

"No, I didn't save her number," immediately shot from his mouth in defense. His thoughts quickly circled his head as he wondered how he could explain himself without telling his wife about the other letters he'd received from Feenie and the fact that he did call her. He reminded himself that he had nothing to hide. "She wrote me like three times, saying pretty much the same thing . . . that she needed to talk to me and all that." He sighed before he began again. "I did call her just one time," he admitted with a matter-of-fact tone that suggested she not question him. At least not at that moment. "Actually I called her three times. The first time was because she kept sending letters, so I called myself, trying to give her a chance to tell me what it was she was squawking on paper about. I got her number off one of the letters and called, but when I did, she refused to tell me on the phone, so I just hung up. The second and third times were when I cussed her out about vandalizing my property."

"So now she has your phone number?" Dominique more stated than asked.

"No. I dialed star-six-seven first so it would show as a private call," he explained.

"Oh." Dominique paused. "So now what?"

"So will you please come home now, babe?" Marvin asked. "This whole thing has just been a crazy misunderstanding all over someone who means nothing to me. I just can't believe that after all these years she was able to waltz into my life and just about destroy it a second time." He paused pensively, then chuckled at the irony. "Jerrafine Trotter got me once and damn near got me again." He paused a second time, then began again. "Anyway, it would be such a tragedy if we couldn't move past this, Dominique. I know what you thought you heard, but I swear to you, I have never been unfaithful. You're the love of my life, and I need you with me. Please come home, baby."

Dominique nodded as Marvin took her hand and kissed it. He ran his hand across her belly just in time to feel the baby stretch and move. "That's my boy there," he bragged. With a wide grin on his face, he continued. "You see how he just knew it was me and started moving?"

"Marvin, he's been kicking and fighting all day." She giggled.

"Not like this, though. He knows this is his daddy talking to him."

"No, he knows that it's time for his mamma to get him something to eat."

"You haven't fed my son today?" he teased. "Don't worry, man," he spoke to Dominique's rounded middle. "Daddy's gonna take care of that." He leaned over and kissed his wife's lips. "I love you so much, baby."

"And I love you back," Dominique answered and smiled between kisses.

"All right, switch places with me." Marvin hopped out of the passenger seat and jetted to the opposite side of the car to open the car door for his wife. Using Marvin's offered hand, she heaved herself up from the seat and fully stood. Marvin wrapped his arms tightly around her. "Mmm," he moaned. "You feel so good. I missed you so much," he added, kissing her forehead.

"I missed you, too, Marvin." Dominique clung to her husband just as tightly as he did to her and laid her head against his chest. They kept the embrace for a full minute before finally pulling away.

Marvin turned his wife's face toward his own with a nudge of his finger and looked her squarely in the eyes. "Dominique, I need you to listen to me. I have been absolutely miserable these last few weeks because you were gone. You are bone of my bone and flesh of my flesh, and I never again want to be without you." His eyes studied her intently. "Never," he repeated. "You're my wife, you're having my baby, and I love you, and because I love you, I am not going to intentionally do anything that would make you want to leave me." He paused. "Let me get you two something to eat." He escorted Dominique to the passenger side, opened the door, helped her get seated, then took the driver's seat. "What do you have a taste for?"

"Mexican," she said, without having to think about it.

"Cool." Marvin wheeled the Lexus onto the highway and drove to Plaza Azteca on Laskin Road.

They slid in a booth together, with Marvin sitting on the same side as his wife, instead of across from her. He dropped an arm around her shoulder and kissed her cheek. "You're still the best part of my day," he said with a smile.

Dominique couldn't help but smile back, although her thoughts were consumed with the question of whether she should come clean about damaging his vehicles or not. Before she could decide, the server approached the table, asking for their orders. Dominique decided on an entrée of grilled chicken breast and slices of tender steak served with an enchilada, *pico de gallo,* rice, beans, and corn tortillas. Marvin ordered a mixture of chorizo, chicken, and beef fajitas with sautéed peppers and onions, served with refried beans, cheese, and sour cream.

While they waited on their food, Dominique dismissed her vandalism confession and thought it best to bring up something that was sure to put a smile on her husband's face. She pulled the images of the baby from her purse.

"You want to see something incredible?" she asked, leaning against his shoulder.

"What's that, babe?"

"Look at your son."

Marvin's eyes filled with tears as he studied the images, but he forced them back before they could spill down his face. "Wow," was all he could say. "Look what we made."

The couple enjoyed their meal, then rode home in silence, with Marvin relieved that he'd gotten this whole episode behind him. He had a partial smile on his face as he drove with one hand on the steering wheel and the other hand on his wife's belly, once again happier than he could ever remember being.

EPILOGUE

Marvin stood by his wife's side for close to fifteen hours while she tossed, moaned, and grunted through her labor pains. He wiped her forehead, gave her ice, held her hand, and repeatedly told her he loved her, planting kisses on her forehead when she would allow. And when the time was right, Dominique pushed forth the most perfect and incredible baby boy he would ever see. Marvin had never experienced anything so incredible in his life.

The miracle of life overwhelmed him to tears, although nothing would erase the proud grin on his face as he looked upon the face of his six-pound, twelve-ounce son for the first time. The newborn squirmed a bit against Dominique's chest, where he'd been placed for the moment.

After finding a comfortable niche, the newborn peeled his eyes open and looked at his her. Marvin reached for his tiny hand, and the baby immediately tightened his grasp around Marvin's index finger.

"You two are the loves of my life," he whispered.

"And we love you right back," Dominique returned. "Don't we, Marlin Jacob Temple?"

Marlin's mouth formed a perfect circle as he inhaled, then let out a yawn, then closed his eyes. Marvin snuggled his head beside Dominique's and looked down in adoration at his newborn son, but then looked at his wife as a lightbulb slowly illuminated in his head.

"It wasn't Feenie. You're the one that messed the cars up."

Dominique's silent smirk was all the confirmation Marvin needed.

Feenie had not anticipated getting fired from her job and initially thought her world was falling apart when she was. There was no way to prove that Celina, in her jealousy, was the author of the inappropriate e-mails, although Feenie knew beyond a shadow of a doubt that it was her. Initially, she was furious and wanted to plot revenge, but she was reminded of the multitude of lies she'd told Marvin, the traps she'd set for Rance, and the life of deceit she'd led for such a long time, for her own selfish gain.

Once the girls went to school, she spent the next week praying and meditating. And in that process, she reflected on how far she'd come and how much she'd changed. Anyone that had known her just a couple of years before would have to admit that she was now a completely different person. Instead of despising them, she now embraced her girls; she'd been able to come clean about her shameful past, making amends with both Marvin and Laiken, having asked both of them for forgiveness; and she'd discovered a talent that had been hidden in plain view all her life.

It had been a hard kick out of the nest, but now was the time for Feenie to test her wings. And with the determination to fly, and God on her side, she had the time, space, and motivation to be the best mother to her girls and fully launch her business, Finesse Feenie's Interior Design.

Visit Kimberly's Web site:
www.kimberlytmatthews.com

Follow Kimberly on Twitter:
www.twitter.com/KimberlyMHooker

Find Kimberly on Facebook:
Kimberly T. Matthews-Hooker

Find Kimberly on MySpace:
www.myspace.com/perfectshoe

Read Kimberly's blogs:
kimberlytmatthews.blogspot.com

E-mail Kimberly:
Kimberly@KimberlyTMatthews.com